Benicia and Letters of Love

a novel

James M. Garrett

Outskirts Press, Inc.
Denver, Colorado

Outskirts Press
http://www.outskirtspress.com

ISBN-10: 1-59800-854-4
ISBN-13: 978-1-59800-854-8

Printed in the United States of America

Introduction

Hello,

One day I felt the need to open the opportunity for anyone, who wished to accept, to submit a letter to me telling of love, in any way, they held in connection with Benicia. I would then include the letters I chose from those received into a compilation titled "Benicia and Letters of Love". With those thoughts, I would purchase a quarter-page advertisement in the Benicia Herald which would run for one month.

After considerable thought I came to the belief there were too many potential problems possible...legal, hurt feelings, lapses in memory on the part of some of the writers of the letters, and misinterpretations. That being the case I decided to make the compilation a work of fiction and write each of the letters myself. The result is the book you are now reading.

I have long held the belief that Benicia possesses many love stories. The loves spoken of in "Benicia and Letters of Love" are as recent as yesterday and as far as decades in the past. People want to tell of their loves and to share that love with others. This compilation is an attempt to share some of the loves of Benicia in a fictional manner.

I write about things I know. Names, dates, and places change, but concepts remain the same. Each letter in "Benicia and Letters of Love" is a scene from my imagination. The finished form of each letter is my attempt at writing in the style I picture the fictitious writer would use. Please remember they are letters, not Shakespeare.

This effort of fiction is dedicated to my wife, Roberta Ann (Marchioni) Garrett. My "Bobbie" is my love. She is my reason for living and for anything I do. She is my port in a storm and my sanity. Much of her presence is included in the letters.

I may add a volume(s) to "Benicia and Letters of Love" in the coming years, as I both search my memory for subject material and also learn more of the situations which inspired "Benicia and Letters of Love". I would try to have the publication of volumes occur shortly before Valentine's Day each year. The story of "Benicia and Letters of Love" is, truly, a never ending story.

Hopefully you will enjoy reading "Benicia and Letters of Love".

Peace
As always before,
Jim Garrett

Table of Contents

Letter 1

The Transfer Student

Dear Mr. Garrett,

It is with surprise that I read your advertisement in the recent edition of a local paper. Your words of "loves of our lives connected in any way with Benicia" immediately touched my heart. I so hope you will select this letter to include in your compilation. Thank you for this opportunity to tell anyone who may read this about my Bud.

Bud was a good man. He was a good boy who grew to be a good young adult and became the good man I eventually married. He was the love of my life, my soul mate, my kindred spirit, my "everything". He is gone now, but I so much appreciate the chance to tell you of him.

We met in the Sixth Grade at the Grammar School. The class was taught by a man whose name I can't recall. He was a little over six feet tall. His hair was dark, with gray at the temples, and he combed it straight back. It bothers me now that I can't remember his name. He often wore a light gray suit with a broad tie. The grounds are the same site for the Benicia Unified School District offices and Liberty High School now.

I was a transfer student from Fairfield. My father had gotten a job at the Benicia Arsenal and moved the family to government housing on Larkin Drive a few days before the school year started. It isn't the same Larkin Drive which is in Benicia now. It was located where the first street north of the I-780 overpass, Vecino, off East Fifth Street is now.

Bud's family lived a few houses down the street towards East Fifth Street. He and I had seen each other in those early days, but didn't speak.

On the first day of school it was as if he had been waiting for me to walk down the street. He was standing on his porch. When he saw me, he walked towards the street and said, "Hello, my name's Bud."

By the time we had gotten as far as the original King's Market, it seemed as if I had known him all my life. I had no way of knowing that I would know him for all of his life after that and keep him in my heart for the remainder of mine.

Of course, on the first day the teacher had to call on me for an answer concerning something with which I was unfamiliar. It was something from the Fifth Grade curriculum in the Benicia School District which I hadn't had in Fairfield. He was a kind man and assumed I knew of what he was speaking. I didn't have the slightest idea, but tried my best to respond.

Some in the class laughed at my ignorance of something so many of them knew. Bud sat across the aisle from me on my left, and he didn't laugh. I remember to this day how bright his face became and the words he said. The words burst from his mouth in a manner which simply wasn't done in those days in a classroom. Later, as a teacher myself for thirty years, that example was many times accepted, granted, and wanted. People grow just as society grows.

He said, "Don't laugh at her! She just moved here. She doesn't know the answer, but I bet she's smarter than most of you!"

Without knowing it, I had found the love of my life, my knight on the white steed, my hero. It didn't seem like it at the time. I was crushed and embarrassed in a hurt which can only come to a transfer student in the Sixth Grade.

Bud and I walked home together that first afternoon as we did most afternoons after that. He never mentioned the incident in school that day and neither did I. Though I lived past his house by about one hundred yards, he always walked me to my house, said "Goodbye", and then turned and walked home.

My parents asked how things had gone at school that first day and I told them what had happened. My mother said, "Bud is a good young man. He's been brought up well."

My father said, "It looks like we have a gallant young man as a neighbor".

I didn't understand exactly what he meant at the time. I simply knew I liked Bud.

That feeling of "like" I had for Bud turned to love. He didn't make any grandiose efforts to impress me. He was just himself, a kind, warm, thoughtful man. I miss him very much.

Thank you, again, for letting me share thoughts of him with you and any others who may read this letter.

Sincerely,
Luanne

Letter 2

An Unknown Brother

Dear Mr. Garrett,

I don't know if this is the type of letter you said you were looking for, or hoping for, in your advertisement. It is a love connected with Benicia, but it is the love for a brother I never knew I had.

My parents moved around quite a bit before finally settling down. They raised me and my brothers and sisters in the same house. It was a wooden frame house near the water on the west side of town. It was cold in the winter and hot in the summer.

For years I thought all of the children were raised there. Long after my parents and a brother and sister had passed on, my remaining brothers and sisters and I learned that we had another brother.

We found out about our long unknown, and lost to us, brother, after the death of his mother. Her attorney contacted us at her wish. He told us of the mother's life and the life of her son. Her son was the only child she had. He had lived most of his life in another state and raised a family of his own. He had been a pillar of his small community, active in his church and a participant in many community activities.

In his youth my father had a period of what some would call "sowing his wild oats". Today it would probably be called playing around. The son he sired at that time was with a woman of whom we other children had only heard through family rumors from aunts and uncles.

Before our father died he told our mother some things which obviously answered some questions she held concerning his life. Our mother told us what our father had told her. He never told her about his first son.

Dad was a wanderer in those days, looking for what work his carpenter's hands could bring. He stopped in the small town of Benicia and was hired by a local contractor to help build some small structures. I've seen his work in the city where I live. There are two houses, which he built next to each other. They are located near a community center which was built long after dad built the houses. He was a very skilled craftsman and could build a house from the ground up with very little help. He wasn't a slap-it-together, nail-bender worker. He was a craftsman.

The contractor's eldest daughter worked in the office doing all of her father's paper work. That included making out the payroll.

Each Friday afternoon after lunch she walked to the bank to withdraw the cash needed to pay the men. Her father always made sure that one of his employees was around at that time and he asked the man to accompany her. The third week my father worked in Benicia he was the one asked to escort the owner's daughter.

My father wasn't bashful. There was a dance at the town hall the next week and he took the opportunity to ask if he could escort her to the dance, as they walked to the bank. She agreed.

They saw more of each other as the time went by, but work ran out for my father and he moved on. For the next couple of years, if it was at all possible in his travels, he passed through Benicia. During one of those times my older brother was conceived.

My dad and mom loved each other, and demonstrated that love to each other, and demonstrated their love to each of us as well. I have no doubt of that.

Sometimes in his later life dad seemed to escape for a few minutes into a scene in his mind known only to him. Looking back at those times, when I happened to see him looking as he did, I wonder if he was thinking of the woman he had loved and the child she bore him. He did truly love her, but it wasn't with the love he and my mother shared. But it wasn't a summertime love, because it obviously stayed in his mind too long for that.

Things happen to each of us in life, as things did to my father. On a trip back through Benicia he discovered that the daughter of the owner of the business had gotten married and had given birth.

They met, and talked, and she told him of his son. She said he would always be the father of her son, but that her son would be raised as the son of another.

After her son married he and his wife gave her grandchildren. He asked her to choose the name of his first son. She did so. She said the words were in loving memory.
Perhaps someday I'll quietly visit your town.
With appreciation,
Kane

Letter 3

A Naïve Girl's Mistake

Dear Mr. Garrett,

You may not receive another letter such as this in response to your advertisement. From what I've heard and read over the years, though, I don't think the story is unique.

I thought I was in love. I was seventeen, had dated a few boys since I was fourteen, but never went farther with a boy than kissing.

One day shortly after the start of my junior year at Benicia High School a senior boy I had always thought was cute asked me to go to a dance with him. He was very popular and had flirted with me in Mrs. Potter's typing class. In the social circles of the day I felt as if I had hit the jackpot. After all, HE was interested in me.

When the boy came to pick me up that night, my father acted differently towards him than he had towards the other boys I had dated. He had never tried to influence me towards whom I should choose as friends or whom I should date. I think he felt that phase of growing was part of my life decisions to make.

Something seemed to blossom in me the night of that first date. He treated me as I had never been treated by other boys. I was too naive to know he had a much practiced approach.
I learned, but it was the wrong way.

My father seemed stunned for a moment and then asked,

"You're what?"

He said the words in disbelief and with a lack of understanding, but he knew what I meant. I was pregnant. It had come about so quickly. I felt naive, stupid, and used.

When he asked if the senior boy was the father, he asked with the voice of someone who knew the answer before the question was asked.

When I told him it was that boy, his face got the darkest red I've ever seen someone's face get. For the only time in my life I heard him swear. He swore not at me, but at the boy and how he had hurt me. The anger came from what he had learned at his workplace of the boy in the community through the past few years.

My father forgave me, but the warmth that was once there between us was gone. I had been his "little girl", and as time passed I understood what that meant to him.

In those days, if a girl suddenly went to live with her older sister, many excuses were given, but nearly everyone guessed the real reason. My son was born in late June in San Francisco. I placed him for adoption with the church. Then my visit to my sister was ended and I came back to Benicia and started my senior year at Benicia High School. My sister didn't need me to "help her through her illness" any longer.

I don't know of the life of my first born. I love him as my child, and wish him and his well, but I don't love him as I love my other children. I guess that is something which often happens. I never held him.

Through the years I came to know my father better as a person, and not only as my father. Years after I had been married I asked him if he had ever had contact with the boy after I told him I was pregnant. He said he had gone to the home of the boy to talk with him and his father. Both the father and the boy denied what I said had happened. Then one laughed, and then the other. My father said that when he showed himself from their home a few minutes later neither was laughing. I thank him for that.

The senior boy with whom I foolishly thought I was in

love, and who fathered my first child, has been very successful in his professional life. His personal life has been just a bounce from one woman to another. He was married once, but the marriage lasted less than a year.

I entered my senior year as if nothing was any different from the fact I had been gone for a few months to help my sister. I was given a few looks by some of the other students, which I knew were questioning. Some were from the boys and some were from the girls. The two classmates of mine, who had always hung around with the father of my baby, almost snickered the first few times I saw them.

The few times I saw the father of my baby through the years after I returned from San Francisco, he turned away as if I was a stranger.

What saved my sanity then was the care and understanding shown by a few of my friends and my two favorite teachers. The girls I had been friends with before welcomed me back to their lives. No boy ever did anything to embarrass me or him in relationship to why I had been gone.

One day after class I needed to stay behind to ask one of my teachers something. She answered my question, reached for my hand and held it in both of hers and said, "If you ever need to talk about anything, just come see me." I appreciated that very much.

The other teacher was one whom I sought out. Some saw him as a rough, tough, gruff, hard-nosed coach. I knew I saw more in him than that. I was right.

He was walking across the quad before school one morning and our paths crossed. The timing wasn't accidental on my part. I needed to tell him something.

We said good morning to each other, as I stopped in front of him.

With a boldness I never knew I possessed I said, "You know I was pregnant, when I left your class and moved away last year, don't you."

He said, "Yes, I knew. I'm glad you're back in our lives. I missed you."

I said, "Thank you." Then I reached out and squeezed his arm and walked away. He hadn't judged or accused. He simply understood.

We never spoke of that part of my life again. The first son, the love of my life and I were blessed with, has as his name the name of that teacher.

I recovered from that long ago mistake. I wanted to share the knowledge that things can change for the better. Young people don't have to live their lives hurt.

What changed me was a young man. I've been married to the love of my life for the last forty-three years. He and I started going to school together in kindergarten, in the building on the corner of East Fifth and East "N" Streets. That building is now the site of a Mexican restaurant. We teased each other then and later on in the other lower grades.

We had always been friends and talked with each other. When I came back for our senior year, we started talking to each other more. During that year we talked and walked, and walked and talked many times. He had always been a caring guy and he became a "hand-holder". I didn't feel damaged any more. I felt accepted again. The Winter Ball was held at the Officer's Club in the Arsenal that year. It was our first real date.

My deep regrets in life are for the child I never knew and for my father. During all the time after I told my father I was pregnant, he was always there for me, my baby, and later the man I truly loved. I wish I could have repaired the hurt and ache in my father's heart. That loving heart failed him one day. He now rests beside my mother on the hill in the City Cemetery overlooking homes, Safeway, and the Carquinez Straits.

Thank you for allowing me to share these memories.

Sincerely
(Unsigned)

Letter 4

A Last Baseball Game

Mr. Garrett,

So many memories came to mind as I read your advertisement. Some were funny, some sad, and some brought questions to my mind.

When I grew up in Benicia, kids didn't have the ease of transportation that they do now. As I drive by the high school, when school is in session, it almost amazes me to see the number of cars in the lots. When I attended BHS, at the old site where City Hall and the Police station are located now, there might not have been that many cars in the entire town.

There may have been an equal number of cars or more for workers at the Arsenal, but most of them came and left with the timing of the work day. The first traffic signal lights in town were at the intersection of East Fifth and East "M" Streets. East "M" is called Military East now. When the Arsenal closed, the traffic signal lights were removed. A number of years later another light was put up at that spot.

My mother and I would drive to downtown Vallejo to shop about once a week. It was a looked for excursion for both of us. Compared to Benicia, Vallejo was like the big city in those days. A lot has changed in both cities over the years.

Sometimes my girlfriends and I would ride the Benicia-Vallejo Stage Line bus to Vallejo for a group outing. We would meet at one of our homes and walk together to the depot. There is a physical fitness center there now.

Once in awhile in my senior year, as a special treat, my father would let me drive to Vallejo with my best friend, Beth. I think part of his reasoning was to let me grow more.

On one of those rides, during the spring semester, we stopped for lunch at the "Eat and Run". It is a fast food restaurant of another type now. It is located at an angle across from the old Ford outlet. There were two boys in another car there at the same time and we started talking. One of them, David, lived in Benicia and Beth and I knew him. In those days every teenager in town knew every other teenager in town.

David and his friend attended St. Vincent's High School in Vallejo and were thus Hilltoppers to us being Panthers. That was long before St. Patrick's/St. Vincent's was founded. B.H.S. and St. Vincent's were long-time rivals. It wasn't like today. Both schools were about the same size and played each other yearly in all the sports the schools had. David was a good athlete and played football, basketball, and baseball for his school. His living in Benicia helped the rivalry in a friendly way.

Also, at times a Benicia boy would invite a St. Vincent's girl to a dance at his school, and at times a St. Vincent's boy would invite a Benicia girl to a St. Vincent's dance. That helped the rivalry, too.

My boyfriend at the time, Bill, played football, basketball, and baseball for B.H.S., but he and David were friends. Bill had graduated from Benicia Grammar School, and David and I had graduated from St. Catherine's Academy. St. Catherine's was located where Safeway now stands. The dormitory, where students from out of town stayed, is now the Youth Center. I can easily remember it being moved down the street to its present site.

During the summer, starting after the sixth grade, David and Bill played on the same baseball team. Before that they would play pick-up games after school and on weekends. The town didn't have Little League baseball in those days. That program started in town the year after they were too old to play at that level.

Being in a small town Bill heard about Beth and me talking at the "Eat and Run" with David and his friend. He was angry about it in a young man kind of way. His actions were cute to me, and I appreciated his concern. I was his girl, and he felt he had to defend me, though the time with David was innocent.

The Benicia and St. Vincent's baseball teams were scheduled to play the second game of their home and home series the next Friday at Benicia.

When David and Bill played baseball during the summer, one would pitch a game while the other caught. The next game their roles would be reversed. If the pitcher needed to be relieved, the pitcher and catcher switched positions. In high school, when one wasn't pitching, he was catching.

It was so funny watching them play that particular Friday. They looked like they were so angry with each other. What made it even more humorous was the fact they lived about a block apart and had played together from the sand box in kindergarten through that day except for high school sports. That they were now high school rivals and that one felt infringed upon and the other felt he had to give a bold front was funny. Perhaps it was one of those scenes someone would have to see and know the background of to appreciate the humor. It made me happy, and it also embarrassed me, when our friends in the stands teased me about how two boys were obviously fighting for my affections.

In that last high school game against each other, each was the pitcher for their team. Every time the other one would come to bat they would glare at each other. The catchers for each team knew what was going on and did their best to make clever remarks to David and Bill when they came to bat. It just made David and Bill angrier, as the catchers intended. David and Bill later told me there was nothing really mean or offensive said.

The game was won by Benicia. I don't remember the score. Knowing David and Bill as I do they could probably give a pitch by pitch account of the game. Both of them played well. Each hit the ball, and each struck some batters out.

After the game each team went their separate way. There was no after the game lineup in those days, as there is now where the players on each team pass each other in congratulations. Teams just picked up their equipment and left.

The visitor's dugout was on the first base side of the field. David was the last St. Vincent's player sitting in the dugout. Maybe he was waiting for Bill, or maybe he was realizing he had just passed the last time he would play a high school game on that field.

Since he lived in Benicia, there was no need for him to get back to Vallejo like the rest of his team. As he sat changing from his spikes to tennis shoes, Bill walked towards the dugout and stopped at the opening. Beth and I saw him walking towards the dugout and came out of the stands.

When we got to the dugout, David and Bill were smiling and joking as usual. We stretched a half-an-hour walk to an hour, which took us all to our homes. We walked Beth to her home and then the rest of us left and continued to walk together. I was flanked by the best boys I knew, as they walked me to my home. When Bill and David dropped me off at my home, Bill gave me a quick kiss and turned to leave. As he turned, I saw David looking at me.

Beth, Bill, David, and I have remained friends through the years. David and Bill are the best of male friends. Beth and I are the best of female friends. Beth married Bill. David is my love. I married him.

Thanks for sparking the memories.

Sincerely,
A.

Letter 5

My Love Handed Me His Glasses

Mr. Garrett,

My daughter is writing this for me as I tell her the story. Arthritis makes it hard for me to write anymore. I don't think she has ever heard this story before.

My love once handed me his glasses.

He was standing by the driver's side door of the car with our eldest son. We were stopped at a small roadside rest stop coming back to Benicia after buying fruit on a Sunday ride near Dixon.

The car was a black 1939 four-door Chevrolet. The window in front of where I sat had been cracked years before when a deer jumped from the side of the road. Our eldest had been sitting in the seat at the time. When my husband hit the brakes, the head of our eldest cracked the window. I have often joked with him about his hard head. I tell him he got it from his father's stubbornness.

Shortly after we had stopped, there was an argument between my husband and some other men who then stood nearby. It was right after that when my husband reached through the window opening in the door and handed me his glasses. I sat in the passenger's seat and held our youngest. She is the one writing this now. She looks surprised, so I'm sure she was too young to remember and has never heard the story. Our two other children sat in the back seat. One was our eldest and the other was our older daughter.

My husband stood six feet tall and weighed 165 pounds most of his life. As he's grown older his body has stooped some and he's lost weight. He's always been strong. He has the long fingers of a piano player, but he never played that instrument. He played the banjo, the violin, the mandolin, and the harmonica, which he learned to do in his youth on a farm in the Midwest. Time has caught up with his music playing days, but he still makes music in my heart. His eyes hold the same twinkle they held when we met picking fruit in the San Joaquin Valley.

At the time by the car our eldest son was just back from the war. He has always been a boy and then a man who supported and defended his family. He showed those feelings a number of times in his life, so what he did wasn't a surprise.

After my husband handed me his glasses, I remember him turning and then I only saw his back and the back of our son, as they stood side-by-side. Our son had watched the argument. When he saw his father returning to the car, followed by the other men, he got out of the car and stood next to his father.

When the other men got near my husband and our son, they loudly said some very mean words. The fight was on. My husband has always been a very self-reliant man. He didn't ask for the help from our son. Our son simply gave it as he knew his father would for him. A few minutes later my husband and our son got back in the car and my husband asked me to hand him his glasses.

When I asked what had caused the fight my husband just said, "Men stuff, it's over now."

Then he turned and said, "You did good, son."

Our son said, "Thanks, Pop, so did you."

Then we drove away. No one ever spoke of the incident again.

My love and I have been together for almost 50 years. He's always been my knight in shining armor. He's always been my love. Our daughter-in-law has the same type of knight in our son, and holds the same type of love.

Respectfully,
Mrs. "Smith"

Letter 6

I Miss My Sister

Mr. Garrett,

My sister died of breast cancer. I miss her. When we were teenagers some people said she was the better looking of the two of us, but that I was the smarter. They were wrong. She was the better looking and the smarter.

We used to trade clothes when we were teenagers. We thought that was great fun. We would sit on the bed in one of our bedrooms and talk of boys long after we should have been sleeping, but it was enjoyable. We were each so happy to run and tell the other when a boy called one of us on the only telephone in the house. We weren't jealous of each other like some teenage sisters are.

Looking at that last paragraph I can see there are far too many uses of "We" to go unnoticed by Mrs. Chorley. If I had turned the paragraph in as part of a writing assignment in her English class I don't think I would have gotten an A grade on it. It doesn't change the fact my sister and I truly were more "We" than we were "she and I".

When we each married, we wound up living about two blocks apart. For a time her death almost destroyed my brother-in-law. I pray for both of them, but I know the ache will always be in him. They fell in love in high school. He was the boy, who telephoned the most often, and with whom she talked the longest.

I miss her. I will always love her.

Mary

Letter 7

Chocolate Covered Cherries for Christmas

Mr. Garrett,

There was a young man I loved as a son, though he wasn't mine. He is a middle-aged man now. He came from a family that was on hard times, because of the father's addiction. His mother had all she could do to take care of the family as best she could.

A couple times a month, for close to three years, he came over to our house to visit. Some of those times I think he just wanted to escape to a calmer place for a few hours. I think he came over some of those times, because he was hungry and he knew we would feed him and not ask questions. He was a really good kid.

Every Christmas for a number of years he would stop by on Christmas Eve with an unwrapped box of chocolate covered cherries. I'm sure he had taken what money he could get each year to buy us the present. He always helped us eat the contents of the box, and I'm glad he picked what was obviously a favorite of his.

After he graduated from high school, he kind of disappeared. We got a couple of letters a year. The letters told of his progress. He had found something he wanted to do and followed his need, and desire, to do it.

He has been very successful in his career. He's made a ton of money, has a nice family, and is respected. I'm very happy for him. He was always a good kid. He tried.

J.

Letter 8

Youth and The Navy's Call

Sir,

I was career military and served our country in the Navy for 32 years. As my expertise grew from my training and experience, I was qualified to be stationed any place the Navy chose and perform on surface vessels or at shore installations. A short period of time served was on one of the last diesel submarines in commission in the Navy, but that was only for training purposes. Through the time of my service I was stationed at many places on the planet.

As time passed I became less "hands on" and more administrator as happens, if you stay in the military long enough. I came to really miss the "hands on" time, but we all grow older and our bodies tell us much of what we can and can't do. I retired as a Master Chief Petty Officer, Gunner's Mate Gunnery (GMG) and was the Command Chief at my last duty station.

My family wasn't the closest of families. My father came to Benicia by train as a child with his family. He met my mother in Vallejo. First Street was only paved as far as "H" Street at that time. Men still hunted deer a little way past where Military West is now. The Military East section of that road was built because of the Arsenal and is probably the best built road in town. It had to be for all of the military vehicles which used it decades ago.

In all the time I served in the Navy I never forgot about Benicia and many of the people I knew there. I graduated from Benicia High School in the early 1960's. I took my senior yearbook with me wherever I went. Mr. Simons was the yearbook advisor and one of my teachers. We didn't always understand each other, but he was a good man.

There were some other good teachers and good coaches there, too. My memory of the coaches is probably strongest.

When I was a senior playing football, Coach Goettel said I would grow to weigh 190 pounds. With my job and the training over the years I weighed as much as 210 pounds in my early 20's but dropped a little over the years and have weighed 205 for the last 35-40 years.

"Old Barn", Coach Corrigan, left good memories to me. Sometimes, when he got a little angry at practice, his face would get very red.

Mr. Lorenz said college would be good for me. I hope he was right. I graduated from college through my time in the military, worked for the Federal Government, and then retired again. The most time I ever had at any one stop for my college education was one year in Maryland. Other than that it was correspondence courses and extension courses.

I still remember most of the people, especially the kids I grew with as they were, though all have long since changed, as have I. I accept that. I think I can say I loved most of them, and still do, as I think I can say I love Benicia. It is hard to use the word love, it is a hard word to understand, but I've always called Benicia home.

Five or six of the boys and girls who were my schoolmates wrote me for the first year or two. Then all but one got on with their lives and probably forgot about me.

The one who continued to write for a few years was the best looking girl in the town at that time. At least that was my opinion, and the opinion of most of the other boys. All we had ever done was grow-up together. She always had male admirers and developed from cute to gorgeous from kindergarten to her senior year. She just got better looking after that.

We had a couple good hours during our year-end eighth grade trip to Vichy Springs. She seemed to spend more time with me that day than anyone else. Maybe she was talking, and I wasn't listening.

Our freshman year some of the boys in the upper classes discovered they had a beauty in their midst. The girl was popular and went steady with four guys in her time in high school. There was nothing unusual about that then. Benicia girls were nice girls, but they were still girls like everywhere else. Hopefully that is still how things are.

I enjoyed being around her, but we never had a real date. Today it might be called hanging out. I don't know. I don't really understand some of the terms and language of these times. Something didn't seem right about asking her to go on a date. Maybe I knew it wouldn't work. The window of opportunity was there, but I didn't see it.

I never understood why she wrote for those first few years, but I was always glad she did. I would write back each time she wrote. Looking back there were times I could have written, but put it off.

She started to write less and less often, and it was obvious she had found someone with whom to share her life. More than one man in the Navy has said the old line of "If the Navy wanted you to have a wife, they would have issued you one".

During that time in my life I didn't spend much time in Benicia. I visited once after Recruit Training, but only a few other times through the early years of my career. It seemed I was always far away on a ship, at a distant shore station, or taking training. Twice I hopped flights on a stand-by basis and had a few hours in town. Another time I rode a bus all night from San Diego to San Francisco and then took the local from there to Vallejo and a cab from there to Benicia. There wasn't much time left to be in town that trip, but I needed to come back so it was worth what time I had.

Those times I did come home were times for special needs. Each of those times was to see the girl. I just wanted to see her and hear her voice. I guess it was like far separate maintenance doses to an alcoholic, or a young boy pulling from home like a yo-yo until the string finally breaks.

She lived with her parents then, and was attending Vallejo Junior College. I would visit for as long as I could, then walk to my parents' home. We spent most of the hours I was in Benicia together.

"Far away places with strange sounding names" kept calling to me. I sometimes wish I hadn't heard them, but what happens in life is what is supposed to happen.

For a few months after Recruit Training I attended two Navy schools for my initial skills training. After that I was assigned duty in Vietnam. It was a far different place on the planet than any other place I had seen up to that time. Since then I've seen some other places which were similar. I've also seen some which were far better, so things even out in the long run, if your run is long enough.

When I re-enlisted, after my first hitch, it helped cut some ties with Benicia. At that time there wasn't much of a future in Benicia for a kid like me. There was no way I was headed for college at that time. I think my re-enlistment made the girl finally decide I was a lost cause, as far as marriage went. It was my error.

She married a scholar she met at San Francisco State. I think it was a good decision for her. It may be foolish, but I still keep the framed photograph of herself she gave me.

I've subscribed to the local Benicia paper for over 40 years. I've read that paper in many far places. One day I read of her wedding.

The newspapers and the yearbook more and more became my only ties to Benicia. I saw names in the paper of kids and then young adults and wondered if they were the children of kids with whom I had grown up and gone to school. I read of births and deaths. I read it all and absorbed it all as best I could, even the advertisements. It was the vestige of an umbilical cord to my youth, and what my future could have held.

I came back to Benicia to visit because of your

advertisement. I stayed at the motel on East Second Street. Some things have changed greatly, yet in some ways not at all, like anyplace else.

Sanborn Field is gone. The post office sits on the site. The girl was a cheerleader in high school and cheered on the local heroes many times at that field. At times I was lucky enough that she cheered for me. Young girls cheer for young boys at another field now.

The weather seems the same for this time of year. Mother Nature rolls right along. People are still basically friendly, even to a stranger.

Some of us boys used to sit on the corner by the Black and White Liquor store and watch the girls drive by. There is a print shop there now. The Chinese restaurant burned down, and there is a hardware store there now. The pool hall, which was across the street, is probably not even a memory to most people in town now.

Kids can't take their dates to the Victory and State Theaters. The Victory site has changed uses over the years. The State has been renamed the Majestic, but movies aren't shown there anymore.

There are so many more houses in town. Places we played as kids have been obliterated. Things happen when the population grows from 6,000 to 30,000, but along the way some good things are lost.

Guys don't polish their cars inside the old sheet metal building at the end of the spit off First Street. The area looks better now, though.

Some young people still meet at the swimming pool, but it isn't a center point for the older high school kids like it once was. That Olympic size pool is located where we used to have physical education classes sometimes and practiced track.

Facilities at the schools are so much better than they were once. Aside from Sanborn our only other playing field, the baseball diamond down town, was dirt.

Someone wrote that the only thing we know for sure is there will be change. Aside from personal belief in religion,

and some people, I think the author might be correct. Time moves on. I remember many things about the town and its people. Most of all I still remember the girl.
Respectfully,
GMG, Retired

Letter 9

She Was Walking With Another Guy

Mr. Garrett,

Liz, my wife, and I got married because I saw her walking down the street with another guy. OK, that wasn't the reason, but that was the point that made a change in my life.

I saw them walking down the street by the fire station as I drove by. He was walking her home from school. We each waved. His wave was given like a social obligation. There was no friendliness in it. Liz's wave came with a quick smile. It was a smile I remembered, and missed. She and I had dated for awhile and then broken up. I thought: "Look what I'm missing. This is going to end." I called her that night. We started dating again.

She's kept me on the straight and narrow path since then. The best day of my life was when Liz stood by my side in St. Dominic's Church and became my bride.

In all honesty, ninety-nine percent of the time, whatever she wants in anything is fine with me. I enjoy being with her and seeing her happy. When I tell people about how "whipped" I am, I laugh, but I love it.

We had three kids who went through the public school system in town and are off on their own now. The "empty nest" is quieter now, but not empty. We have our memories and our photo albums. We wouldn't have any of it if it wasn't for her smile and the love she brought with it. She gave that love for a

lifetime to a young guy. That young guy is older now, but still holds her hand as he did then.
Yours,
Hank

Letter 10

Jon and I Are Lovers

Mr. Garrett,

I'm glad I saw your advertisement. When I read your words about not caring what form the love took, it touched my heart.

Jon and I met at Benicia High School. My name is Ron. Jon and I are lovers. We've been lovers since we met. A few months ago we were married. Thank you so much, Mayor Newsome.

I think some of the teachers guessed about Jon and me. Two of the "jock" coaches were mean in what they thought was their sly contempt.

It was funny at times the way some people at school acted. There were two teachers who were gay and two who were lesbians, to anyone who understood people. One of the gays and one of the lesbians were coaches.

The gay acted so straight, but some of the things he said and did were revealing. The woman would joke with the guy teachers, but she wasn't flirting. They later openly showed their preferences, but it wasn't in Benicia. It is hard to say you are straight, when you've been seen at certain venues. Trust me on that.

Some kids joked concerning two teachers being gay, but they weren't. They were just towards the feminine side. They were always sweet men.

There were teachers, who were so ignorant about

differences in people, it was sad to watch. It took a lot of effort to get through their classes. The majority of teachers just went with the flow. A few teachers understood. They were the most human in the larger meaning of that word.

Being gay doesn't mean you don't love sports or aren't good at them like some guys said. Some of them on the football teams for four years would be surprised to know they had at least two gays on their teams. There were times after practice when Jon and I laughed as we talked about how a gay knocked some prejudiced ass on his "ass".

I feel sorry for those prejudiced people I knew in high school, those who were my classmates and those who were my teachers. There will always be some like them I guess. No one has to agree with anyone else about anything, including lifestyle, but everyone should try to work at understanding difference.

Jon and I have lived in San Francisco for years. Even in these "enlightened years" we are safer living here. I think people generally seek to live in an area where they feel most accepted, if they can.

We have a small business, but it is steadily growing over the years. We come to Benicia now and then and never miss the Peddlars' Faire. There are still a few familiar faces to see, stories to share, and questions to ask about those others we remember.

I took you for your word. I hope you print this letter.

In care,
Ron

Letter 11

Flashing Brake Lights

Mr. Garrett,

Great advertisement in the paper!

You might not print this letter in your book, but I thought I would send it in anyway.

The woman I love and I had our first kiss on the hill where Francisca Court is now. We had gone there to watch the submarine races in Carquinez Straits. It was towards the end of our first date.

The area where we parked had been the site of government housing. The houses were all gone, but the road which circled the little area was still there. It's gone now too, with the new construction being added to the hill. Grass and anise weed had grown up a lot around the area and there were still a few trees.

The car of one of our classmates was parked down the road from us. My date and I guessed who he was with. Later conversation between me and the other guy proved we had been correct.

The flashing brake lights on the other guy's car were annoying my date. There was no way I was going to let those lights keep flashing. I wanted all her attention. I got lucky up on that hill a couple times with other girls, and you can never tell what can happen.

I walked down the hill to the other car. When I started to knock on the driver's window I saw two butt cheeks that looked like white melons moving up and down. I didn't knock, but went back to my car. I thought it would be best if I didn't disturb the occupants of the other car.

I walked back to my car and told my date what was going on and we both laughed.

My date told me she wouldn't have anything to do with that type of activity that night. I love her more because of that.

Good memory! If I sign this my wife will kill me!
(Unsigned)

Letter 12

The Last Bus Trip to San Francisco

Dear Mr. Garrett,

How sweet! Your advertisement was like a light shining on memories and a wind blowing dust from paths!

My mother took her three daughters to San Francisco one day. It was the only time we all went as a group, and the only time she did as she did.

That trip she took all of us to see where she had grown up as a young girl in the avenues west of where Geary Boulevard crosses Park Presidio.

Through the years she would take one or two of us a couple of times a year, but that trip was the only time she took all of us. It was the last trip any of us took to The City with her. I think she was trying to tell us some things and pass on more of her heritage to us. We were all teenagers at the time and perhaps she thought we would all be married and gone soon and would not know as much about her as she wished us to know.

We took the bus from Benicia to Vallejo and another bus from there to The City. We rode a bus out to the avenues. When we stopped, she led us down a street and pointed out who had once lived in almost every house on the block. She described each member of each family as if she was turning the pages in a book. In her mind she was.

We took another bus downtown and had lunch at the

counter of a large department store on Market Street. I can hear my mother's sigh when she said it was time for us to go back to the bus station for the ride home.

We returned to Benicia from the trip to San Francisco with an even greater love for our mother than we had before. I think my father knew and understood the reason and meaning of the trips to The City with our mother, and especially that last one. He met us at the bus depot in town and we all walked the few blocks to our home. It truly was a home. I hope the people, who reside there now, also have it as a home.

One-by-one the number of the older generation has passed on until I am the only one left. At each yearly gathering of the clan we all talk of that trip. The younger members of the family mainly talk of news of the day, and their children play as children have always played.

When any at the gatherings ask about my mother, their grandmother and great-grandmother, it is easy to remember the love we all shared growing up in Benicia. Part of that love she gave us was taking her three daughters on the trip to San Francisco to tell of her youth. I have tried to pass on her love of us and her childhood to the next two generations by telling of my youth in Benicia. From the seed, the acorn, the seed, ad infinitum.

Respectfully,
Opal

Letter 13

J. J. Lucky

Mr. Garrett,

After my wife died, I married the woman who looked out for me for the last few years.

All three of us worked in the Arsenal starting out of high school in the late 1950's. Joan had been my first love and wife, and Jane became the second.

There was a big government housing project called Woodbridge Circle off of East Fifth Street in those days. That's where we all lived. We went to and from work together. I lived farthest up the hill. Next down the hill came Joan and then Jane. I would pick them up in that order each morning and drop them off in reverse order.

We would often be found together after work and on weekends as a trio or with other friends. We went bowling and when I played on one of the Arsenal or city ball teams they would be at the games. We went fishing together. When Pete moved to town and started working at the Arsenal, we all seemed to get along so well together. They were friends to each other and they were my friends.

One Thursday after I stopped to drop Joan off after work we sat and talked for a longer time than usual. I asked her if she would like to go to a movie the next night. She said she would love to go with me and had been waiting since high school for me to ask her out. She reached over and squeezed my hand before she got out of the car. For the first time in all the times I had driven her home I got out and walked her to her door. She had suddenly stopped being just a friend.

Every time after that when I brought her home I always walked her to her door. That Thursday she said "Thank you" before entering her home. Friday night she said "Thank you" and kissed me. She kissed me every night after that whether after work or any other time I walked her to her door. A few months later we kissed, as I opened the door to our home for her, and carried her over the threshold.

Joan, Jane, Pete and I remained friends. When Pete got ill, Joan and I would often go to their home to see if there was anything we could do for either of our friends. Pete passed after a short time.

When Joan got ill, Jane would often come by the house to see if there was anything she could do for her friends. Joan lingered for almost three months before passing.

Jane knows I'll always love Joan in a way I can never love her. She loves me just the same. We are more than simply companions fading into the twilight. What a lucky, lucky man I have been to have two women, who have loved me, and to have had two women to love in return.

Signed,
J-J Lucky

Letter 14

Distant Friendship

Dear Mr. Garrett,

I very much enjoyed your advertisement.

Sometimes loves are as strong as loves can be, but are fulfilled in different ways than might be usually thought. The love in a good marriage is a good love, and I love the man I married and have no regrets.

There was another young man than the one I married, whom I knew would always be there for me in anything I needed.

I think he knew I loved him, but he was married before I was married. He never made a move towards me other than to be a caring gentleman. I never made an outward show of my love for him.

He was in Benicia for almost two years, and then life took him and his lovely wife elsewhere. He sends me Christmas cards from Northern California year after year. Each year with the card he sends a photo of his family. I've saved all of the cards and photos. There are seventeen cards and photos now.

I've seen his family grow from just he and his wife to group photos of children growing and adults aging. Other than those from my children, the contents of the envelopes he sends each December are the most welcome holders of love I receive in the mail at that time each year.

It may sound strange, but we haven't seen each other since

he and his wife moved. Still, a connection is maintained. I know I could call on him at any time for any help I might need, and be sure he would do his best to help.

I will always love that man in a way only he and I can know. I live without him in my daily life, but feel love from within him.

Thank you,
Ada

Letter 15

High School Misconceptions

Mr. Garrett,

At Benicia High School I was called a lesbian. I wasn't then and am not now.

I loved sports. In that aspect, when I was a child, I sometimes wished I had been born a boy.

I played volleyball, basketball, and ran track. It was in track my freshman year I met a special boy. I had seen him at some of my volleyball matches and basketball games, when we were freshmen. He seemed to always be at the volleyball matches and basketball games when we were sophomores and juniors. The more I saw him, the more it seemed he was always looking at me whenever I was looking at him.

Along the way we became friends and were just friends until our junior year in track. Something came together then which I came to realize had been building step-by-step since we were freshmen. We started spending time together then, and by the time we graduated we were a couple.

He and I are both seniors in college now, but not at the same schools.

A week ago he drove to my college and proposed to me. I accepted. So much for the concept of high school stereotypes holding true. We'll be married in June following our graduations. Then we will join the Peace Corps.

Some of those people at Benicia High School were so

hurtful, and some were plainly ignorant. I feel sorry for them and hope they will develop a broader perspective.

The majority of those at the school were good, bright, friendly people. My thoughts are strongest with them.

Thank you for letting me share with you these thoughts on love and understanding.

Be well,
He and Me

Letter 16

Put Beans on the Table

Mr. Garrett,

My husband Amos is a stubborn man, but I love him so much. His stubbornness is part of his charm. If he said he would or wouldn't do something, anyone would be hard pressed to change his mind, including me.

In our younger married years he would come home and tell me he had just told the boss off and we were moving someplace else. He is a highly skilled craftsman and could find work almost anywhere. Where there was no call for his skill at the time he was usually able to find some other type of work. The man can repair, fix, or build anything. All you have to do is tell him what you want done and leave him alone.

He is semi-retired now, though he still does some projects. His joy in doing them now is in knowing that he doesn't have to do them to "put beans on the table" as he often has said through the years. It is his belief that a man's duty is to take care of his family, "put beans on the table". My husband has always done that for his family.

Some people might say that "putting beans on the table" is only being a provider, and has little or nothing to do with love. I believe they are so wrong. If the man didn't love his family, he wouldn't get up in the dark of morning and return in the dark of night for years to insure his family had what it needed and much of what it wanted.

I hope others stop to think of what it costs the man, or the woman for that matter, who is the provider for the family. They could choose the easy way out. The results of that attitude are seen around us each day and depicted on television and the movies.

I think much of my husband's stubbornness is actually determination. He has told each of our children "What's yours is yours, and what's mine is yours". He is a man of his word.

Thankful,
Sarah

Letter 17

The One Who Got Away

Mr. Garrett,

My love is "the one who got away". He was my high school love, but I didn't know it. He became the love of another. I still sometimes see him around town, or at the movies in Vallejo, or shopping with his wife. They are always at the yearly Peddlars' Faire. I make it a point to look for him without seeming to look for anyone. Sometimes I've seen him alone and we shared a few moments in talk, which meant nothing, but which was filled with understanding.

My head was too far past what I thought he offered to get as close to him as I should have when we were younger. That is my life's one regret.

When we grew up, he lived on the west side of town and I lived on the east. In grammar school he would ride his bike around the block where our house stood. One day my mother made a point of watching for him after he had ridden by for what seemed to me like the millionth time. She invited him in to have cookies and talk. She liked him. I think her life experiences allowed her to see things then I didn't see until later. When I saw them, it was too late.

In high school, if there wasn't assigned seating, he would usually be seated by me in any class we shared. So many times, when he appeared in the hall or in the quad, I was also there. I was so foolish to not see it. Other boys were around, and I missed the best.

That went on for four years. I thought we were just friends. I saw later it was more than that to him. Later still I understood it should have been more than that to me. I was simply stupid. He kept being persistent in a shy, bashful way, but he was so strong. I didn't see as deeply then as I should have.

We went on two dates in high school, but they were just double-date, hand-holding times. After he walked me to the door at the end of our first double date, I kissed him on the cheek and said, "Thanks, I had a good time. Goodnight." The second time I teased him with a quick squeeze and kiss on the lips and then pulled away and went inside. I was so stupid.

The moment of our times together that I remember most was during a summer day our senior year. We had some redwood water towers in Benicia in those days. One was near my home. He "just happened to be around" and asked if I wanted to go for a walk up to the tower and see the sights. It was a nice spring day, and I wasn't doing anything else, so I thought it would be a good idea.

When we got to the top of the hill, we looked up at the tower and that was when I learned to never dare him in anything. I dared him to climb the tower. He looked at me for the longest second of my life and said, "OK". Then he started to climb.

The first part of the climb was actually the hardest. The tower wasn't designed as a pedestrian's path to the sky. When he got to the walkway around the base of the tank of the tower, he looked down at me and told me the view was great.

Then he looked straight at me and called out, "I love you." That was all he said. It was as if he was calling on the world to know how he felt. He kept looking down at me for a few moments and then started back down the tower. I watched him all the way and said nothing.

When he got next to me he said, "You can see a lot from up there." He was deeper mentally and emotionally than I was at that moment.

He walked me home and then walked away. I think he kept

waiting for me to say something he very much wanted to hear, but I didn't.

After high school he joined the military. He went to Vietnam three times, three times! He wrote me, but I didn't write back. I meant to, but I was busy. No, I was stupid. He didn't write again.

He never called on me again after high school. As often happens, you can read it in books and see it in movies, at times an understanding comes to people and they move on. He got married.

He's well known in town, in a quiet sort of way. He's like a rock in his living of life, as he sees it should be lived. I envy him. Others make adjustments in life just to get along, he doesn't do that. He has grown to be such a good looking man. He was always good looking, but some of the boys of the youth of all of us never got better in looks, he did.

Once some of my colleagues and I went to lunch in a restaurant in town, as we often do, and he and his wife were sitting at a table we passed. I stopped and talked for a few minutes. I turned to his wife, who is a wonderful woman, and said, "If you two ever get divorced, he's mine." She laughed, I didn't. I told them I would see them later and went to join my colleagues.

I've never married. It seemed pointless. I'm very successful in business, many people know me, and I'm active and popular without writing that egotistically. It is simple fact. There is emptiness within me though. I think it is the emptiness of, "What if?"

I was so, so stupid. And, people have told me how smart I've been in life. They just don't know.

I can't sign my name. Thanks for the "venting time".
(Unsigned)

Letter 18

Grace is Happier

Mr. Garrett,

In your advertisement requesting stories of love that in any way dealt with Benicia you wrote it didn't matter what type or form the love took. You gave some headings you would like. One was interracial love.

I grew up in Benicia. When I was in the service I was stationed for a time in the Philippine Islands. In that time I met and fell in love with Grace.

At the time and place we couldn't get married. The commanding officer wouldn't give his permission. He said some things with which I didn't agree, but I had to take it. One of the things he said was I was too young and that I might just be lonely. He said I should wait until I got out of the service. Then if I still wanted to marry Grace, the military wouldn't be involved.

Grace and I kept our correspondence to each other going while we both worked on getting her to the United States. It took some doing, but Grace and I finally got married. In fact we got married twice. The first time we exchanged vows was in a Catholic church in Manila. The second time was in Benicia.

We made our first home in Benicia. It is where I had always wanted to live. I had told Grace so much about it that she wanted to live in Benicia too.

Most of the people in town seemed to accept our marriage. Some didn't. Grace felt more uncomfortable as that first year of our married life was coming to a close. She wanted to move from Benicia to Vallejo. She has family there.

We moved to Vallejo, and I think Grace is happier. I am happier because she is happier.

Maybe we lived in the wrong neighborhood in Benicia for acceptance. Maybe we went to the wrong stores or gas stations. I don't know.

I still love Benicia. I think Grace loves my love of it. We go over there occasionally. We would have liked to have made our home there.

John

Letter 19

Benicia Has Been Our Home Forever

Mr. Garrett,

Ken, the love of my life, and I got married right out of high school. Some people said it wouldn't last, but we've hung in there pretty well. We celebrated our Fiftieth Wedding Anniversary last June.

There have been ups and downs. The first was when he got drafted. He was gone for a year. We had just gotten started on our life together and he was gone.

His being gone made each of us stronger in our love, and it made the love of our marriage stronger. There are two boxes full of letters and postcards from that year he was gone. One is full of words from me to him and one is full of words from him to me.

There is another box of letters and post cards from him. When he got out of the Army, he went to work for the federal government. The letters from him, which are in the second box, were sent from the various places the government sent him over the years. Counting his time in the Army he worked for over 30 years for the United States government.

We started out renting a small place in Benicia out by the Arsenal. Then we were able to build our one and only home on one of the many open lots in Benicia at that time.

There were times when Ken had to be stationed at a facility too far away from Benicia for him to commute. During some of those periods I was able to go with him. We kept our home in Benicia. There were good neighbors all around us. They knew the situation and were volunteer caretakers for our home in the times we were gone. I think it was a much different time then. People generally looked out for one another then. You knew your neighbors and they knew you.

When I started having children, I had to stay in Benicia regardless of where Ken was assigned. The children were teenagers when Ken was sent to the Midwest for a year. We were able to spend most of that summer back there with him. To tell the truth I was never so appreciative of the cool breezes and summer fog of Benicia as I was at that time.

Our Fiftieth Anniversary celebration was such a joy. Everything was taken care of by our children and friends. One of our children manages a select hotel in Monterey. It was felt by all of our children to be the best site for the celebration. The location would be the most convenient for almost everyone. I so regret that some could not make the trip.

A very nice suite with a balcony and ocean view was reserved for us for three days. All of the nearby rooms were occupied by our children, other family members, and friends. Many of them were able to stay the three days.

Our son drove us on a tour of parts of that beautiful city of Monterey and the coastline. He drove us in a restored model of the same type car which Ken and I had been loaned for our honeymoon trip to the mountains. That was so thoughtful of him.

When we returned from the tour, we dressed for the evening and took the elevator down to the banquet room. When we walked in, the people were standing in a horseshoe formation which closed around us as the doors closed behind us. It was so nice.

There must have been over one hundred people in the banquet room. The faces we saw and the stories we told were like a history lesson of our lives. So much Benicia lore was revealed and legends explored.

Scenes and times forgotten by one or more in attendance

were remembered vividly by another or more. Those scenes and times sparked still other memories of other scenes and other times.

Benicia has been our home forever. When we depart the flesh, our souls will rest here overlooking the water we have seen for nearly every day of our lives. To others there are better places to live than Benicia, but not for us.

Sincerely,
Margaret

Letter 20

They Chose to Adopt Me

Mr. Garrett,

I'm writing of the love for a couple in Benicia. They opened their hearts to a baby, when they didn't have to do it. They chose to do it. They chose to adopt. They chose to adopt me.

Mary Jo chose to give birth to four children and she and Tony selected me. They gave me a good life growing up in Benicia. I'll love them forever and am so thankful.

I don't know all of the background of my biological parents. They never married. I was informed of where they each live and have been able to visit them. The visits were more out of business and curiosity than anything else. I wanted to know any medical information or family history I might need for myself or my children. There was no desire to reconnect in any other way with the two who brought me to life. The love I hold for them is in giving me life so I could be raised by Mary Jo and Tony. They are my real parents. They are Mom and Dad. Their children are my only brothers and sisters.

One night, when I was very young, my sisters and I were in the bedroom we shared. Today that room seems so small, but it was a lovely "girl" room when we grew up. I started crying and couldn't stop. Thoughts of guilt about what I must have done to cause me to be put up for adoption wouldn't leave my mind.

My sisters tried to console me, but it was no use. We all loved each other then and still do, but I needed Mom and Dad then.

It seemed as if they and my brothers magically appeared to join my sisters and me. I blubbered and sniffled and felt sorry for myself. My family embraced me and said words of such importance. They proved I was loved. I have been loved by them from the moment Mary Jo and Tony held me. Mom said they told my sisters and brothers, when they held me that first time, there was another love in the family. They meant it.

Sincerely,
Jan

Letter 21

For the Love of Benicia

Mr. Garrett,

I'm sitting here in Iraq. In the mail today I received the issue of the local newspaper, which includes your advertisement.

It may sound strange, but a lot of us are over here for the love we have for the people in Benicia, wherever our specific Benicia may be.

We have to keep our "heads on a swivel" over here, but there are some quiet times, like now, when I can sit and write. Often in these times the thoughts, which come to mind, are of Benicia. I remember the people.

For anyone who doubts, we truly are at war. Semantics are semantics, but bullets, bombs, and death are just as real no matter what the terminology from where they come.

In classes in high school we learned some about this part of the world, and we learned some about war. I don't think any of us ever thought then that war and this part of the world would come together in our lives, and that we would be a big part of it.

There is a certain feeling of individual and team pride in just being here doing what we are doing. I don't think anyone loves being here. I think they all believe in duty, honor, country. Part of that belief for me is to protect Benicia. I think I have to be here at this time to do it.

Some of those with whom I serve have chosen to make the Corps a career. I've chosen to give four years to our Corps and then become a teacher. If I can take some of my experiences back to a classroom for a few years, maybe I can do a little to help change the world for the better. Maybe then fewer people will see what some of us have seen.

I send my love to Benicia and thank all of you there.

Semper Fi
Matt USMC

Letter 22

I Love My Dog Duke

Mr. Garrett,

You mentioned love of an animal in your advertisement, so I was inspired to write.

I love my family. That being stated, I also love my dog, Duke. There is a lot in him of the image John Wayne projected in movies.

It may be anthropomorphic to some, but I think someone can love a dog. It isn't the same love one human can give another human, but it is love just the same.

My dog has been more loyal to me than most humans in my life, apart from my family. That loyalty is love.

He doesn't ask for much, but appreciates what he gets. He has care, food, water, and shelter and gives his love in return. He doesn't pay for what he receives by giving his love. His love is given in respect. He knows he is important to me and the others in his family.

If there is a sound in the night, he knows it before I do, and if he thinks it could be a problem, he lets me know.

If the doorbell rings, he sits by my side as I answer the door. If he knows and likes the person at the door, his tail is swishing across the carpet before the doorbell rings. If he senses something isn't right with the person coming to the door, he seems to grow a little bigger as if he's prepared to defend all of us and his home.

If I have to leave, he shows he missed me when I come back.

If I had a bad day, he wants me to feel better when I get home. He lets me know everything is OK.

It would be nice if more people had more of the qualities of dogs. We could use more courage, respect, care, and love in this world. My dog is a good example of qualities to emulate.

Fred

Letter 23

The Teacher Who Understood

Mr. Garrett,

I thanked a teacher, for being the person he was, for letting me be me.

When I got in his class, I had an attitude. I thought no one knew what I felt and that no one understood. I was proven wrong, because he knew, though he didn't say anything directly to me, and he understood.

One day we had a class discussion on love. He said he felt it didn't matter who someone loved, because everyone needs someone. He said as long as his children understood what repercussions can come in life, who they loved was their choice. There were some things he said he wouldn't allow in his home, but that once his children were 18 and out of high school and living on their own their decisions were their decisions. Something else he said, which sticks with me, is that his children would always have a safe place to sleep and food to eat if anything ever went wrong in their lives.

In that class I was able to speak my mind. He wouldn't let anyone laugh at anyone for what they said. They could laugh with, but not at.

He wanted us to think. He felt that was his purpose as a teacher, not to try to make us agree with him.

The first time someone saw my girlfriend and me kissing on campus people told him about it. In class that day the subject of showing affection on campus came up from one of the other students. I think the teacher knew it was coming and used it to teach.

I watched that teacher so closely when he talked about it. He told about the school policy, but he was honest. He said kissing has gone on at the school forever. He was honest. He said times have changed. He was honest. He said girls kissing girls was more acceptable to society than boys kissing boys. He was honest. I'll always love him for being honest, when so many others weren't.

In Honesty,
Lana

Letter 24

They Live Together But Live Apart

Mr. Garrett,

Long ago a man told me that sometimes a person can love someone, but not be able to live with them. He also said sometimes people love and live together, but live apart. I didn't understand then what he meant, later I did. My husband and I live together, but live apart.

Sometimes things happen to people, which they live to regret the remainder of their lives. In my case I fell in love with another man, but it was only for a short time. At the time I commuted from Benicia to where we worked together in San Francisco.

I thought the other man had facets my husband lacked and they drew me to him. I was wrong. My husband had all of the same facets and more. I didn't see at the time that he demonstrated them differently than the other man. He showed his love repeatedly, but I was blind to the depth of what he gave.

When my husband discovered I had been with the other man, he felt embarrassed and betrayed. He asked what he had done wrong. All I could answer was, "Nothing". His reply was, "Then why?" I had no answer to give other than I had been stupid.

My husband forgave me for my stupidity, but nothing else. I don't think it is in him to ever forgive me for my lack of trust.

I've begged, cried, screamed, and pleaded for him to forgive me, but he just looks at me with no emotion.

He trusts me with our finances. He trusts me in decisions with our children. He trusts me when I leave the house to go shopping. He trusts me when I'm late coming home from work. But, he doesn't trust me.

I love him and I know he loves me, but what we had is gone. I pray that love, time, and understanding will bring back what we have lost. I love him.
Laura

Letter 25

Ferry Boat Rides to Martinez

Mr. Garrett,

You wrote you wanted letters of any form of love connected with Benicia. I love many things about Benicia. One love I had is no longer possible. That love was ferry trips to Martinez with my friends when we were teenagers. The love of those ferry trips was because of the love of my friends.

The ferry slip was at the end of East Fifth Street. On some warm summer days we would ride our bikes there and wait to board. Sometimes the ferry was already in its slip and sometimes we got to watch it work its way back from its previous trip to Martinez.

When the cars had been driven on board, we would move our bikes to the railing near the bow of the double bowed ferry, which was pointed towards Martinez.

Sometimes we would go up to the passengers' area and put our nickels and dimes in a vending machine for a bar of candy.

The day could be warm, but once the ferry got underway any breeze there was increased. If there was no breeze, we got one. Getting that cool breeze on a warm summer day was one of the rationales for the trips but the real reason was the friendships.

When we got to Martinez, we rode our bikes to the downtown area and explored. Along the way we always stopped at a burger stand for refreshments.

It worked out that we were never late for the return trip. We got home in time for dinner after having a really nice day.

We also took the ferry with some of our parents to watch our boys' summer baseball team play games against a Martinez team. There was usually a chilly wind blowing when we came back from those trips.

Over one summer I warmed to one of those baseball players. He became my boyfriend and later my husband.

Fondly recalling,

S.

Letter 26

The Baby-sitter's Boyfriend

Mr. Garrett,

It may sound wrong, but it happened and everything turned out fine. One night when I was baby-sitting at a neighbor's home, my boyfriend came over. The rest, as they say, is history.

It wasn't accidental that he came by. We had originally planned to go to the movies in Vallejo at the El Rey Theater that night. The baby-sitting job was really a favor for a young couple, who had been nice to me. I asked them if it was OK if my boyfriend came over that night and they said it was. I think they understood, since they had only been married about two years.

My father didn't exactly like Nick, when he was my boyfriend, but he came to like him after he became my husband. Nick sort of grew on him. It wasn't the same with my mother. I think she was close to being a marriage arranger at times.

Mom and I could always talk, but I think Dad thought boys were boys and that what they wanted was girls. With some of my dates, he was right. He wasn't right about Nick.

Dad joked about being scared to death about having a daughter. I think his big dread was me coming home pregnant some night. Mom was more understanding. She told me to be careful and to not go any farther with anything than I wanted.

She said the right boy would understand.

Nick understood. That baby-sitting night was the only time we made love until our wedding night almost five years later. He said it took him a lot of cold showers, pushups, and long runs at night for him to wait, but he did.

We were both virgins before that night of baby-sitting. I think, for both of us, that night was the sealing of faith between us. I'm not saying that is how it is, or should be, between anyone else but that was how it was with us, and it worked.

Married and loving it,
Martha

Letter 27

Love knows No Boundaries for Age

Mr. Garrett,

It pleases me that you realize love knows no boundaries for age.

My wife is much younger than me. She's in her thirties, but still that is much younger than me. Some people might say I robbed the cradle or she was just a gold-digger in marrying me. I would disagree.

She has her interests and freedoms. Some of the things, which interest her, I can't do anymore, but I love watching her enjoy them. She has times away with her friends and that brings me joy.

She knows every investment I have and where all the money is. She is the only beneficiary in my will. If I didn't trust her, none of that could be. I love her.

I was straight with her from the start, and she said she appreciated it. When I told her I didn't want her to give up her friends and that it wouldn't be right of me to ask it, she seemed a little surprised at first. Love knows no boundaries. If she loved me, and I loved her, things would work out regardless of the age difference.

I enjoy her, and the way she sees things through eyes which don't yet wear glasses as mine now do. When that time comes for her, I don't think I'll be here.

She is much more mature for her age than many of her

friends. I think she must have always been so. That makes our marriage even easier, and better.

I make no demands on her and she makes none on me. We share and care.

The love of my life chose me. I asked and she accepted, but she chose me. I have been honored to have her choose to be in my life.

Chosen,
J. J.

Letter 28

Once There Was a Woman in Town

Mr. Garrett,

Nice advertisement. Once there was a woman in town with the looks of a goddess and the actions of a whore. Her payment wasn't in money or gifts. Her payment came by the hurt she hoped she gave her husband for hurting her. She wasn't a whore. She was a good woman, who was hurting.

The woman had a carriage to her that said, "I'm good looking, and I know it". She was the wife of a professional, who worked in town for a few years. He basically ignored her until he needed her to smile and hang on his arm at some function. He knew what was going on, though. Maybe he thought it would help his career.

She wanted to be only his, but he had another woman in town. She took it out on him by seeing the other guys. Her idiot husband had it coming. He didn't care about his wife.

That woman could turn a guy on by accident. When that was what she wanted to do, it was almost like the guy was drugged for the time she showed interest in him.

Those guys she was with may not have been loved in whole or in part by her. What they thought was love may have been just lust that's turned to a memory of love over time. I don't know about them. I do know there are those around town who remember her and the brightness she brought to their lives, even if it was for a short time.

A number of guys in Benicia thought they had each found love with her for awhile. Maybe they each did, but she left Benicia and isn't with any of them. She's with her husband for all I know.

I hope she's found happiness. I thought she was a good woman. I still do.

Ian

Letter 29

Love for Eternity

Mr. Garrett,

Thank you for your call for letters of love connected with Benicia.

There can be shared love between people. Two can love one, one can love two, and three can love each other. An example would be when one, who loved and was loved, dies and the survivor later falls in love with another. My question has long been, when those two pass, with whom does the survivor spend eternity?

I believe in one wife for life, one true love for Eternity. We may love more than one person in our lifetime but in a different manner than the love of our life and Eternity.

My brother and the two women he married each loved the other. I loved the three of them, each in my own way. After my brother's first lady died he married again. Each of his marriages was truly a marriage of love. Shortly after my brother's second lady passed, my brother did also.

I wonder which lady my brother is with now. I wonder what happened to the other lady. Did my brother become two in heaven so each lady could spend Eternity with him? I don't know, but I don't think I'm supposed to know.

I do know that I also loved one of the ladies with a love for Eternity. She was my brother's second wife. Had she become my wife she would have been my wife for Eternity. What is meant to be is meant to be. I know she loved me as a brother, as I loved my brother. She couldn't love me to be my love. That love was held for my brother.

If we meet in Eternity, would I have the chance to win the love of my life for all of Eternity? Who is with my brother? Is it my love?

Love never dies. It is rekindled in our hearts, minds, and eyes. I know my brother and the two ladies are happy. That's what matters.

A Brother

Letter 30

I Once Loved a Woman Who Was Older

Mr. Garrett,

I once loved a woman who was older than me. When I was almost nineteen she was twenty-seven. I'll always remember her fondly.

When the high school was located downtown, it was within easy walking distance from the homes of most of us. Some, who lived a little farther away, would walk to the house of one of their friends and they would walk to school together. If they played on the same teams, they usually walked home together. A few of the students had cars and would pick up their friends at their homes and go to school.

If you walked, you got to see the neighborhood and know it a lot better than if you drove. That was how I met the woman. She lived a couple blocks from my house and a couple more blocks from the friend with whom I usually walked to school.

One bright spring morning she was in her front yard. She said she had seen me walking by many times and thought she would say "Hello". Mom and Dad taught me to be polite. It didn't hurt that the woman, I was talking with, was so beautiful.

At first I was just a little nervous. Here was this good

looking "older woman" talking with me. She had a calming effect on me as if we had known each other for a long time. It was like we talked every morning.

Her husband traveled in his business for weeks at a time. During those times things happen around a house like they do any other time. She asked if I ever had time to do some odd jobs around her house. I said I would like doing them.

She asked how much I charged. I told her that, when I finished whatever job she wanted done, she could pay me what she thought it was worth. She laughed at that. She thought that attitude was very unusual and that she might cheat me. I told her I didn't think she would. She never did.

Going to and from school after that I always looked for her. If I didn't see her, I slowed my walk but not enough to make it obvious. Later I discovered she watched for me and my slowing down had been obvious.

One afternoon she was again standing in her front yard. She asked if I could help her with something and I agreed. It was just a five minute job. I think it was a test for her. It was the first time I was in her home.

As time went on, she introduced me to coffee, some great music, and to her.

She was the first "college girl" I had ever met, other than my female teachers.

We became very close. She was good to me and I think I was good to her. We needed each other at that time in our lives.

After high school I joined the military and wasn't around for much of the next four years. She wrote me a few letters and I wrote her back. She liked reading of where I moved around the planet and what I did.

I don't think what she and I had, when we became close, was wrong. Some others may disagree. People are people. It was only for a few short months, but each memory is clear.

It wasn't a fling for her with a younger guy because she was lonely. For me the first call was to my hormones, but that fell within moments of speaking with her the first time. I enjoyed being with her. It didn't matter if she handed me a nail when I repaired her step, we talked about which branch to prune, or when she held me in her bedroom. As happens with people, that time was only a chapter in our lives.

We see each other in passing now and then. We both have gray hair now. She lives with her husband and I live with my wife. She'll read this, remember, and know I did care for her. She cared for me.

Seth

Letter 31

Martin Kept Taking Me Back

Mr. Garrett,

Martin kept taking me back. He did it over and over. I love that man, but I just couldn't keep living with him. I hold his love as he holds mine, knowing the love will be permanent, but the togetherness will be apart. I've loved Martin more than I have loved any other man in my life.

For short periods we have lived in Benicia as man and wife. Then it would become time for me to leave again. There was always some kind of call for me to leave. Each time it was a tug-of-war at my emotions.

Martin could see the signs that our time for sharing each other in the same home was coming to an end. He would be rational and use logic, but he knew after I had left the first few times that it was no use.

He asked me to marry him so many times. He said being married would keep us together though we were apart. I couldn't do that with him or any other man. In my heart I know he didn't look on me as his property. He simply wanted stronger ties. He told me he knew I would leave again, if we were married, as well as if we weren't. Being married would make him feel better.

I know the man very well. Getting married wasn't something he wanted to do to keep people from talking about our arrangement. He didn't care what they thought or said.

In the early days of our arrangement he introduced me to his friends and others as his girlfriend. He later often referred to me as his lady. I was flattered and charmed by both titles.

During dinner at a restaurant in Benicia, he said he wanted to introduce me in the future as his wife. He had to have known the chances of that ever happening were far from coming true. I would live with him when I wished, and come to him if he ever needed me, but I wouldn't get married.

It would be easy to say I wish I wasn't as I am, but that would be a lie. I enjoy who I am. My professional life has given me freedom and financial success.

Three years ago I flew into San Francisco, rented a car and drove to Benicia. I was supposed to fly on to Seattle, but was pulled to see Martin.

I surprised him, but he accepted my arrival as if I hadn't been gone for a moment. It had been almost four months since we had seen each other. The house was just as I remembered. Everything was as if I had just stepped from the house, turned and reentered.

He knew that visit was going to be different. That evening he made dinner for us. We had a long talk while we sat watching the flames in the fireplace. There was no anger or animosity. He accepted better than most men I know would have accepted, but he is better than most men I've known. The next morning we kissed and I said goodbye to him.

Martin is there in Benicia waiting for me now, knowing I won't be back. If this is published in your book, he might read it. There are many women who must think I am stupid and self-centered. In the fact of what I could have with Martin, they are probably correct.

In time I may regret what I've given up. I don't know. I think it would be wrong to stay in the relationship Martin and I shared. It would be unfair for him. He wanted children. I love children, but I don't think I could give them all of what they might need. I think in time Martin will have children of his own, but it won't be with me.

If I was to have ever married, it would have been with Martin. He is the one by whom I judge all men. He is my love. He kept taking me back, but we are apart.
Paula

Letter 32

A Soldier Serves to Keep His Country Free

Sir,

My wife Barbara helps keep our lives together and connected to our home in Benicia with the many things she does. One of the things she does is e-mail clippings from the local newspapers, which she thinks might be of interest to me. That is how I found out about your advertisement. I think it's a great idea.

Many times when I look around over here, all I see is brown. It isn't the brown of the dry grasses of Benicia in the summer time. It is the brown of sandy dirt.

I see signs of violence. I see destruction. I see what hurt and death have done to children, adults, families, and communities.

"Over here" is Afghanistan. The things I see every day make me appreciate the United States and the specific part of my homeland, called Benicia, more.

From our home in Benicia Barbara and I can see the water and the hills across the Straits. The leaning tree standing all alone against the skyline is a favorite of ours. One day age, wind, weakened roots, and its eastward slant will cause it to fall. I pray that nature is the cause.

From where I'm sitting now, and with what is in my power if the need arose, I could destroy a tree like that in one flash.

At times the trains, going east and west along the shoreline beneath the hill where that tree grows, draw the attention of Barbara and me.

If I was sitting on my back deck, I could fire a weapon at any train passing by on that opposite shoreline and probably kill everyone aboard. If the train was an enemy means of transport and I was ordered to destroy it, I would. I'm good at my job. The government taught us well and we've gotten practice and experience.

The depth of different places and different times is amazing. I am so happy that Barbara and I have our home in Benicia. I'm so happy to be able to see the water, the hills, and the trees. Being here makes me appreciate more what we have. It gives me a better understanding of the lives some others are forced to live. Seeing what I've seen makes me understand why I and others are here. Maybe we can make things better for some others, keep things good for our families, and make things better overall in the world. That may sound like dreaming, but at least some people are willing to try.

I don't like being here, but be here I must. I remember a poster I saw in a classroom in high school. The words stick in my head: "If not you, who?" The teacher talked about each of us owing something to our country. He said the first thing we owe is to be a good citizen. After that, how we repay our debt to our country, and those who have come before us to make it what it is, depends on the interpretation each of us makes in life. He talked of "duty, honor, and country" as a calling of love. It was a calling of love for each other, our country, and Benicia. It was a love of the tree across the Straits on the hill. It was a calling of the hope that those on the trains arrive safely at their destinations.

I'm giving my country four years of my life. My job classification isn't applicable in the civilian world. What I'm learning is definitely applicable.

You can read about things like destruction and poverty in

books and see them in the movies, but you can't get the smell from them.

I don't want to see and smell in Benicia what I have here. If, in some way, that means I have to be here for this time in my life, then so be it.

I want Barbara to be safe. When I get back this time, we're going to start a family. I want my children to be safe. I want to sit on the back deck with all of them and look at the hills across the water in the cool of the evening.

Respectfully,
Craig

Letter 33

Pop Had a Doctorate in Life

Mr. Garrett,

I love my father. He was a strong man. He taught me to be polite and have good manners, and how to treat my lady. He taught me about tools, how to shoot a bow and a rifle, how to make a fire, how to drive a car, how to stand my ground when I was right, how to put up with pain and discomfort, and how to give my best in anything I do.

He was a quiet man but always got his point across. He never pushed any of his kids to do anything, but we all had expectations put on us.

If there was a question on a decision we should make, he explained things to us and pointed out all the options he could think of. For example, he said none of us had to help out in doing any of the household duties, but that if we didn't, we couldn't expect others to help us in what we wanted. He said the same thing applied in life outside the home.

There was no curfew, though he openly worried about his daughters as the clock ticked farther along on a Saturday night. If any of us got home late, we were expected to get up at a normal time the next morning. After that, when we had done anything which was needed, we could take a nap. He didn't care if the nap lasted until dinner time. Once or twice over the years we each took a nap, but like most young people recovery time was quick.

He understood more than his children thought. There were times when we told of a happening in our lives or how someone had treated us and his opening comment was often, "I know. Things like that happen". Or, "I know. There are people like that out there. You have to be aware of them, and work at understanding them, but not be upset for long about them, or be afraid of them." Then we would continue talking of what had happened. I think I can say that each of his children felt better after the talks, though we may not have always understood the message at the time.

Pop loved Mom and showed the love daily. It was cutely comical at times the way they treated each other. They had their own little routines and methods in so many little things. At the start of every meal they would touch their wedding ring against the other's wedding ring. Then they would toast each other by clinking their glasses together and saying, "Chin, chin."

The thumb on Pop's left hand had been injured years ago. It had gotten infected before it could be treated. The result was the top joint of the thumb made a 45 degree angle away from his hand. It never stopped him from having a master's two hands in whatever he did.

When he ate spicy foods, his head shone with drops of perspiration. That is one of the traits I inherited from him. I've been told I also inherited his stubbornness, but I'm too stubborn to admit that inheritance.

One time we walked out to Ninth Street and fished from the point. Our only catch from the water was a flounder. For hours we just sat and watched the water as we talked. When the sun was nearly level with the top of the Carquinez Bridge, he said it was time for us to "head for the barn" because my mother would be expecting us.

What my father, Pop, and I brought back from that time walking, talking, and fishing, wasn't just the flounder, it was a greater understanding. He told me more about himself, his history and feelings, his dreams as a youth, and his hopes for the future, than he had ever done with me before. I think he saw that time together as a rite of passage, father to son, though I don't think he knew the term "rite of passage". I think he simply saw the time as closeness with one of his sons, whom he was getting ready to release to the world.

I hope I've honored him with the life I've led. I've made mistakes, but he said people will make mistakes in life. He said when you make a mistake to ask for forgiveness from God, and He will listen and understand. He also said to ask for forgiveness, in any way you can, of those you may have hurt, even if you can only ask in your mind. He also said we need to forgive ourselves.

Pop never graduated from college, but he had a Doctorate in Life.

Yours,
Joe

Letter 34

Mom Was the Glue

Dear Sir,

My mother was a good woman. Her family was cared for, her home was loveably well kept, clothes were clean and neat and were sometimes patched or made by her, and along the way she loved her husband and children. That's a pretty good tally sheet for any mother.

Mom could "bake a cherry pie". She could feed any number of people---"Put more water in the soup" was her call to add more food to the meal for any unexpected guests who would appear. They could be family or neighbors, it didn't matter. No one at our home ever went hungry. Everything might not have been the tastiest all the time, but bellies were as full as their owners wanted them to be.

I didn't know what a pizza was until I was a senior at Benicia High School. Much of the food Mom prepared was based on what was available from the store or our garden and always with cost in mind. There were always potatoes and onions around. Steak was cheap in those days. When that was the meat for the meal, there would be a big black skillet full. Garden vegetables in a cream sauce were about a week to ten day staple. Winter meant an increase in root crops like parsnips, turnips, and celery root. I didn't care for some of those items then, but have found them to be tasty, as I got older and cooked more myself. There is a lot you can do with them.

All her inherent attributes became more developed because she married Dad. Mom and Dad loved each other and wanted to please each other, so they helped each other.

Mom and Dad were born before the turn of the 1900's. When they married, she became his partner in everything. That meant she cared for the home and the children wherever the home was located and however many children there were. It meant, if there was a project around the home, where he needed help, she was there. If it meant taking a hot meal to him at work, she did it. If his work kept him from home for a time and something needed a nail, she hammered it home.

Dad taught Mom to shoot, and she was good at it. She could "shoot the eye out of a gnat at one hundred yards". It surprised me the day I learned she could shoot. She brought that lever action rifle to her shoulder and popped away. I was impressed.

Mom was the glue. She bandaged Dad when he had gained an injury in his work. She consoled him when things looked a little bleak. She loved him all the time.

Along the way Mom raised four kids. If there was a function at the school of any of her kids, she was always there in support by her presence, by bringing a food dish, or by loaning something needed. And, she stood up for her kids when they were in the right.

I'm her son. As her son, I know her as my mother, always there even when I thought I didn't need her. As a man I look at the few pictures made of her in her younger years and see a beautiful woman. In her youth her long black hair was pictured held in a bunch which descended half way down her back. Her head was held modestly, but with the look of someone who knew more than she revealed.

On their wedding night Dad had to leave to go to work. Not much of a romantic time maybe, but their marriage lasted almost fifty years. Dad went on ahead of her to get a place settled for her and the family, as he had done a few times in their lives to follow his work.

At one time his work led him to be caretaker of a large

piece of property in Northern California. Part of the deal was that he be married. That was no problem. A little bit of a problem occurred when my older brother was set to arrive in this world. Mom had to take a train to a hospital in San Francisco to give birth to him. The minute she was able to leave the hospital she wrapped her first child safely and got on the train back to the home she had with Dad. Dad was Mom's love and the point of her life. With that came the love they shared for their children.

A few years after Dad died I asked Mom if she had loved him. She looked at me like she wondered if I was ill.

She said, "I've always loved your father. I've loved him from the moment we met at a dance, I love him now, and I'll always love him. Why did you ask that?"

I replied, "Because you didn't seem to show it."

She again gave me the look concerning my health. She told me that I'd understand as time passed. She said to give it a few years because I was still in that younger stage of love with my wife. She said that would stay as time passed, but it will grow. She said my wife and I would hold hands more often and longer like Dad and she had. She said I'd understand the caressing of his head, when the lion of the house thought life was a little against him. She said I would be there for my love as she had always been there for Dad. Then she said that some day she would be with him again.

She was so correct. I didn't understand some things at the time. It takes a few decades sometimes to understand some things. I know Mom is with Dad now, and will be forever.

When Dad passed, Mom was alone in the house they had shared downtown. Each of her children would invite her to their homes for visits of a day or two or longer. Each Christmas and July Fourth celebration found as many of us as possible together at the old homestead once again. Mom loved seeing us all back together again. She loved seeing grandchildren.

Mom may have had her dreams of which none of us knew. If she did, I don't know how many came true. I hope at least some of the dreams she might have had did.

I know Mom wanted what was best for her children. None of us turned out to be perfect, but she wouldn't have expected that. Her words of correction, when one of us had done something thoughtless: "Don't let that happen again." That's pretty good advice.

Mom wanted us all to be caring and considerate. I think we've each been that in our own way. It might not have happened, if she and Dad hadn't met and fallen in love.

Thanks for the chance to share words about my mother.

Robert

Letter 35

A Wrong Number Changed My Life

Mr. Garrett,

In the "old days" in Benicia the telephone numbers were two to four digits, sometimes with a letter after them, if it was a party line. I started dating the girl, who became my wife, because I wasn't used to the new system.

It was our junior year and I had been dating another girl. That was who I thought I was phoning. When Laura answered the phone by saying "hello", I thought it was the other girl. I started saying some things and I heard laughter. Laura said my name and then said that I had the wrong number. She said it happened every now and then, because the other girl was so popular and their phone numbers were so similar. Then she told me who she was.

Laura and I had gone to school together forever, it seemed. You could feel that way in Benicia then. I don't think the kids have the same feeling now. She and I had danced and been involved in school activities over that time, but we were only friends, there was no boy/girl connection.

We talked for about twenty minutes. I liked what I heard, both the voice and the words.

Finally, she said I should phone the other girl, since that had been my intention in the first place. We hung up and I did phone the other girl. We went to a movie at the Victory Theater that night, but Laura kept coming to my mind.

There was nothing bordering on permanency with the other girl. We weren't going steady. She was a good person, and we enjoyed each other's company, but she dated other guys and I dated other girls.

The next day I phoned Laura on purpose. I had two high school connections with girls before that phone call. Laura is the only girl I phoned for any boy/girl connection after that.

Once, when I jokingly asked her where she had been all my life she answered, "Sitting behind you waiting. You just didn't see me." She was right. Looking back on our school years, there were so many times we were together in the same class, or at some social or sporting event, or at the pool in the summer.

We were a certified couple by the time our junior year ended. There were little tidbits about us in The Prowling Panther gossip column like with other couples. I was told the name of the Benicia High School newspaper was changed, but it will always be "The Prowling Panther" to me.

Our senior year was a special time to remember. It seemed like so many things came our way. It seemed like a culmination of things we had unknowingly prepared for had happened.

After high school I got hired as an apprentice shipfitter at Mare Island and Laura was hired as a typist at the Arsenal. We both started at ground level, but had good and successful working careers.

We continued to date after high school, and grew closer. When I got drafted, we wrote regularly. I was sent to Germany for a year and I think the distance increased the depth of the letters we each sent. I knew I had a special thing going with Laura that I didn't want to lose.

When I got back to town on leave, I asked Laura to marry me. As soon as I got separated from the Army, we got married in St. Dominic's Church. There were a lot of familiar faces at the wedding. For our honeymoon we drove up the coast to a place by the Noyo River.

Sometimes mistakes in life can lead to problems. My

mistake in dialing that day so many years ago opened my life. It led me to be with the love of my life and to share all that goes with that with her.

Last night, when I sat with Laura, I looked at my dialing finger and jokingly thanked it. She asked why I did that. I told her it guided me to the correct numbers on a telephone dial, when I at first thought I had made a mistake.

Yours,
Lee

Letter 36

How Serious Can You Get in Fifth Grade?

Sir,

He said, "I wouldn't take her to a dog show, even if I knew she would win First Prize!"

At that time in my young life I didn't understand what the other boy's words meant, but I understood their meaning. His parents raised a dog which they took to contests. His vocabulary wasn't mine. He was talking about my girl, the woman I loved (at least at that time).

I guess Grammar School hormones were running strong in me, both for the girl and for my youthful manhood in feeling I had to defend her. She was an early maturing female. What she was born with continued to develop from then through high school and later.

As with some other times in my life, I didn't know what else to do, so I hit him. It was a good shot for a kid at that age. I hit him on his left cheek, partly overlapping his cheek bone.

When it was part of the school district system, the only green on the field was seasonal grasses and weeds. Those were soon worn down to where the field was mostly dirt. That playground is Duncan Graham Park now. Mr. Graham was my Algebra teacher in high school. I gave him a little annoyance in that class I'm sure. He was a good man, and I was just being a kid.

The guy I hit that day fell backwards in the dirt on that playground at the Highlands School and started crying. Even a dumb kid like me knew I had won in defending my girl's honor.

The teacher on yard-duty at that time saw me hit the other kid. She came over, helped him up, and wiped away his tears. The bell rang about then and she escorted the two of us, followed by my girlfriend, to our classroom.

The bell to start class rang as the other teacher told our teacher what she had seen. Then she left. Our teacher told me to apologize. She, the other boy, and I were standing in front of the classroom. I stood there with both of them looking at me for a lot of seconds. Then it dawned on me that I was supposed to say, "I apologize." I had never done that to anyone before, so in my ignorance I hadn't known what to do. After I apologized, the teacher told us to get back to our seats.

If what happened that day were to happen today, I probably would have been taken into custody for assault. Back then things were handled differently, and in many cases better.

The girl I thought then was the love of my life stopped paying attention to me shortly after that. Anyway, how serious can you get in the Fifth Grade?

Love like that quick Grammar School romance can never be lasting. It is kind of a trial run or practice game, though. You may have only one of those in your life or you may have many. If you are lucky, they are only preludes to finding the one you truly do love. That's how it was with me. I eventually found her in college, or she found me, and we have been happily married ever since.

The guy I hit and I had never been enemies, but we had also never been friends. Still, we got along well enough through the years. We had some classes together and played on some of the same sports teams. There were times along the way when I got a little angry or acted like it, around him

and he backed up just a little. I think he thought I might hit him again. There might be some truth in that, though I now know how to apologize, if I do have a slip back into immaturity.
Kirk

Letter 37

"I'll Be Seeing You" Was Their Song

Mr. Garrett,

Your advertisement brought back memories of my mom's mother. I wish it could have brought the same kind of memories of her husband, my grandfather.

From family history, reading, documentaries, and film I've learned a great deal of the patriotism my grandparent's generation held so dear. I would like to see more of that type of expression today, but times were different then than they are now.

There is a photo of her in high school wearing the cutest outfit. It is easy to see how she would have appealed to Grandfather or any other boy. She graduated a year ahead of what would be her high school graduating class. She was in love with that big, good-looking guy a year ahead of her in school. She was determined to graduate when he graduated. Grandmother was so smart, and so good at so many things.

When the war started, Grandmother and Grandfather were attending college. They had gotten married almost as soon as they stepped off the stage at their high school graduation. Grandmother said of those college times that they were two people living on the poverty program. They didn't have much money, but they had each other and they had their goals.

Grandmother said she and Grandfather would ride for hours if necessary, to get to that certain spot where the big band would play. She said that sometimes they got home later than they should have, but that it was great fun. I believe her totally, because Grandmother was great fun.

Grandfather was a big man for the times, and he would be a big man now. I've looked at the college football programs many times. He was 6'4" tall and weighed 220 pounds. Grandmother said he could run like a deer.

He was a model for the good-looking, smart, intelligent, and patriotic image of a man. He loved Grandmother and what they had together and what he hoped would be their future. He didn't see that continuing or happening unless the enemies of their country were defeated. The day after Pearl Harbor he enlisted in the Navy.

The Navy saw what others saw in life, and which I see still in the photographs that have been handed down to me. They placed Grandfather in a program to become an officer. His training was as a gunnery officer. Part of his life had been on a farm and he enjoyed hunting to put meat on the table and for the time in the outdoors. The matching couldn't have been better for the Navy or for him.

Grandmother told me she wanted to be as close to Grandfather as she could. Since he was in the Navy and the closest Navy installation to Benicia was Mare Island, she joined the work force there.

She started out as a "Rosie the Riveter", but her background and skill moved her from a blue collar position to wearing skirts in an office.

As luck, fate, or the alignment of the stars decreed in 1944, Grandfather's ship came into Mare Island for upkeep and repairs. Grandmother said she fell to her knees and thanked God for having that happen.

The ship needed a paper pusher from the shipyard to handle that need. Grandmother's efforts at the yard, her continued expression and support of her husband, and her ability made her the choice for the assignment. Along the way it allowed her to spend more time with her husband than she would have otherwise. That was part of the thought of the man who assigned her the duty, along with knowing he was sending the best he had. I have often thanked that man in my prayers, though Grandmother never told me his name.

My husband has told me many times of how men in the military make sacrifices for their buddies. Grandfather's buddies did for him. They allowed him to have as much time off the ship they could for as long as they could. Grandmother and Grandfather would ride the bus from Benicia to Mare Island in the morning and return in the evening. They spent every moment they could together. Ben Franklin may have said, "Early to bed and early to rise makes a man healthy, wealthy, and wise". It also keeps young couples, who are in love, close. In that time of 1944, in Grandmother's youthful bedroom at her parent's home, is where my mother was conceived.

Grandfather's time at Mare Island was for only a few precious months. Towards the end of 1944 the repairs and alterations to his ship had been made. The ship steamed down the channel, turned to starboard slightly and finally passed under the Golden Gate Bridge headed for Pearl Harbor.

Grandmother watched the ship from dockside as it moved down the channel. Then she rode one of the many bicycles the yard held at the time to the farthest point she could and watched from there. Then she walked until a Marine sentry told her that he understood, but that he had to keep her from going any further. Grandmother said the walk and bike ride back to her office area felt cold, though the sun was shining brightly.

After she had kissed him goodbye, before he walked up the brow and disappeared onto the ship, he said, "I'll be seeing you." He said those words whenever they parted regardless of the occasion. He had done it since they had first started going together in high school. It was the title to "their song". Many couples have a song they call their own, and that was theirs.

They were the last words he ever said to her in this world.

Grandfather's ship stopped at Pearl Harbor before heading farther towards Japan. The ship was attacked many times as the fighting grew closer to Japan's home islands. In one of the battles Grandfather was killed. Like so many others, he was buried at sea.

My mom's mother never remarried. From everything Mom told me about her mother she was a one man woman. Mom said men were often interested in gaining her attention, but Grandmother was polite and social, but never romantic with them.

Mom said that after the war there were a lot of Navy ships tied up along the Mare Island docks. She said some were of the type on which Grandfather had served. Once a week my mother would drive my Grandmother to Vallejo to look at those ships.

They would park where they had a good view. Mom said sometimes they sat there for an hour or more. One by one the ships were towed away. Shortly after the last one departed, Grandmother died. Mom said she thought her mother had held on until the last vestige of something Grandfather had been connected with, from the time she last saw him, was gone.

My Grandmother loved my Grandfather. That love began in Benicia and holds here still. Mom wishes she had known her father. I wish I had known him also.
Sherry

Letter 38

He Was the Last Person I Wanted to Date

Mr. Garrett,

Well, you see, there was this guy. Sean was probably the last person in the world I wanted to date, but he was so persistent!

In truth he was a little gangly and awkward in school, but he was cute. I liked him because he was a good guy. He was polite and a good student. In sports I, and some others, thought he was a little too hard-headed. When he was playing, the whole world was just the field or the court. That has to happen I guess, if you put your full effort into something. He put his full effort into everything I've ever known him to do.

Finally we did go out. We had a great time. He had a facet to him, which I hadn't seen before.

When I told some of the other girls that Sean and I were going out, they gave me a jokingly bad time. One said Sean had asked about me a couple of times before, wanting to know if I was serious about anyone. I'm glad she told him I wasn't.

Sean was one of those physically late blooming boys, who matured into a big, lithe, strong, coordinated man. Along the way he kept his intelligence and increased his knowledge. He went on to college, became highly skilled in his profession and has been very successful financially.

That first date with Sean was the best date of my life. We went to the Winter Ball. Six years later I married him.

Sincerely,
Sue

Letter 39

The Couple Down the Street

Mr. Garrett,

The couple down the street is in love. They live in Benicia, and have for years, so that qualifies them to fit what you were looking for with your advertisement.

I've watched them drive down the street from the day I noticed them as strangers on the block looking at a house, which was for sale, until as recently as this morning.

They bought the house and as time has gone on they have completely made it their own in style and structure. I've seen him teach their children to ride bikes and play catch there. They help each other washing their cars. They often work in the yard together. At Christmas, Easter, and other times of the year she decorates the outside of their home and the front yard with seasonal decorations.

They have always been friendly. They talk with me every time I walk by their home. They do that with most people, I think. She once told me that he will talk with anyone like he's known them all his life, though they may have just met.

Every couple of months or so a number of cars appear around their home on a Saturday evening. There is never any noise or disruption of any kind other than what would be expected for people arriving or leaving. When I go to bed around eleven o'clock, some of those cars are still there.

They often go for walks, hand-in-hand, down the street to

whatever their destination is and return. At one time they would go jogging, at times with their children, but time has caught up with their bodies as it did with mine long ago.

I've seen them leave their home together about mid-morning many times over the years. Often he wears a dark suit and she wears a dark dress. It seems those times occur more often in recent years. The car is in their driveway two to four hours later. One day when I passed by, the subject of funerals came up. They had been going to say goodbye and give last respects to someone they knew.

It probably seems like I'm a nosy busy-body, but I don't think I am. The couple and I live on the same block. We like living where we do. It is our block, in our neighborhood, in our town. We try to look out for each other the best we can. He and I joked one time about how much we knew about the block from the year someone moved in to what time someone gets home from work. I don't think that is being nosy. I think that's being aware. More of us should be.

Other neighbors have told me how they are friendly with them. They have told how they have helped them out, given unexpected gifts, supported their children's fund raisers for dozens of different causes over the years, and always cared for each other. One woman told me the couple was "joined at the hip". I easily understand what she meant.

Their children have been married for many years and the couple has grandchildren. The grandchildren have grown as the couple's children have grown. I think each of them has spent some time playing catch on the street in front of the couple's home. I think each has helped out around their home, as the couple's own children have through the years. I would bet that each has had milk and her chocolate chip cookies many times, as well as her potato salad. The cookies and potato salad are the best I've ever eaten.

They aren't perfect, no person is and certainly no couple is. I've heard him lose his temper once or twice in the front yard, when something didn't go right for him. She doesn't seem to get frustrated at anything, but at times there must be things which annoy her.

I don't know what goes on in the privacy of their home and have no desire to know. I know they are in love. They couldn't have acted, as they have for as long as they have, and not be in love. They're cute.

Respectfully,
Ruth

Letter 40

A Good Bunch of Guys

Dear Jim,

We've known each other for a long time. I knew your Mom and Dad. I knew you when everyone called you Jimmy.

Your advertisement brought back many fond memories, which may have been your point, whether you knew it or not. Maybe you were looking to rekindle some memories. I don't know. I do know that I'm old enough to say things that others may hold back. That comes with age, and a little introspection.

I fell in love with a team. I refer to it as one team. Actually it was four years of Benicia High School football teams. There was a core of us who started on the junior varsity that first year and stayed together for the next three years we played football. There were others, who were attending B.H.S., when we got there and graduated before we did. Others either moved into town or moved out through that time.

The boys on that team are long ago grown men. A few have passed on, a few have disappeared from our lives, a few are still around the area, and a few more of us keep in touch the best we can.

That team has seen about all there is to see in one form or another. They have "been there and done that", and suffered all the trials and tribulations life brings any group, and gained all the benefits of their time on the planet.

You had some of the sons and daughters of those men in

your classes at Benicia High School. If you are like me, it surprised you some. The world keeps going around, Jim. Things happen and things stay the same.

It was a pretty good bunch of guys, that team from decades ago. It showed through school and later on in life. I was, and still am, proud to be a teammate. The love for my wife comes first, the love for my country second, the love for some guys I served with in the military comes third, and the love for that team comes fourth. People, who don't know, don't know. There is a symbiosis among people depending on time, place, and, I guess, the alignment of the planets. I think I know what love is.

Many of the guys on that team have known each other most of their lives. They know the girlfriends, who really pulled a particular prank, and who could be counted on when things were on the line in a game. Some of that knowledge carried over into life past the football field.

They were a wonderful team. One became a naval aviator. Two became college professors. Five became public school teachers. Some own their own businesses. A number of them became skilled tradesmen. The two, who became attorneys, were the ones who would talk the most. Some became law enforcement officers.

There were some from the team who found drugs irresistible, and one ended his life by taking his life. Some have developed heart problems over the years and there have been deaths due to health problems.

A number of the guys served our country. One lost his life in that service. There were privates and officers, pilots and cooks, Good Conduct recipients and those who didn't quite meet that standard.

I'm sorry to say some have met with divorce, one guy three times. Maybe he'll finally get it right, when the right woman tells him "this is how it is". He was a good dependable guy on the team, but outside the locker room he had his moments.

Together, all those guys formed a good team. They were dependable and solid on the field. You could look around in a huddle and know everything was going to work out well. We didn't win every game those three years most of us spent on the varsity, but we came close. If you get to know any of the guys well enough, they'll tell you they didn't all like each other all the time, or any time for that matter. When it came to the team, they were all brothers.

Our parents influenced us in life and so did our coaches. They all guided us. Some of the things we were taught and told later proved to be wrong or misguided, but those people all helped us and we know it. When the coaches told us to run, we ran. When they talked, we were quiet.

Memories of "George" Drolette quietly leading with knowledge and humor, "Barney" Corrigan leading the exercises and grass drills, and Mr. Goettel leading and overseeing all are clear in my mind. They were three intelligent and dedicated men. They were winners, and wanted winners, but above all they were good men. They wouldn't be remembered so fondly by so many, if that wasn't the case.

Those three men taught more about the real world on Sanborn Field than many people have learned in a classroom with walls. If you get knocked down, get up. If you knock someone down, and you get the chance, help them up after the play. Don't grab the jersey of a teammate to slow him down when you're all doing wind sprints. Show some style when you play. Act like you have "been there before" when you do well. Don't complain when things go a little wrong, just try harder. He won't score if you don't block and you won't score if he doesn't block. All were life lessons.

We gave all we had as we learned. We learned about football, sportsmanship, team concept, and most of all being there for your teammate.

Nostalgia isn't living in the past, or wishing for its return. It is fond memories of a time and place, smells and sights, aches and laughter. The short steps from the locker room to Sanborn Field, the aroma of that locker room and the grass of the field, a sore muscle and the joyous sounds of boys growing to be young men, are all parts of each of us, who played on that team. About once a year I get out the old yearbooks and the scrapbooks. I see photos and read stories and wish those pictured and written of well.

It was an honor to be part of that football program, which helped make so many good young men what they became. I thank Coach Drolette, Coach Corrigan, and Coach Goettel and the team they formed through the years. I love that team.

Respectfully,
A teammate

Letter 41

He Was a Sailor Who Did Sailor Things

Mr. Garrett,

My father died when I was eighteen so I never knew him as a man knows a man. Last year I learned a lot more about him.

I was sitting on the park bench on our front deck overlooking the street below and the Carquinez Strait in the distance. From my right a black limousine slowly moved down the street and stopped in front of the house opposite of the home my wife and I share.

The man in the front passenger's seat got out and walked around to the back door on the street side of the limousine. As he was walking around, the driver of the car got out and stood on the other side of the door. Both were dressed in obviously tailored black suits, which didn't leave any guess work to the fact the men were well proportioned.

They stood at the military position of 'parade rest' for what seemed to me to be a minute, but I could be wrong. It looked like two admiral's aides standing by their officer's automobile, while they waited for him to exit. While the men stood there, they scanned our home and in seconds the eyes of both men were on me. I could understand they were checking the lay of the land to see if it was safe for whoever was in the backseat to exit. The side glass of the limousine was tinted, but I could easily imagine someone leaning over and looking through it.

I think I'm a friendly guy, but some have said I'm a little confrontational and competitive. I stood up and stared back at the two men shifting my eyes from one to the other. Then the man farthest to the rear of the limousine turned his head slightly towards one of his suit lapels, while still looking at me, and appeared to be speaking.

When he was done speaking, he turned to face me again. At that time the man nearer the front of the door reached for its handle and opened the door.

The man, who stepped from the back of the limousine, is known by sight to a lot of people on the planet, including me. I had seen him in person once and only heard his voice that one time, other than through the media.

My father, and some other men, and I had stood in the background at the funeral of the father of the back seat passenger. At the time I didn't know who the man was. I only knew my father was showing respect for someone, but that was all I knew at the time. They spoke alone with each other for a few minutes outside the church. Then my father and I drove home in silence.

When the three men started to cross the street, with the back seat passenger in the middle, I walked from our house to meet them. One of the flanking men introduced the three of them to me, and each showed identification confirming the information. I invited them into our home.

My wife met us at the door. I told her who our guests were and she offered to bring iced tea. We all accepted her offer and I escorted our guests to the living room where we sat down.

It is my home, and I also like our guests to be comfortable. That being the case, I leaned back in the sofa where I sat. The man from the back seat did also. The two escorts sat on the edge of their chairs opposite each other. Each gave a brief look at the 180 degree perimeter behind the other. It was obvious they were on guard duty.

I told the man that my wife and I were honored to have

him, and his companions, in our home, but that I couldn't understand why they were here.

That was when the man told of the love he had for my father.

He said when he and my father and some others were younger they were sailors and did sailor things. He didn't elaborate and I didn't question him for answers. It was obvious to me he was the kind of man who would tell you just what he wanted you to know, and nothing else. I know he told me what he could and left the remainder to my imagination. It started to get easier to put facts he gave and memories of my time with my father together. My father had told me a lot over the years, I just didn't connect all the dots. The back seat passenger provided a pencil which helped connect some of them.

I told the back seat passenger my father had told me, when we were alone and he was on his death bed, about a group of men with whom he had served. He said he never told anyone else, not even my mother or any other of his children. He said he told me because there was chemistry between those men and him, and that he saw that chemistry between him and me.

The back seat passenger told me he was a friend of my father, and that my father often spoke of growing up in Benicia. He said my father was the next to last to pass. The back seat passenger said he was the last torch bearer for the small group of which they had each been a part.

When I asked what happened to the others it was almost a litany of heroes. "Ding-Dong" drowned. "Fritz the Cat" couldn't handle the memories and died an alcoholic. "Slim", all 6'-6" and 260 pounds of him, led a quiet life in retirement, but he had no way to release what was inside him and that led to the heart attack which killed him. "Bop" lived alone until one day the memories couldn't be pushed back any longer and he went for a long swim in the Atlantic Ocean. "London" disappeared into the secret black world of the government, or died, no one will ever know.

He said that, through their organization, two of the children of the group contacted him through use of the computer. Their

Dads had told them of that means of connecting, as many Dads did in their later years, but they also told them little would be revealed. Two of the children saw photos of their fathers on the web site showing them young and tanned and asked him about them. He said he sent, by a multiple route, what information he could.

The visit lasted almost half an hour. I don't expect to ever be face-to-face with any of those men again in my life. They did their duty in coming to see me. I appreciate that.

There have to be others like my father, the back seat passenger, and his companions out there in society. They have to be around us without our knowing. Some things couldn't work in the world, as they do, if it wasn't for men like them. I have no doubt other countries have the same type of men.

My father so often talked of words to live by. The love some men showed for a man from Benicia is proof the words he so often spoke were true.

Love connections with Benicia come in many forms. You asked for letters of love in any way related to Benicia. The letter you just read is one.

Peace,

Respectfully,

Son of a Veteran

Letter 42

A Rape Victim Finds Love and Understanding

Mr. Garrett,

The love a man can have for a child, which isn't his, and the woman, who gave birth to that child, never ceases to amaze me.

My husband is the man I love, and the one I most admire. The child he helped me raise isn't his child by birth, but it is his child by love, care, and responsibility. Of the two choices of biology or dedication, I'll take the latter.

My husband knows who fathered the child we call ours. He knows it wasn't him, but he loves our son as if he were his by nature. He loves him as the gift from God he is. I thank him so much for that and love him so much more for it.

When I became pregnant, some people didn't understand. They acted as if I had done something wrong. I hadn't. I had been raped. My religion forbids abortion.

Some of those people, who didn't understand, were from my church. I thought, so much for Christian understanding from them. I have attended my church all of my life, but when I was pregnant and not married some who had been friendly turned against me. Some of them were my classmates.

One, who didn't turn against me, was a man who had

attended our church for a few years. He was a regular attendee at the church and its activities, but wasn't always there. There were occasional times when he wasn't around for a couple weeks.

He said hello one Sunday as my family and I entered the church. We sat in the same pew, but he kept separate a few spaces from my family and me, as he sat nearest my father.

As the weeks passed, we each talked more. He was easy to talk with and we found ourselves sharing more words before and after the services. At the time it was obvious I was pregnant. He was a quiet gentleman. He seemed to be aware and understand things. A feeling of warmth came from him. I hoped he felt similar warmth going from me to him.

When we were leaving church on a cool fall day, my father said he needed to prune the trees in our backyard. The man from church said to let him know when my father would do it and he would come by and help. It was apparent my father and the man had come to like each other.

My father gave him our address and asked if the following Saturday morning would be good. The man said it would. He arrived ready to work. He brought clippers, a lopper, and a box of fresh doughnuts. He brought something else, too. He brought a bouquet of flowers for me.

That man knew I was pregnant and that there was no man around in my life. He didn't ask any questions, and he brought me flowers.

It was a sunny day with the coolness of the fall breeze pushing leaves across the ground. My father and the man worked all morning and by lunch time had the work completed. My mother invited the man to stay and have lunch with us and he accepted. When he had arrived, he saw our apple tree. My mother heard him say he liked apple pie. We had sandwiches and homemade apple pie for lunch. Mother liked the man too.

After lunch we talked for awhile and then the man left. I walked him to the door. I thanked him for helping my father and for giving me the flowers. When I extended my hand to shake his in saying goodbye, he said I was a good person. I shut the door and watched him drive away, but his parting words kept moving through my mind.

The next Sunday he arrived at church with an older couple. I thought it must have been his parents and that thought was proven correct when he introduced them. We all sat together. After the services the man and his parents exited the building before my family and me. They looked as if they were waiting for someone as they stood apart from the others leaving the church. We discovered they had been waiting to talk with me and my family out of the hearing of anyone else.

On the sidewalk in front of our church the man said his existence was the result of a rape. His mother stood proudly by his side holding his arm. The only father he had ever known held an arm across his shoulders. The man said he wanted me and my family to know. He understood.

For a moment it seemed we were all part of a living photograph. No one moved, no one said a word, there was no wind pushing at bushes, and there were no background noises. Then my father invited the man and his parents to our home for supper.

The evening was revealing in the words and tears which came from each of us. My father's anger came to the surface as well as his love. When I had become pregnant, we had talked, but he had never expressed himself as he did at that time.

My mother's face was beaming. She and my father would have stood by and defended me against the world, if anyone called me a slut or the whore of whores. At that moment she had the look of a soon-to-be grandmother.

The man talked of his life. His mother showed no shame, as no shame was hers. No shame was mine. His father showed pride in a son he had helped. No shame was his. No shame was his son's. The man and his parents showed true care.

When my baby was born my family, the man, and his parents were at the hospital. The man was the last one to leave. He spent most of the next day at the hospital. He didn't care if some might have thought of him as the father of a child of an unwed mother. Without ever touching me he gave me the care a true husband gives his wife.

Before the man left that day he leaned slightly over the bed and said he loved me. I told him he had months before become my love. He picked up my hand, kissed it, and left.

The baby cradled in my arm then was not named at that time. The name I gave him later that day is the name of the man who kissed my hand.

My love accepted me as I was. Eighteen months later we walked down the aisle with no more than forty people watching. I didn't care if everyone in the world, or no one, was there because I held his arm and in a stroller in front of our parents our baby slept.

With respect,
(Unsigned)

Letter 43

Mom and Dad were Hippies

Mr. Garrett,

Some people would have a hard time believing it today, but in the late 1960's Mom and Dad were hippies. Look in their yearbooks and it can be seen. If you are a friend, they'll show you their scrapbooks of things in which they were involved in those days.

I love them both so much. They haven't given up on some of the beliefs they held then, but the practical side of being employed and raising a family took precedence.

Mom and Dad graduated from Cal-Berkeley. You can see them in photographs in a couple of clippings from newspapers that are in their scrapbooks. They were believers, not rent-a-mob people. It is really funny to see them in a past light. By the time we kids came along Dad was in the corporate world and Mom was a photo journalist. Pony tail, beads, sandals, and tie dye were out.

Over the years I've known the son of the sinner, who was a great person, and the daughter of religion, who fell from parental grace. I think, in similarity, the same could be said of our family. It is all perceptions. Judgments should be made on the person, not the stereotype or the expectations. All of Mom and Dad's kids have gone to college and we are pretty successful.

Mom's and Dad's families gave them a chance to

express themselves and supported them when they did. One of my grandfathers was not the happiest man in the world with some of the things they did, but he loved them just the same.

When Dad told his parents he believed in free love, he said the room got real quiet for awhile. Grandfather said what consenting adults did was between them, but he asked Dad about what would happen concerning bastard children. Dad hadn't considered that. Grandmother said children need a name and a family, and with free love they may be lost and have none, but she agreed with Grandfather. I think it was so cool that all of them could talk about it.

One time Mom said she told her parents she had smoked pot. She said they thought she would become a marijuana junkie. In high school I smoked pot once. Mom and Dad always said I could talk with them about anything, and we always had, so I told them at dinner that night.

At first they got mad. It was like I didn't understand things. Then we talked. They said they understood my curiosity, but that they hoped I wouldn't use parts of the life they had led in their youth as examples. One of those parts was smoking marijuana or anything else. Mom said they didn't want their children to make the same mistakes they did.

When they talked about always trying to prepare their children the best they could to leave them, and not live their lives at home, I almost had an epiphany. They were telling me a warm nest would be there for me if I ever needed it, but I was free to fly when the time came. They had worked on that aspect of my life all along. It was done in tiny increments like when I first paid for something at a store and bold moves like when they encouraged me to attend Cal. When Mom and Dad said they would each always be there for me, like they would with their other children, it really touched me. The last part of that conversation was when Dad told me it was my life and wished me luck with it, and Mom agreed. Then Dad excused himself from the table and started clearing the dishes to be washed.

I had always known they loved me, but that conversation at the dinner table was like a rite of passage. It wasn't planned, or expected, but spontaneous and flowed from adult to adult.

Mom and Dad now live in Benicia.

Respectfully,
Janice

Letter 44

I May Be an Old Prude

Mr. Garrett,

Benicia was at the end of the social change back when I was a kid. We didn't get the hula hoop until 1962! That's a joke, but it isn't too far from the truth.

We did always have a cute bunch of girls. At one time or another I guess, like the other guys, I "puppy loved" them all. I truly loved one, and married her.

Girls back then walked and rode bikes more than girls seem to do today. They were also more like girls than a lot of the young adults I see today.

Some of today's girls look to me like they are 14 going on 40. I feel sorry for them. I've been to a few places in the world in my life. Some of the girls I see in town now dress like hookers. The saying is true that if you walk and quack like a duck you ain't no chicken hawk. Their parents just must not give a damn about what others think when they see their daughters dressed like that. Either that, or there aren't any adults in the family.

I'm probably just an old prude. I remember seeing my wife as she grew from a little girl to the young woman I married. There was a steady progression. By the time she was a senior at Benicia High School she was an accomplished young lady.

She dated other guys than me when she grew and went to college. She wasn't in the date-a-week contest like some of the girls I hear about today. I'm tired of hearing people talk about their latest love, whether it's a girl or a boy, like they've just changed their choice in ice cream.

Like I wrote before, I may be an old prude. I still believe in love at first sight. There is something to be said, though, for long term connections and relationships.

I worked in construction most of my life. Without a good foundation a building won't last as long as it should. The same applies to love.

Brian

Letter 45

Hello Gorgeous

Mr. Garrett,

You said in your advertisement that you wanted letters of love concerning Benicia. This is an open letter to "Gorgeous".

Hello Gorgeous,

I know you're out there. I see you and your wife a few times a year at public functions or in public places. I'm getting to know her better. I like that. It is easy to understand what you see in her.

There was time when I did truly love you, but you didn't see the same love in me. It is amazing to me that we have remained friends all these years. Our love now is the love of friendship.

We used to laugh about how you first caught my attention because of the way you looked in your letterman's sweater. The bulging biceps look was you. You were simply a doll.

That first attraction, when we were freshmen, led to knowing you, and for that I'm so grateful. We joked, and laughed, and danced and went to the movies from then on. I watched your games and cheered you on. When we were seniors, you asked me if I would go steady with you. I thought I was in the land of dreams. I was as proud to be your girl then as I am to still know you and call you my friend.

It was so easy to part with you because I knew you didn't love me as I then loved you. Still you called, and we still danced. That was nice.

I just wanted to say "Hello Gorgeous" again in a public manner as I once did. The love I had for you as the boy of my dreams has been replaced by the warmth of the love of our friendship. Thank you, Gorgeous.

With fond memories,
Beverly

Letter 46

The Prettiest Girl at the Party

Mr. Garrett,

I thought I was in love one time, so I guess I was. It turned out to be one-sided and didn't last.

When I was about eleven, I was invited to a party at a friend's house on the west side of town. There was no significance to it like with a birthday party. I think some parents just wanted some kids to socialize more.

Everyone at the party knew everyone else, the same story in small towns. One of the games we played was spin-the-bottle followed by ten seconds in heaven. Everyone playing got a chance to spin the bottle. They would spin it until the head of the bottle wound up pointing to someone of the opposite sex. Then the boy and girl would step into the next room. Someone where the game was being played would count: one, two, three, go. Then everyone in that room would start counting from one to ten while watching the second hand on a watch. During that ten seconds some guys, and some girls, got the first kiss in their lives from a non-family member.

I know it is impossible, but I think one girl had a magnetic attraction for the bottle. She went in that other room so often I think her lips were wearing out. They must have at least been raw.

I had my chances with a couple of the girls that night, but not with the girl who was getting most of the action. She was the prettiest girl there and, even at eleven, I was feeling a little frustrated.

As it always seems to happen in life, one of the guys was more advanced in his approach than the rest of us at that time. When he got a girl in the other room, he stuck his tongue down her throat as soon as she opened her mouth to say something. She ran screaming into the other room like her dress was on fire. Parents don't like to hear screaming girls, so the spin the bottle game ended. I never got lucky enough to kiss the prettiest girl at the party.

Advance the scene to my freshman year at Benicia High School and another party. Along the way to that point I had kissed more than one girl.

The prettiest girl at the party, when I was eleven, was the prettiest girl at the party when I was a freshman. I think she always has been the prettiest girl.

There were a bunch of us sitting on the floor in one of the rooms of the house watching television. The prettiest girl came in the room, walked over to where I sat and sat down beside me. We stayed there until the party was over. Other kids entered and left the room, but we sat there.

We talked about things humorous, silly, and serious, and watched television. After a time she moved closer to me. Then she reached for my hand. Hormones were jumping in me.

We sat there holding hands until the father of the house came into the room and told everyone it was time to end the party.

The prettiest girl at the party had come to it with some other girls. I had come alone. When we stood at the bottom of the porch, she put her arms around me. Then she said she had enjoyed being with me that night and kissed me on the mouth. I kissed back, and tongues touched tongues. Then she left with her girlfriends.

At the moment of the kiss I thought I was in love and that she loved me. I had been kissed by the prettiest girl at the party. Life couldn't be better.

The next day I phoned her. We talked for awhile and,

shock of all shocks to me, she said she wasn't doing anything the next Saturday night. When I asked if she would like to go to the movies with me, she said "yes"!

Saturday evening finally came, but it was by way of Siberia pulled by a slug in molasses. At her doorstep, when I took her home, she kissed me as before. I told her I thought I loved her. She said she had kissed a lot of guys on the mouth, but that didn't mean she loved them.

I had twice kissed the prettiest girl at the party.

Thanks for bringing back great memories.

Mike

Letter 47

We Met in a Benicia Antique Shop

Mr. Garrett,

Neither my husband nor I have ever resided in Benicia, but we met there. We now live in Seattle. We subscribe to the Benicia newspaper to keep in touch with the place where we met.

A couple times a year, before I got married, I would come to Benicia to walk around and see the sights. It was a great escape from San Francisco, where I lived at the time.

I met Alex in an antique shop. We had exchanged pleasantries in the store as I passed by the counter where he stood when I entered the building. At a glance it was easy to see he was a good looking man, but I've seen a lot of good looking men. I wasn't looking for one.

As we each wandered around the store, we happened to stop by the same area. He pointed out a very nice looking item and we started talking again. He was pleasant.

It may sound corny, old fashioned, or quaint, but he offered to help me place in my car a purchase I had made. He was nice and I saw no harm in accepting his friendliness. We walked outside and I opened the car door. He leaned in and placed on the floor the small mahogany box I had purchased.

After he stood up I thanked him and he said I was welcome and that he was glad to help. Then he looked around and said it was a nice warm day and asked if I would like to walk up the street and get an ice cream cone. I hadn't had an ice cream cone, especially with a man, in years. Alex was the right man, at the right place, at the right time in my life.

We sat at a sidewalk table in front of the store and ate the ice cream as we watched the street traffic and the people walking by. All that time we also watched each other.

After about twenty minutes I told him I had to leave. I didn't really have to leave then. Maybe I was testing him.

He said he came to Benicia a couple times a year from his home in Pleasant Hill. I told him it was the same with me. When he said perhaps we might meet again sometime, I told him I would like that.

Then I did something I have never done in my life, but it felt so right to do it. I said yes when he asked if he could have my telephone number. I had met him less than an hour before, and it was out of character for me then to give my number after just meeting someone. Life had hurt me a little in the past.

Alex walked me to my car. I unlocked the door and he held it open as I got inside. I started the engine and lowered the driver's window and said goodbye. He said it wasn't goodbye, because he would telephone me. He did. There was a message waiting on my answering machine when I got home. He said he knew I wouldn't be home yet, but wanted to phone then to keep the memory of the time we spent together fresh. He said he would phone later at a time when I should be home. He did. We talked for over an hour as if we had known each other forever.

That day in Benicia started the time from which Alex and I will know each other forever. It was a "Benicia" connection and it is still going strong. Two lives came together that day, and I am so grateful they did. That day gave me the love of my life.

This summer we'll fly down for the Peddlar's Faire. We would both like to have an ice cream cone again.

Yours,
Georgia

Letter 48

A Velvet-Covered Irritant

Mr. Garrett,

I will always question what he saw in her that he didn't see in me. We had been high school lovers for over a year until a few days before graduation. Then he broke up with me and we went our separate ways. The breakup was quiet, but it bothered me, as it should any girl of that age. The feeling of that breakup is now a velvet-covered irritant and has been for years.

We seemed to drift farther apart after the breakup. There was no attempt by either of us to avoid the other. We had some of the same classes together and he was always himself. Neither of us was looking for someone else in our lives at that time to fill what we had from the other. It is like when you are in a small boat and two pieces of flotsam follow alongside. The pieces are there, but they keep their distance because that is the way Mother Nature wants it to be.

He later started dating another girl and they eventually got married. People have told me the other girl and I are a lot alike. I still have the question.

He seems happy, and I am happy with the man in my life. The question is still there for me. Now it is more an academic question than an emotional one. I think that at times when relationships change, someone can't help but ask why, unless the answer is obvious. With us, the answer wasn't obvious. After our breakup we drifted almost side-by-side for the year and a half we had left together in the small town Benicia was then.

My high school classmate met his lovely bride when they were in college. I met the man I married in college. Our first taste of love came in Benicia.

I loved that boy in school with all the heart I knew I had at the time. Since then an expansion has come to my heart. Still within my heart is, and always will be, a tender place, where thoughts of him reside.

Rachel

Letter 49

A Young Man Defends His Sister's Honor

Mr. Garrett,

I started dating the man, who became my husband, because I saw him beat up a guy. That may sound a little strange, but that's what happened.

There was a party (yes people of Benicia, there are parties in Benicia where kids drink) and a guy started doing something he shouldn't have with a girl.

The next thing anybody knew, the brother of the girl was on the guy like stink on stuff, as my basketball coach used to say (Yes, you know who said it!).

He didn't just pull the guy away and hit him. He hit him, and hit him, and hit him. Finally there was almost a cloud of guys covering the brother and pulling him off. The guy he had been hitting was basically carried out by some of the other guys at the party.

I had never seen someone stand up for another person like that in my life. I've been around guys who talked a lot of smack, but when it came to doing anything about a problem, they always seemed to be looking the other way. I was impressed by the guy who came to the aid of his sister more than I had ever been impressed by anyone. Seeing what he did that night made him my hero.

Before that time the girl's brother had just been someone I knew and had some classes with over the years. Girls know what they want in life just like boys. I knew that after what I had seen, I wanted to get to know better the boy who had defended his sister.

I "just happened to be around" him and talked with him enough until he finally asked me out. He probably still thinks it was his idea, but I tell him it was mine. I was one scheming female, but I'm glad I did it. I know he is glad. We seemed to hit it off well. Anyway, it must have been pretty well. We've been married for close to thirty years now and I've loved every moment of it. He is still my knight and always will be.
Allison

Letter 50

Benicia Is Still a Small Town

Mr. Garrett,

People have said things about me for years. Some of what they say may be true, and some of it definitely is. On the other hand, some is definitely not true.

If a woman doesn't want her man to look at another woman, then she should change her habits. I'm happily married to the man I love. Others should hope the same is true with them.

I've done nothing with men I'm ashamed of. Before I accepted the proposal of the man, who became my husband, I dated who I wanted when I wanted. There is no difference in that than with a guy. When I agreed to marry, all my dating ended except with him.

Too many people out there still don't understand that Benicia is a small town. When you talk in a restaurant, or the grocery store, or the gas station there are ears all around. Some of those ears are straight pipelines to other people in town. A lot of people in this town are related to their neighbors. Word gets around fast. I know, I've heard it and know the sources.

I dated men in this town who told me they loved me. I think two actually did for awhile. I felt the same for them. For the others our time together was for fun. That was mutually agreed. That doesn't make me or anyone else a whore. People would call a guy like that a stud and praise him for how many babes he bedded.

There are a couple women in Benicia who could be called "The Bitches of the Ball". They've had more sex with more guys than porcupines have quills, even after they have been married.

I kept my word to the man who proposed to me. Those other women should do the same and keep their mouths closed. They should prove they love their guy.

Sammy

Letter 51

An Unexpected Good Night Kiss

Mr. Garrett,

Catherine and I didn't actually meet. There was no introduction. We had the same class together when she was a junior and I was a senior out at the high school. I saw right away that she was cute.

We started going out when she asked me to take her to a Sadie Hawkins dance. We had a good time at the dance, though I admit I have never been a good dancer. She was light in my arms. Every time I looked at her after looking away for even a second, as we danced, her eyes were always on mine. It was a good feeling.

I thought I would get a little peck on the cheek when I took her home. After I unlocked the door and handed her back her keys, she asked if she could have a goodnight kiss. I said sure. I don't think I've ever been a complete idiot.

As I like to say, she tickled my tonsils. That was one of the few surprises life has given me. It was totally unexpected. I think that is what made it so nice.

Our next date came soon, believe me. She didn't do any more asking. I had her telephone number memorized before I stepped off her porch.

When I ask Catherine what she saw in me, she always says such nice things and they are always the same. I thank her so much for seeing what she saw, for saying the words, and for being persistent. Persistent she was. Six years after that first date we were married.

Through our decades together we've had some stumbling blocks, caused mostly by my ignorance, stupidity and temper. She says I've been mellowing over the years. What mellowing I've done is because of her.

She is an amazing woman. She is my love. She is my lady.
Robert

Letter 52

I Thought Mary Would Be My Daughter-in-law

Mr. Garrett,

I thought for years Mary would be my daughter-in-law. That didn't work out. Our son and Mary are still friends, but they are each happily married to someone else. Things work out as they are supposed to.

Mary was so loyal to Mario, and he to her. Thinking of their names it is kind of strange, because if they had gotten married their initials would have been the same.

He used to play with her in our backyard sandbox. It was the typical next door relationship, though she lived a block away.

Mary's dad and I worked together. That made things nicer with family connections. We exchanged Christmas cards and were there for each other at the special times for each family. A saying I learned in the military, in reference to a buddy, was, "I got your back". They were always there for us as we were always there for them.

When Mario graduated from college, the Vietnam War was still going on. He joined the Marines. He was always the kind of guy who felt, when there was something to be done, he was going to get into the thick of it and get it done. He wasn't looking for medals, but he received some.

Mary sent him perfume-scented letters and packages of goodies all the time he was gone. He wrote her back.

When he got back, it wasn't the same between them. I don't think they ever had sex before he left. I think they did after he got back. I think it was more out of a strong friendship-love than for the love of a lifetime with marriage. I don't belittle or begrudge them anything they had. They were good for each other all their lives before and have been since.

Somewhere along the way, though I guarantee they loved each other dearly, they each came to understand what they thought they had felt, wasn't what they truly felt.

A father,
Jose

Letter 53

A Chance Meeting on a Street in San Francisco

Mr. Garrett,

A girl who gave me her high school love disappeared from my life for years after that time. It was something stupid, which caused what we had then to end, but end it did.

Then one day I saw her walking up the sidewalk towards me as I approached her on that hilly street in San Francisco. Her head was bent slightly forward as she walked. I recognized the movement of her body before I could see her face.

When she had gone away to college I wrote her once, but she never wrote back. That hurt me, but I could understand. When we broke up, both of us were ignorant of some things, and assumed some things. There was passion and dreams shared between us, but not much in-depth talking. We were young. Each of us had plans and aspirations. We each thought the other would understand and always be there.

When I said hello to her, it shocked her a little for a moment. We stood there, neither of us knowing exactly what to say. As close as we had been, how we broke up and the time between seeing each other again, would make it difficult for anyone.

Then Tami said it was good to see me again. She said it with a blunt honesty and gave a little sigh like she had just gotten over some hurdle in life. I told her it was good to see her, too.

The years had only made her better looking. She was a full-grown and developed woman. I don't mean just her body, but her carriage, the way she looked at me, and how she spoke. I hoped right then that I wouldn't come off looking like the slightly tongue-tied guy I felt I was. I admit when I was first attracted to her in Mr. Simon's history class it wasn't because she was smart. I just lucked out that she was both good looking and intelligent.

I didn't know if I should dance an Irish jig or say goodbye. I didn't want to hurt her again, or do anything she wouldn't like, or put pressure on her. A moment later she was in my arms.

Over and over again she said she missed me, as she pressed the side of her head to mine. I said the same thing back to her and pressed my head to hers. It all seemed so natural and right.

I've seen guys debark from ships and airplanes bringing them back from far distant places, where they had been stationed by the military for long periods of time. The feelings of some of those men embracing the woman in their lives couldn't have been any stronger than mine at that moment. If I wasn't in love, and had been in my heart all along for Tami, I don't think I can ever know what love is.

The smell of her hair had been kept recessed in my mind by only the thinnest veil of protection. When we stood on that sidewalk and embraced, the veil vanished instantly. My mind said I didn't care if I got hurt again with her, I was going to hold that young lady as long and as firmly as I could. She returned what was more than a hug from me with equal strength.

We stood there on that street and held and kissed each other like we were the long separated lovers we actually were.

Tami bought a house in Cordelia after graduating from college. She only came to Benicia occasionally after that to see her parents and friends. I had never seen her on those occasions. If we hadn't had business in San Francisco that day, fate would probably have kept us apart. Fate gave us a chance again, and we took it.

We had finished our business in The City. I walked her to her car and she drove me to mine. I drove behind her escorting her to her home. She was the one for me, and I was the one for her. From that time until late into the evening was our time of returning to a feeling in our lives we had each missed so much.

There is something to be said for teenage love, but it doesn't compare with the love which grows over the later years.

John

Letter 54

Ronald Treats Me Like a Lady

Mr. Garrett,

My husband, Ronald, is almost 20 years older than me. We married five years after his first wife died. I never knew her, and he rarely mentions her except in fond memory.

Ronald treats me like a lady, unlike how I see many of the younger men treat women. It both makes me angry and makes me feel blessed when I see how some of those men treat their ladies, and know how my love treats me.

I don't understand why the women who are treated with such discourtesy accept as they do. Good for her, if her man opens the car door, or any door for that matter, for her. Good for her, if he carries a package into the house. Good for her, if he takes the garbage to the trash can and the can to the street on the appointed day. Good for her, if she gets to be part of making decisions which affect the lives of both of them.

Those men and women had to have seen something in the other which made them want to be together. It must have ended after the initial sex passed or one or the other, or both of them, felt they had a mate and thus had it made in life.

Ronald has never been that way with me in anything. I am truly blessed that he chose me to be the one with whom to share his life. Our marriage vows included "love and honor", and he has done that with me and me with him.

I've been mistaken for being his daughter. One woman

even said she saw the family resemblance. That was so funny, but I was polite with her. I've even been mistaken for Ronald's caretaker! I doubt the man will ever need a caretaker. When the woman said I was Ronald's caretaker, I had to turn away and fake a sneeze to keep from laughing out loud. The woman, who said that meant well, but she didn't understand that two people with the age difference Ronald and I have could love each other as man and wife.

When Ronald proposed to me, it was in the old-fashioned setting of a booth in a dark, wood-paneled restaurant. There was a candle off to the side between us and two red roses in a vase. I later learned that he had made arrangements for the flowers.

He was caring and careful with his words, but he was also blunt. He said he loved me, as I knew he did, but it was obvious he was much older than me. It was almost like he was proposing to me to not propose to me, if that makes any sense. He wanted to make it easy on me, if I rejected him, but he wanted to tell me how he felt and to propose.

There were two things he said which would never happen again. The first was that he would never have any more children because he was too old to start another family. The second was that he would never propose to another woman again.

I told him I couldn't have children. He told me he was sorry, but never has asked why I couldn't have children. That added to my respect for him.

The best words to ever exit my mouth were those when I told Ronald I loved him and would love to marry him.

When I told Ronald I couldn't take the place of his first wife, and wouldn't try to, he said he didn't expect or want me to. He said he was asking me to marry him, not trying to live in the past. Ronald said that I was who I was and that was with whom he wanted to share the remainder of his life.

Some younger guys tried to make time with me, but they were just boys to me. Ronald understood. He once told me, if I wanted to have an affair with a younger man, he would understand. He said he knew he might disappoint me because of the difference in our ages. It has been the only time I've gotten angry with him. I didn't care about that. I understood. If there was something I couldn't handle at the moment, I could take a cold shower.

When I told Ronald I loved what we had together, the love between us, the sharing, the caring, he thanked me. I thanked him for choosing me. I've been honored.

Respectfully,
Elizabeth

Letter 55

My Future Husband Winked at Me

Mr. Garrett,

Tim, my husband, and I met after he winked at me. I'd never been winked at before. It was friendly and made me feel comfortable. I smiled at him, he walked over to where I stood on the fantail of the Vallejo ferry coming back from San Francisco and we started talking.

We had seen each other for the last few months, usually every Monday through Friday, on the ferry as we went to and from work but had never spoken before then.

Many of the other men on the rides to SF would spend the trip time reading a newspaper, working on their computers, or listening to something on their headphones. Tim never did those things. He sat with a confident, well prepared, under control look about him and seemed to enjoy the ride, looking at the people on board, and watching the sights we passed. It was the same on the way back, except sometimes, like when we started talking, he would stand outside. I liked that.

I had actually been hoping there would be some cause for us to start talking, but it hadn't worked out until that day.

He told me he liked San Francisco but no longer wanted to live there. I told him I liked it, but wouldn't want to live there.

He had lived in Benicia for almost two years and at first commuted to SF by car, but thought he would give the ferry a try and was glad he did. I told him I had lived in Benicia a little longer than he had and I was glad he had decided to take the ferry. He said he lived by the marina and I said I lived by Raley's Shopping Center. It was just getting to know each other.

We decided to give car pooling from Benicia to Vallejo a try. That led to dinner. The dinner led to marriage, and we couldn't be happier.

Tim and I now own a home in Southampton.

Kellie

Letter 56

I Wrote My Wife an Anniversary Poem

Mr. Garrett,

On our last anniversary, our thirty-fifth, I gave Kathy a poem and held her. I couldn't think of anything else to give her.

I'm not the cleverest guy at giving gifts, but I've tried over the years to get her things she would like and want. Sometimes there are practical gifts included with the personal gifts at Christmas time, like the vacuum cleaner with the headlight so she can clean the floors at night! We needed a new one, so it was an obvious purchase anyway but I enjoy joking about it.

For Christmas I've always tried to get her one gift that is something special. It is the last present she opens.

As the Christmases we've shared through the years have grown in number there have been less presents, but the ones given are just as meaningful. Like with anything else, getting presents for someone you love is a learning experience.

Our Christmases are just the two of us now. Family has passed on or are scattered in one way or another. It is still such a nice time. I wouldn't want to share it with anyone else.

For us the usual birthday presents are a thing of the past. Now we pick what we want for the evening meal and enjoy it together. Then, as every night, we snuggle on the couch.

We have everything we need or want in life. The gifts of material things are nice, but the gifts from the heart, from the time, from the thought are the best. People have said it for centuries, but it truly is "the thought that counts".

Kathy has given me the best present I've ever had. Kathy gave me Kathy.
Terry

Letter 57

Love Finds Us in Different Ways

Mr. Garrett,

Love finds us in different ways, even when it was there all along.

It was almost three years after we had walked on the grass at Drolette Stadium to get our diplomas before a young lady and I talked again. I had kept the love I felt for Maria hidden in my heart since we had English together with Ms. Finn.

During the conversation she asked me why we had never gotten together in high school. She said she had liked me and wondered if she had ever done something wrong towards me. She said, "You didn't seem to like girls, or at least you didn't seem to like me."

Her words made me almost weak as I stood there. All I could say was the only answer I had to give her: "You weren't my girl. You were always Wayne's girl. I've liked you since we started high school."

Maria said she had never thought of herself as Wayne's girl, though she had dated him more than any other guy in school. She also asked why I had never let her know how I felt.

I told her I, and others thought they were an on-and-off-again couple. They were often seen together around campus and they dated. They held hands and put their arms around each other. They often went to dances and parties together. They sat near each other in class. It seemed they were a couple.

Maria stood listening and then nodded her head. Then she said she understood. She said that during all those years Wayne was just a great friend and still was. When she said he was like a combination companion, big brother, rock of comfort, and willing escort, I felt like a door in our lives had opened.

We've been together since that day, and so much regret the time we missed.

Matt

Letter 58

Lisa Just Likes to Shop

Mr. Garrett,

I love my wife dearly, I truly do, but sometimes that woman makes me question if I'll remain as sane as I think I was when I married her.

Lisa can shop until I drop, and many times I've thought that time was fast approaching. She has a combo Ph.D. and black belt in shopping.

It is a good thing we always have a good breakfast either at home or at a nice restaurant. That keeps me going until I can sit down and eat lunch at another nice restaurant. When lunch time nears, I tell her she'll have to feed me pretty soon.

I don't mind going shopping because she enjoys it so much, and I enjoy being with her. However, it is absolutely amazing to me how many of the same type of article she can look at in one day!

There are times we come back home with a number of purchases and times when we have none. On those times when we are empty handed, believe me, we have still been shopping.

I've always told her to buy anything she wants. She never exceeds needs, and never over indulges in any way. Many of the purchases she makes are for us. Many are for me. I thank her for all of that. Lisa just likes to shop.

We've now covered most of the antique stores in California and we know where the bathrooms are in a number of malls! If there is a sale or if a store is going out of business, we know about it because she has a sensing and homing device, which places the information in front of her in an instant. I don't know how she gets all the information on the site of sales events or how she knows if something is a good buy or not. The woman is amazing.

I'll match my Lisa against any shopper on the planet. She knows what we need and knows what we want. I have it made with that woman. All I have to do is drive and eat.
Eric

Letter 59

A Man Loves His Wife Quietly

Mr. Garrett,

The image of me being what I picture in the movies, as a man who loves a woman, eludes me because it isn't me. In a way that bothers me. Sometimes I wish I had more of that image in me, but I don't. We each are as we are.

My wife receives all I have to give in everything I have to give. At times it may not be what she wants or needs. Or she needs or wants more, but what I give is all I have to give at the time.

On screen there has always been the image of the man calling out his love for his woman in demonstrative ways. That just isn't me. Maybe it is that way with most men.

My wife knows I am and always will be there for her. That isn't a cliché. It is a fact based on who I am, who she is, and what we have built together between us in our lives.

Theresa says what I give and how I show love is fine. I'm glad she feels that way, and I know she isn't simply being kind.

Part of love is simple duty. Things need to be done in lives shared by two. I do what I know needs to be done and what she lets me know needs to be done. I help her, and she helps me. I know that is love.

The kindnesses of touch, and the feel of an embrace, are each part of love. Each may be given only for a specific moment in time or given for no reason. That's all love.

I'll never be a movie idol, and I don't want to be one. I am my Theresa's love, and she is mine. I give my love for her as I can. As long as she says what I give is what she wants, that is all I need. If the time comes when she tells me she needs more, I'll do the best I can. I think that shows love.

Yours,
Gene

Letter 60

Live and Let Live

Mr. Garrett,

I won't tell you my name, or my husband's name, because some might make fun of us over what I write about below. I wouldn't like that, and I know it would upset him. He would then want to confront anyone who did, and that wouldn't be good for any concerned.

My husband and I were both virgins until our wedding night. So many of the other kids we grew up with in Benicia gave up their virginity so easily and so readily. I wanted to give the man I loved and married what no one else could. He felt the same. The stars aligned to allow us each to give the other that gift.

I don't mean to have this read as if I'm preaching. "Live and let live" is a good motto and, as my husband says, "You don't kick my dog and I won't kick yours". I've seen him have to put that concept into action both in high school and after.

My husband has told me of guys who bragged about how many times they have had sex and with how many girls. He has also told me how he believes some of it is simply untrue.

The same has happened with me. When I was in high school, I was a cheerleader and absolutely loved it. I didn't appreciate some of the comments that were made about cheerleaders and how sexually active some were supposed to be. Some of those girls I was with must have had sex at least once. I think some regretted it. I think some thought having sex made them more likeable and appealing to guys in general. I think some were scared little girls, who lacked confidence, and didn't know what they wanted out of life.

Some of those girls with whom I was a cheerleader, and others of my classmates, have been divorced one or more times. One must be a confirmed alcoholic.

I'm very thankful for what my husband and I have shared, from meeting, to dating, to wedding night, and beyond.
Appreciative

Letter 61

Our Newton Loved Baseball

Dear Jim,

I hope you are doing well. I knew your mother and father. They were good people. My husband and son are with them now.

You know that what is now called Fitzgerald Field was just called the baseball field in those days many years ago. Our son, back from the war, and other men in town, built the stands.

There was no grass on the field, except for a few patches of naturally provided weed ground cover, which faded with the season. Most of the field was the loose powdery dirt of the summer. In the winter the field was a lake, like it is now. I saw it that way then and I see it that way today in January after the heavy rains we've had. I don't walk much, or very often, but when I do from my home in the mobile home park, I stand across from the field and look at it.

As the field dried the dirt got very hard. As the weeks progressed the sun cracked the dirt. The infield was dragged by a man driving his old car around in circles pulling a piece of wood. I'm sure the boys, who play there now, think it has always been as it is. I hope they appreciate what they have.

Our Newton loved baseball. It was his third strongest love. His first was his young wife, Mary Jo. The second was his parents. The third would always be baseball.

He was one of those boys who could tell you every pitch

thrown in a game in which he played and the batting average of most major league ball players. That might be a little crazy, but he enjoyed it.

At one time our son was one of the youngest players on a baseball team of various ages which played teams from surrounding towns on Sundays. During one game an opposing player had yelled something bad about a member of our family. After getting a hit, that man was on second base when he yelled it. I remember seeing our son look at him from his position at third base and nod. I never knew what started the bad feeling between the two. I think the man was just a bully and was trying to intimidate someone he saw was young.

The next batter hit the ball to right field for the final out of the game. The man on second base started running towards the third base area. He ran directly at our son like he was going to run him over. Our son turned to face the man and dropped his glove. The man started to raise his right fist and our son hit him in the middle of his face and knocked him down. The field was just dragged dirt like most of the baseball fields in those days. When the man hit the ground, there was a little cloud of dust which appeared all around him. Picture a man falling backwards into a pond, but the water, which splashed up, was brown. It was like a picture held by time.

Everything got quiet for a moment. Then our son picked up his glove and walked off the field with the members of his team, while the other team gathered around their player, who was on the ground.

Cancer took my husband and took our son. I miss them. Cancer is taking me. One day we will all be young again. My Amos and I will sit in the stands and watch our son get a hit and strike out. We will all love it again.

Blessings to you and yours,
Inez

Letter 62

My Business Brought Me to Benicia

Mr. Garrett,

The woman I love and I met at work at a business in the Industrial Park. She worked at the site. I flew my plane in and out of Buchanan Field in Contra Costa County on business connections with her company, and still do. I rented a car for the time I thought I would be around and got on with business.

Martha attracted me enough to start extending my time in Benicia on those trips and delaying my departure as long as possible. Eventually I came to Benicia only to see her every weekend, or other times as I could.

Eventually I did my sly best to entice her to have lunch with me. For over the next year we got to know each other better. We would email and write snail mail and telephone. As time passed, the telephoning between us increased until no day went by without one of us phoning the other. Then it became more than once a day.

If Martha is the example of the women, who live in Benicia, you have a very lucky community. The remainder of the world should envy the women who reside there.

I have a cabin by a lake. Before I met Martha, most of the off time I had was spent there alone. After I met her the time I spent at the cabin became less and less. The time I would have spent there went to coming back to Benicia and staying as long as I could. My business suffered a little, but I didn't care.

Martha and I spent time getting to know each other for over a year before I asked her to fly away with me to the cabin for the weekend. We've been flying and spending time at the cabin ever since.

We aren't married yet, but we soon will be. It was a chance encounter when I walked into that business office in Benicia. Without that, I never would have discovered the happiness I now know.

Ed

Letter 63

I Love My Daughter

Mr. Garrett,

I love my daughter. I've loved her from the moment I first saw her.

When Kim told me she was pregnant again, I thought I was going to be the father of another son. The thought of having a daughter had almost scared me senseless. I had often said to others how happy I was to only have sons. I said I would be scared to death to have a daughter. I was just so worried about her because of so many bad things which I've seen and heard of happening in life. Then I saw our daughter. I love our daughter as I love our sons.

Bringing her home from the hospital was like presenting royalty to the neighborhood. Her two brothers had been informed there would be an addition to the household. They waited with their grandparents at our home. All came out to the car when Kim and I introduced them to the latest member of the family.

It seemed that within days she was on her first date. In what became a permanent routine, I met the young man at the door. Our daughter understood. I had told her to delay appearing, for a few minutes, for any first date she had with any young man, while I conversed with the lad. I think I may have scared some young men off, but they all knew where I stood in my care for my daughter.

She and her escort went to a school dance and had a fun time. She went to a lot of dances and parties over the years. Planning for that first date kept her and her mother busy for over a week. Everything had to be just perfect. Our daughter didn't have to worry, she looked great as always. It was the same with her all the time. She planned ahead, made sure everything was done, and most of the time had fun on her dates.

Every time after the first time I met the young man, it was fine with me if our daughter answered the door, when he called. I had made my point. I did want to see him each time he came over, because I thought that was the polite thing to do and to keep connections strong between us.

Prom dress time her senior year at Benicia High School was my big contribution to her dating life as far as wardrobe was concerned. I remember so well all of us going shopping for the dress. I didn't care about the distance traveled, the time spent, or the price of the dress. She was my little girl, it was her last high school prom, and I was going to do right by her.

We each gave our opinions on which type and color dress would be best for her. Then her mother and she would go into the fitting room and try on the dresses. She would come out and show her brothers and me some of the dresses she wore and ask our opinions. At one store when she exited the fitting room area she walked towards us and said she thought she had found just the right dress. She couldn't have been more correct. It was a beautiful dress on a lovely young lady.

All three of our children were in high school at the same time. I never had much fear for her safety or for her being embarrassed by anyone then. Her two big brothers would kick the butt of anyone who messed with her.

Along with her brothers being around was the fact I had taught her self-defense, the same as I taught the boys. It was partly to counter any bullying while she grew up. In part it was fear on my part of her being a little girl, then a young girl, and then a woman. I had fear of abduction, date rape, and death. It all figured into it. The world has changed greatly since I grew up.

Our daughter could release an unwanted grip of her hand, a frontal choke, or a grab from behind just as easily. We spent some time one day talking about what her response should be if she ever got in a sexually or life threatening position with anyone. I was afraid she might be harmed in some way. It may seem wrong to some but I taught her and my boys, how to kill someone if necessary. I don't care how this reads. I love my kids and want them to come home safely. If that means an attacker gets hurt or dies, that is on the attacker.

Once during her high school years another girl was being unkind to her. Our daughter ended the annoyance very quickly, and then offered the other girl her hand to assist her in getting up and in friendship. They never became good friends, but they became friendlier. The confrontation helped my daughter's "rep" in a number of ways. She wouldn't back down from anyone, neither would our sons. If the other person wanted it, things would work out well between them. High school had its rough moments for all of our kids, including our daughter. Overall it was a time which flew by with fun times and good memories.

She took after her mother in the intelligence area. Some of the classes were a challenge, but she was on the Honor Roll every semester all four years. She also scored very high on her SATs.

Taking part in school activities and being the holder of offices during her high school years was simply part of the equation of who she is. There were times at home when she fell asleep with a book in her hands, but everything got done and got done well.

As with our boys, our daughter is a fine athlete. She played volleyball, basketball, and softball at the school. She swims like a fish, has a great forehand in tennis, can run all day, and glides across the dance floor. God granted her natural grace with a competitive spirit. I think my wife and I helped to develop those qualities. She was the epitome of the female athlete. Before and after the game she was the good looking girl and during game time she was a tenacious competitor but also a fine sportswoman.

Our daughter was highly recruited athletically and academically. She was granted various forms of scholarships in academics. She accepted an athletic scholarship at a very prestigious university, but it was really the all-around person all the schools recruited. Even if she hadn't received an athletic scholarship her grade point average, the classes she had taken, and her extracurricular activities in general made her a catch for any institution of higher learning.

When the kids were younger, and we were too, we would go backpacking in the mountains. Many times some of their friends would come with us. Our base camp was the cabin where many fine days were spent. Then we would hike to the trail head and start exploring. Our daughter was a mountain goat in her ability to climb in those mountains. She fished with the rest of us, and when we set up our night camp, settled in to tell stories and listen to tall tales. She could rough it with the best of any of us, her father included. There was a surprise snowfall one night. She woke up laughing about it, she enjoyed it so much.

Her mother and I introduced her to wine, as we did her brothers, when we thought it was time. The cork remover gave her a little problem the first time. When she came back from college during her senior year, she said she had to teach her roommates how to use a cork remover. They only had a corkscrew at their apartment and one of the girls held the bottle between her legs and fought the cork out. The next day our daughter bought a cork remover for all of them.

Part of her education from her parents was introducing her to people who could help her. As she grew, she met those we had known in our youth. Some of them were teachers. Parents do what they can to smooth the path for their children.

In her senior year in high school our daughter was brought home after a date by her long-time boyfriend at 5:00 a.m. Though I knew they would be late, because it was a special occasion, I think they were both a little worried about how I would react. I "just happened to be up early that morning reading the newspaper" when they arrived. My daughter kissed me and her date thanked me for allowing them to attend the function from which they had just returned. I told them both that I knew he would always defend, protect, and honor her. He had proven that to me in the time I had known him and seen them grow together.

When our daughter graduated from college she married that fine young man. They live out of state now as they follow their careers. I miss them both, but especially my daughter.

The one who I wrote of as my daughter is an illusion. Thanks for giving me the chance to write about the love I could have had for a daughter. My daughter is the daughter I never had. I miss her.

Scott

Letter 64

We Talked

Mr. Garrett,

Anna pounded on the door until I thought the glass would break. I heard her say, "Open the door. If it's over that's fine, but talk to me. This isn't right."

I pulled back the curtain, opened the door, and let her back into my home and back into my life. I had been very, very, stupid. I had felt sorry for myself and felt I had nothing to offer. Economic times laid me off. I had enough money for about a month. After that I would be living under a bridge somewhere.

We had only been able to see each other when we could, long weekends, times we could make special arrangements to get off, and holidays. For each of us special efforts were made to see someone special. She spent days and nights with me at my home, when she could, and I did the same with her.

I had sent her an email telling her I couldn't marry her if I didn't have enough financial stability in my life to care for my wife as I thought I should. In about a heartbeat after I sent the email she called me. I let the phone ring and the answering machine picked up her message. She said she knew I was by the phone and pleaded for me to pick up the receiver. I couldn't do it. She hung up and sent back an email reply saying things would work out, but that we had to talk.

It wasn't in the plans for her to drive to Benicia then, but that is what she did. It was a Thursday evening. She filled her travel bag and started driving that night. When I found out she did that, I ached that she drove alone from Arizona starting at night.

She called in sick the next morning from a coffee shop. Later that day she was in Benicia at my front door.

I got another job Monday, when she was driving back after calling in sick again. We aren't married yet. If things go right, Anna will be my June bride. Spending my life living under a bridge didn't happen. We talked.

Sebastian

Letter 65

A Father's Sin

Mr. Garrett,

My father raped me. He said he was teaching me about sex and breaking me in for when I got married. He said it was a custom for fathers in his country to do it. I later found out he lied about that, like he did so many other things.

Being raped by my father affected my relations with boys and then men. I think some guys thought I was shy. I was deeply confused and didn't know what to think or say to anyone. I got through high school the best I could. My grades were always good. I think I put extra effort into them to escape memories and because I felt I had nothing else.

I started dating a man when I was twenty-two. We didn't even hold hands until almost a year had passed. He didn't force anything. It was like he knew something was wrong in my feelings and emotions.

Once when we were alone, I started crying and couldn't stop for what seemed an hour. He didn't reach for me, but he opened his arms and let me come to him when I wanted to. I told him what had happened with my father. He listened. He didn't say anything except that he was sorry for the hurt and pain I had gone through then and all the time since.

I got angry with him and told him sex was probably all he wanted from me anyway and he was just playing me along. He said that if all he wanted from me was sex, he wouldn't have been spending so much time trying to get to know me. He became my friend, my lover, and finally my husband.

I'll never forgive my father. He hurt me, but he didn't destroy me. I'm not under his control. When he died, I didn't even attend his funeral services.

I'm with a man who truly loves me. He is a kind man, an understanding man, and the man I will always love.
(Unsigned)

Letter 66

Two Pregnant Women

Mr. Garrett,

I had two women pregnant at the same time. It wasn't being studly, it was being stupid. Yes, it was in Benicia.

One may have been trying to trap me. Maybe that isn't what happened. We were alone one night and she wound up getting pregnant. The other woman loved me, but I was too stupid about a lot of things then to understand.

I told each of the women about what was going on. It wasn't macho bragging, I just thought they should each know. I wasn't proud of what I had done or of having to tell them.

Nature terminated one of the pregnancies. That woman forgave me. Then she said things probably wouldn't have worked out between us anyway. She is a nurse and helps bring a lot of babies into the world. I hope she is capable of having children when she wishes to have them. She has no children now, and I've found that kind of strange.

The other pregnant woman felt sorry for all of us involved. She felt sorry for the other woman's suffering and the loss of the child she was carrying. She felt sorry for me because I didn't see that she really loved me. In something, which was strange to me, she said she felt sorry for herself, because she didn't think she and I would be together as man and wife.

That woman was wrong. I don't know what you would call it. It might be a spark or something, but a change came over me. I had dated a number of women, and lived with two of them. The woman who carried my child was different from all of them, but I hadn't seen it until that moment.

We started our relationship fresh right then. We've been married for almost five years. Our son is almost five years old now, and a baby sister is on the way. All of our life together is because of a forgiving woman I love very much. My only regret is that I didn't see sooner the love she held for me.
Jerry

Letter 67

You Told Me She Was a Good Girl

Hey, Big Jim,

You told me about that girl, but I wouldn't listen, like usual. You said you knew she was a good girl and wouldn't play around, and you were right. I had to find out for myself.

After that first dance, we were parked up in the hills where they were building some of the Southampton homes. I was trying to put my magical moves on her. The local gendarmes patrol saw us parked there and ran us off.

Hey, I can always improvise. I drove us down to the Clock Tower and we started watching the submarine races. I know I told you about the time I removed that double-barreled slingshot from that one girl's bosom. I thought I would at least get the same action from this girl.

She had snuggled up next to me and I had my right arm around her. We started kissing and my left hand casually dropped down to see what type of material her blouse was made of and she slapped the snot out of me. I mean, the girl hit me!

She said she would kiss, hug, and hold me, but I wasn't going to touch her there, or anyplace else she didn't want, unless we were married. She meant it.

We must have sat there and talked for a couple of hours. No girl had ever sat and talked with me for that long. Maybe I didn't give any of them the chance, but I know none of them did.

Jim, that girl got me to cut my hair shorter, slow down my driving, and spend all my free time with her before we got married. Now, my free time is her free time. Our SUV has school stickers on the back.

I won't sign this because I know you know who I am and because I don't want to embarrass my wife. I love that woman, Jim. You were right about her being a good girl. There should be more like her.

Thanks for the advice.

(Unsigned)

Letter 68

It Seemed As If Her Eyes Were Always on Me

Mr. Garrett,

When I was freshman at Benicia High, I was at a dance and a senior girl asked me to dance. She had walked over from where she was standing with some other girls. The guys I was standing with started making the usual comments guys make at that age and in similar circumstances. I admit I was a little nervous, but also excited. Part of what I felt was challenge and the need to show the guys I could handle things.

She knew what she was doing. Her smile was natural, friendly, and relaxed. Being three years older than me helped. She had a lot more experience than I did in social situations and boy-girl relations.

We spent most of the evening together. We spent a lot of time after that together too. She opened some avenues in my life. Through the years I've heard of and read a number of stories about the "older woman" in the lives of some men. In most cases things worked out well between them. That's how it was with us.

When I asked her why she had asked me to dance that night, she answered that she had seen me around school and I looked like a nice guy.

I was "in love" for the next two years. We went places and did things together. We spent as much time together the summer after she graduated as we could. Then she went off to college in another state. We kept in touch with phone calls and letters, but gradually time did what it often does in situations like ours. She came back to Benicia for Thanksgiving, Christmas, and Spring Break, but things had changed. Distance was good for us. It gave each of us a wider view.

She was always supportive of me and I was the same with her, but our lives pulled farther from each other. It took her being out of high school for a year for me to get over her.

My junior year I quietly dated six girls. When my senior year began, I became very aware of a girl in the junior class.

It isn't an uncommon story, I guess. Sharon was there all along for the last couple of years, but the strength of my vision was directed elsewhere.

The first attraction I felt towards her was her eyes. It seemed as if they were always on me. It wasn't that her eyes were simply beautiful and were held in a beautiful face. What I saw was a veil which protected the beauty and depth behind them. I felt something lovely and deep passed through those eyes to me.

For the remainder of that school year, if either of us were seen at a dance or party the other was probably there too. When I played ball, she was at every game, home-and-away that her schedule would allow. If she was involved in an activity, I was there if I had any chance of making it. Sometimes our schedules clashed, but we phoned each other as soon as we could after the conclusion of the games.

We never went steady. We just were so often around each other it probably seemed like we did. It was so natural for me to assume she would be my date as often as she could, would help me wash my car, and would help me with class work when trigonometry was just a little hard.

She regretted not being able to be my date once, when her parents had a family outing planned. Once she wasn't feeling well, so we didn't go to the movie like we had planned. Once I was too late in asking her to a dance, and she went with someone else.

At the dance she gave the other guy the friendliness and respect he deserved and earned by his invitation and her acceptance. He was a good guy, and we both liked him as a friend.

I went to the dance alone, but we all talked there. She danced all the dances with him. I danced with a couple of girls, but mainly watched her, while trying not to show it.

The next morning I phoned her. I told her that if she helped me wash my car, I'd buy her an icecream float. She said she would be happy to be with me, but I didn't have to buy her an icecream float.

We had a good time washing the car. I managed to "accidentally" squirt her with the hose a couple of times. She paid me back with a soapy sponge up side of my head.

We went to the Royal Bakery for the icecream floats. The talk there led to thoughts of the dance the night before.

I told Sharon I was sorry I had waited too long to ask her to the dance.

She said if I wanted her for my own, I had to tell her. I did. We became a steadily unofficial steady couple after that.

High school came to an end for me and I thought of how the other girl and I had been. I didn't want to put any holds on anyone. I knew I wouldn't be around a lot. Sharon and I agreed neither had a hold on the other, but that we each liked each other very much.

I went to college and the next year she joined me in the same state. I made some long drives between her college and mine over the next few years.

When Sharon graduated, I gave her a compass. I told her it was to always guide her to my heart. She said her heart was mine. Then I gave her a ring and asked her to be my bride. She said “yes”.

Our kids have gone through the school system here in Benicia. We've never told them how to live their lives, but we have told them to always keep their eyes open in everything.

Sharon and I still wash the car together.

Jon

Letter 69

I Loved My Husband and His Brother

Mr. Garrett,

I loved my ex-husband's brother. It cost me my marriage and the love of both men.

My ex-husband and his twin brother grew up in Maryland. I was raised in California and I met them at a party in Florida. Such things happen through institutions of higher learning and career paths.

The brothers are military men. Each looked great in his uniform. My ex-husband is a naval officer and his brother is a Marine officer. Their father was career Navy. It was a natural move for them to become officers.

I doubt there are many brothers as competitive in everything in life, and especially against each other, than those two. It wasn't just the everyday things, or the pick-up games, it was everything. Maybe that was the problem.

An example of the competitiveness between my husband and his brother happened one year at the annual Marine Corps Marathon. It was unbelievable. I was near the finish line and it was hurtful to me to see how hard they ran against each other. Believe me, they were running against each other, no matter how many others were out there that day.

"My husband and his brother" that reads so strangely to me now when I see it. Once they were, but that was centuries ago it seems.

When we got married, my husband's brother was the best man. It seems kind of ironic now, since I later came to think of my then brother-in-law as the best man.

We had a nice house in Norfolk, Virginia. My husband's brother lived on base at the Batchelor's Officer's Quarters at the time.

My husband was deployed to the Persian Gulf, in the first war, shortly after his brother rotated back from Iraq. I missed my husband desperately. My brother-in-law tried to help me through that time. We started going to the grocery store together and sharing Saturday evening meals. One night he didn't leave. I didn't want him to leave and he didn't want to either. We both knew what we were doing. As foolish as it seems now, it seemed like the right thing to do then.

Any branch of the military is actually a small community. Within each of those small communities are still smaller communities. Word travels quickly anywhere, especially within small communities. The people who informed my husband did the right thing.

My husband and I divorced for "irreconcilable differences". He and his brother kept what had occurred concerning all of us to just ourselves. Some people have an idea of what happened, but it didn't affect the careers of my ex-husband and his brother. I'm glad of that.

Who was to blame, some may ask? I don't know. Perhaps it is only me. Perhaps it is all three of us and our parents.

I moved to Benicia and live alone. Maybe I subconsciously needed the small community and the water and a continent between me and the East Coast. There is love in my heart for both of those men I knew. When I sit in my living room watching television in the evening after work, I wonder if I'll see either of them again. I don't date. I drink too much alcohol. I go for walks with my dog. I did love them both, each in my own way.

Mr. Garrett, I thought your advertisement was nice. I hope this letter isn't too much of a "downer", but you said you wanted letters dealing in any way with a connection of love with Benicia. This is mine.

B.

Letter 70

The Bag of Sand Was Really Heavy

Mr. Garrett,

The things guys do in the name of love pass all boundaries of what they would do for someone they didn't love. My wife, Betty, and I could have gone to a store and bought prepackaged bags of sand, but she wanted sand from a specific beach, Ano Nuevo. It had been "our beach" until it became a regular public attraction. It is as popular now as Ninth Street beach here in town.

When we first went to Ano Nuevo beach, we parked on the side of a back road along the cliffs. Then we walked down a pretty steep grade to get to the beach. Once there we walked north until we found the spot we liked. It was the same spot each time.

Years after we were married, the love of my life decided she wanted a bag of sand from that beach as a memento of the memories we had shared there. Her idea of a bag was one the size of a navy sea bag or a barracks bag. Anyone, who has ever lifted one of those puppies, when it was only packed tight with uniforms, other clothing, and other gear, knows how heavy they are. It isn't like in the movies where the star studly easily picks it up and carries it like it's a briefcase.

I got out one of my old sea bags, quietly complaining all the way, and told her she had no idea how heavy that full bag would be. Blessings on her, when she told me she just thought it would be a sturdy bag, and whatever I carried in it would be fine.

We drove to Ano Nuevo beach the following Saturday morning. There were already more people there than there had ever been totally in all the other times we had been there.

We walked down to the beach, and I thought the road had gotten steeper over the years. We sat and looked at the water for awhile. Then I loaded the bag about half full and almost got a hernia when I tried to lift it. It is amazing how sand weighs more the older you get. My love laughed and told me to take some of the sand out. I blessed that lovely child and told her what a nice person she was.

Carrying that almost half-filled bag of sand up the road was an adventure in itself. I swear, if I didn't work out, Betty could have rolled me into the drainage ditch, used the sand in the bag to cover me up, and let me rest in peace.

I got the bag to the car, put it in the trunk, and told my lady we needed to talk about ever doing that again. My legs were heavy, but my breath was rapidly returning to normal. Then she took the cooler out of the trunk. Our lunch was in that cooler, and I was definitely ready for it.

We walked to one of the empty tables at the south end of the parking lot and laid out our meal. Tuna fish sandwiches, as only she can make, and which were the main part of our meal the first time we went to that beach, again were eaten. Potato chips, an apple, a cookie, and a carbonated beverage each complimented the sandwich. It was a great meal as they have all been.

As we sat there, we were back in a time and place of our youth. The girl with whom I fell in love sat there with me for almost two hours as we looked at the water and talked. We weren't sitting or lying on a blanket on the sand, and we weren't alone. It didn't matter. She was with me and I was with her. When the sun was nearing the horizon, we repacked the cooler and started the drive back to Benicia.

The sand was placed in a special container in our back yard. Sea shells and small pieces of driftwood were added to the surface. That magical piece of artwork sits there every day bringing each of us memories we cherish of days on a stretch of empty beach.

We often walk to the Ninth Street beach. Betty and I also watched the sunset there in our youth. It was "our first beach" and will be our last.

Yours, Jack

Letter 71

If Love is Real, It Will Last

G-Man,

When I had you for Military History you told us a lot of stories. I think that was a great way to teach because it really got to a lot of us.

What you did most was talk WITH us. That was important.

There were things you wouldn't, or couldn't for one reason or another, talk about. I think if we had been closer in age and each "18 and out of high school" like you always used to say, you would have told us more.

Your love for your wife came across so much in the class, and in the times we talked after class, and at your home.

You didn't encourage any of us to join the military and you didn't try to discourage us. You always said it was our decision, and that you just tried to inform us of what to expect. You joked about it, but you were also being truthful, when you said a recruiter's job is to recruit. My recruiter was one of the guests in our class that year and he definitely recruited me. It was good for me, though.

I wanted to tell you that a girl, who was in one of your other classes at the high school, and I have been married for almost seven years now. You said one day in class that if love was real, it would last.

That young lady and I made love for the first time in a parking lot at the San Francisco airport before I went back to base and shipped out.

I don't want anyone else to know about that evening between my wife and me. I wanted you to know, though, that you were right. If love is real, it will last against time, distance, youth, and opinion. You were right. Our marriage is proof.
(Unsigned)

Letter 72

Unrequited Love is Still Love

Mr. Garrett,

The last thing I told him was to take good care of her.

We had all gone to good ol' B.H.S. For about a year of that time she had been my girl. We broke up, as most high school couples do, and went our separate ways for a few years.

Each of us went off to college. Her school was about mid-way between the school of the other guy and mine. Whenever the other guy, or I, got the chance we would visit her. The only times were all together for the next few years was during school vacations and breaks.

She kept entering my thoughts, and the depth and length of those thoughts got longer and longer.

It came down to her choosing him or me. She chose him. I'm happy for her happiness.

She knew I loved her, because I had told her. I only did it once. Maybe that was the problem. Maybe he told her many more times, and in ways I couldn't.

I was a long way away when they got married. They invited me, and I could have been there. I just couldn't deal with the idea of sitting there and seeing her at the altar marrying him.

I still think of their life together, and probably always will. They have two nice children, and I'm not even married.

I have enough business in my life to keep me busy, but

some of the nights are long. It takes two or three cups of coffee to get started the mornings after those nights. I still picture our Senior Prom. Some doctor would say I was mentally ill, but I still hold a love for her.

Unrequited love is still love, though the depth of it is stronger from one to the other than it is returned.
Jason

Letter 73

Loving Care Makes a House a Home

Mr. Garrett,

I love my wife, and I love the home we've made together. Our home is the best looking place on the block, as I tell anyone who will listen. It wouldn't be that way, if it wasn't for Allison. No one can love a thing as they can love another, but they can love what they build together. A building is just a structure, if there isn't loving care applied to it. That loving care of a home can't be with thoughts of a house being an investment. The souls of people are expressed in many ways. One of those is in how they care for their home. The loving care helps to make a house a home. The memories of laughter and sorrow are as much connectors and binding material as nails and glue.

Time is creeping up on Allison and me as it does for everyone. We have everything we need in life. She has my love, and I have hers. When it comes time, we are prepared to lock the doors for the last time and move on to the next stage of our lives. We are also prepared to each live on here alone as we wait to join the other again. Whatever happens, as always, will be as God wishes.

Our home was never a monetary gamble, as we looked for the best time in the market to sell it. It is better at this moment than many newly built houses. The money we've spent on maintaining and improving the structure of the house, and the grounds surrounding it, has been for our enjoyment, protection, and pride.

We could have cut corners with the house. We didn't have to use the extra nail, or the best paint, or install the solid brass door knobs throughout our home. A home reflects who lives there. Ours reflects us. It is cozy, comfortable, functional, and truly has a "lived in" feel. It is a home, not just a house, an act of love, not number-crunching for potential gain.

In time our home, and all in it, will be given away. That may sound silly, stupid, or even crazy. We don't care how it sounds. We can't take it with us, and we want our home and its contents to be useful and appreciated.

There are those, who we know, who will be given specific items or items in general. What they do with them after that is on them. The point is they will be given things which have been cared for and appreciated. The man, who enjoys camping with his family, will receive articles my wife and I have used. Men, who enjoy being handymen and building things, will be given sets of tools. The hunter will receive the rifle, the fisherman the fishing pole. The collections, the books, and the mementos will be given to those to whom those items have special appeal.

It is set up to will our home to a good young couple, who will appreciate it, take it for theirs, and make it their own as time passes. We would enjoy, so much, the knowledge that we have left the home we've built to a couple just starting out. The gift wouldn't answer all their questions and settle all the problems which come with starting out in married life. It would give them a solid home footing foundation. They would have their struggles, as everyone does in life, but they would know they lived in a home which shared love. Their love would only make the love shared with that home stronger.

We keep on the lookout for that good young couple. There are those we see who meet what we seek. Perhaps someday an attorney will ask to meet with them.

George

Letter 74

She Was Clean

Mr. Garrett,

The first kiss at the end of our first date is what got me. I've heard some line in a movie, where a woman said something like, "you had me at hello." I understand that completely. As soon as I could, I made sure we had a second date.

I've been asked many times what the attraction was between my wife and me. I admit she saw me before I saw her. Once when I was asked what attracted me to the girl, who became the woman I married, I replied, "She was clean." She truly was, and is.

Things went wrong in my head for awhile, and we didn't see each other. Then the light started to come on in my head and she kept coming back into my mind. It wasn't just because I was in a hot, smelly place far away.

When I got back from that place, she still wanted to be with me. When I went back to that place, she sent me letters and packages. She sent her love care of Fleet Post Office, San Francisco.

When I came back the third time from that place, she and I were well established on fulfilling the life to which fate has led us.

I've been as good to her as I could possibly be and loved her with all the love which is within me. I regret I haven't been good enough all the time and haven't been able to give her more, because she deserves more. I've given what it is within me to give. She tells me that is great, and I thank her for that.

My love was a sweet, caring girl. No one ever talked badly about her, and she had a lot of dates. Some girls get a reputation of being very friendly on the first date. Others get the reputation of being a good person with whom to be.

My love was, is, and always will be clean. There is much depth and breadth to that word.

Mark

Letter 75

Summer Love

Dear Mr. Garrett,

Summer love can be sweet or bitter-sweet, a few days of youthful play, or something which lasts. Even if the two never come to be together, the love can be lasting.

I fell in love with a Benicia boy one summer between my freshman and sophomore years in high school. He attended Benicia High School, and I was visiting my uncle and his family in Benicia.

My uncle worked a lot of hours. He wasn't against hiring a local boy for yard work, or car washing, when he felt the need. That's how I met Jon.

I had made friends with another girl, Carol, at the swimming pool. She pointed out a boy, who I immediately thought was very cute. We laughed and joked as teenage girls did then and I'm sure do today. I may be old, but I think our outlook, and expectations, were different then than those of most teenage girls today. I think ours was more of a romantic era with those feelings attached to boys who came into our lives.

A little before 1:00pm the next afternoon Carol and I were sitting in a swing on the front porch of the home of my uncle's family. The boy from the pool walked up, and I think my heart "skipped a beat", as the saying goes.

He had come to do some yard work for my uncle, and I

couldn't have felt luckier, or happier. We talked for a few minutes, after Carol introduced us. Then he talked with my Aunt and started doing the work my uncle wanted done. The last job he did was scrape the grass and weeds off the front yard. Many yards in Benicia in those days were scraped clean of spring growth. There were very few lawns.

Carol and I had watched Jon work in the back yard raking leaves and doing some cultivating. When he said he was going around to the front, we followed and again sat on the porch. This time we sat on the steps. It was a better place to watch.

Jon got to work on scraping the yard and, in all honesty, lost thought of us. He had a job to do and he was doing it.

After about fifteen minutes, he took his shirt off and laid it over a bush. You could see in his face that his concentration was on his work. I truly don't think he knew we were there at the time. His body was lithe and muscular. The day was bordering on hot and his body glistened in the sun. The little rivulets of sweat ran down his chest and darkened the tops of his pants. He simply kept on working until the yard work was completed. He didn't take a break for water or anything else.

He gave a look around, as if to see that everything he was being paid to do was done. I learned that was just his way. Things were done. Then he put his shirt back on and came over to where Carol and I sat. I was really a little embarrassed when Carol said I had been watching his sweaty body for the last hour. I had, but so had she.

Jon laughed. We all talked for a few minutes and then my aunt came to the door. She paid Jon for his work and commented on what a good, and quick, job he had done.

I think Jon was a little embarrassed. To him life was pretty simple in some ways, but I learned later, very complicated in others. He had merely been paid for what he had been hired to do. That's all he saw in it.

As Jon was getting ready to leave, after my aunt had gone back inside the house, he asked if Carol and I would be at the pool the next afternoon. We blurted out with far too much enthusiasm for decorum that we would be. He said he would be there, too, and would like to see us then.

Later, Carol told me she was as giddy as I was between then and the time we saw Jon at the pool the next day. We were first in line for the opening of the pool door.

We saw Jon walk out on the pool deck and then look around. I think he was trying to look casual, but he was definitely looking for a familiar face or two.

Carol and I talked with Jon for most of that afternoon when we weren't splashing around in the pool. Jon and I seemed to have a connection, and I think Carol understood.

When the pool closed, we walked away together, none of us had cars. We walked Carol to her home, and then Jon walked me to my uncle's home. The world could have been coming to an end, during the time of that walk, when Jon and I were alone, and I wouldn't have known it.

When we got to the door, Jon asked if I thought it would be OK with my uncle, if he asked me to go to the movies with him that night. At the time I wasn't greatly experienced in dating, but I also knew my uncle would approve. I told Jon it would be OK with my uncle and great with me.

So, Jon asked me to go to the movies. We went to the State Theater that night and the Victory Theater the next night. Even if you threatened me with dire bodily harm, I couldn't tell you at this time the names of the movies we saw those two nights.

It was a walk of less than ten blocks to my uncle's home from either of the theaters. I tried to make that distance last as long as I could, but each night we finally got to my uncle's home. The second night we kissed for the first time. It was a romantic, sweet, soft, tender kiss.

I was only in Benicia on that trip for a few more days after that. Jon and I spent as much of that time together as we could. We played a board game on the front porch, sat in the backyard and watched the birds playing in the trees, rode bikes, and walked to Ninth Street, where we sat and looked at the water and the bridge in the distance. It was a good time.

In those few days my aunt and uncle got to know Jon better. I guess they couldn't help it, because it probably seemed to them he was around about every waking hour. I didn't mind.

My aunt was a sweetheart person, as was my uncle. They are both gone now and their home has long been converted and modernized. Another family makes memories there now.

Seeing how I felt about Jon, my aunt asked him to have dinner with us the night before I was to go back home. Jon was surprised, but quickly said he would like to have dinner with us. It was a great evening. Six of us ate homemade raviolis, salad, and sourdough bread. I didn't think my nephews could eat as much as they did, for as small as they were.

Later, my nephews went to bed and my aunt and uncle sat down to watch television. Jon and I were alone on the front porch, and on the seat swing. As the fog came in to cool the night air, we naturally found ourselves snuggled close to each other. When we kissed, our kisses were as romantic as our first kiss, but they were closer in feeling.

About 11:30pm the lights in the living room were turned off. I knew it was time for me to go inside and Jon knew it was time for him to leave. Our summer together was almost over. We kissed once more and then he walked me to the front door. Then tears started running down my face and I put my arms around his neck and told him how much I would miss him. Jon was a tough boy, but his eyes glistened and there was a quiver in his voice, when he told me he would miss me, too.

Jon and I wrote each other a few times over the next year. The following summer I was able to visit Benicia again and he and I started together again as if there had been no parting. It was a closer time for the two of us than the previous summer.

Jon had his driver's license and a car by that summer. My uncle's home became basically a rest stop. Jon and I were almost always doing something and going somewhere. As with all things, that summer came to an end.

My father's work took our family even further from Benicia. I met another boy who reminded me so much of Jon. As the months passed letters between Jon and me became fewer. In one of his last letters he said he was steadily dating a very nice girl. In one of the nicest compliments I've ever received, he wrote that she reminded him of me and that was what first attracted him to her.

I had always liked my uncle. He was so much like my father. When he became ill, my father got airplane tickets for all of us and we flew to San Francisco. He rented a car and drove us to Benicia.

In my heart I needed to tell Jon something in my personal life. I needed to tell him I was getting married. I telephoned him and he came over to my uncle's home that evening. My family was impressed with Jon. After all I had told them about him, I think they felt they knew him. He was accepted into our little gathering as one of the family.

After about an hour, I excused Jon and me with the reasoning I would like to see some of the sights we had known before. As we drove around town, the space between the words we shared grew. I sat close to him, as I had before. I felt nothing wrong in doing it, and I know he didn't either. From our letters, and our conversation that night, he knew what was happening.

Jon parked the car at Ninth Street where we had shared some moments, which were very tender. I put my head on his shoulder, he wrapped his right arm across my shoulders and we sat looking straight ahead and not speaking.

Finally, he said he hoped I was happy and would be all my life. When I told him I was going to be married, he said he knew and understood. We kissed once. It was a long, tender, sweet kiss of young lovers saying good-bye. Then I pulled back from Jon and told him I needed to be getting back.

The porch light was on when we pulled up to my uncle's home. The seat swing was empty.

Jon sent the nicest and most thoughtful wedding gift. He had collected a small box of mementos from places we had been in Benicia. Among other items were a photograph of the swimming pool packed with kids on a warm summer day, two ticket stubs from each of the two theaters, a receipt from the Park and Shop Market, a napkin from the Royal Bakery, a eucalyptus seed from a hill where we once sat, and a small plastic container of sand from the Ninth Street beach.

Jon and I kept in touch through the years. He married a few years after I did. He never once missed sending my husband and me, and later our growing family, a Christmas card. Two photographs were enclosed with each card. One was of a different scene in Benicia each year. The other photograph was of the Carquinez Bridge, taken from the exact same spot each year, the spot from which we each knew our lives were moving on.

Carol and I keep in touch. We also exchange Christmas cards and once or twice a year we send a letter. If something either of us feels is important occurs, we telephone each other. Lately we've started emailing each other about once a week.

Two nights ago I received a telephone call from my friend Carol, who I met at the swimming pool that summer long ago. She said Jon, the boy who captured my heart that summer, and has held a place in it since, had died. Jon had suffered a stroke which, Carol said, probably killed him before he hit the floor of his kitchen.

For what seemed a time without end I couldn't speak. My friend's voice kept coming through to me asking if I was alright. Finally, my voice answered that I was, but I didn't tell her my heart wasn't. I told Carol I was so sorry Jon was dead. I told her he was such a nice person.

Jon was my first real boyfriend, and he was my first love. I hope there is one like Jon in the life of every young girl and a young girl, who cares, in the life of every young boy. When those connections occur, they sometimes lead to a lifetime together for two people. In the case of Jon and me that didn't happen. But, we had such sweet memories of those few days that summer and the few times we shared after that.

I've talked with my husband of how I felt about Jon. He understands. Jon was my summer love who warmed my heart and opened it to the man I later married.
Susan

Letter 76

That Night on the Couch

Mr. Garrett,

It was just a boink to me, but she took it as a lifetime commitment. I'm glad she did.

My wife and I had dated a few times, but hadn't gone any farther than making out. She was a good kid and I liked her or I wouldn't have been taking her out.

One evening after her parents had gone out to dinner, she and I curled up on the couch. I went to kiss her and she came into my arms like she was part of my chest. She had never done that before. I was surprised, but at that moment I was one happy guy.

I can't say that before I knew it we were making love. Believe me, I understood exactly what was going on. I could describe the blouse and skirt she wore that evening. My surprise was in not thinking anything like that would happen with that girl. I thought maybe she felt she would have to have sex with me to keep me around. She wouldn't have had to, and I've told her that many times over the years. We still joke about being on that couch when we first learned of each other.

Some of my friends at work started saying I was whipped, but I didn't care then and don't care now. That night on the couch solidified something, which had already started to grow, between that girl and me.

One Saturday afternoon, when we were walking out to my

car to go to a movie in Vallejo, she had her mind in an upset about something. I had commented that I couldn't wait to get her alone in a darkened theater and she said the only reason I wanted to be around her was for sex. We stopped right there on the sidewalk leading from her front door. I told her that if that was the only reason she thought I was dating her, she was wrong. That was when I asked her to marry me. She accepted.
Fred

Letter 77

Red Lights Run in the Name of Love

Mr. Garrett,

Love is shown in many ways. One way is to get your husband to medical attention.

It started one day when I was home alone. I discovered the years had caught up with me, and I wasn't as quick as I had once been. I had cut the tip of a finger almost off and was in the kitchen trying to stop the bleeding. As I stood there, I wondered how well blood stains would blend in with oak cabinetry. A couple of the splatter marks on the paint work by the sink actually looked kind of attractive. It was a rosette-like pattern. I guess you had to be there.

I applied direct pressure and elevated my hand like some red cross instructors had taught me years before, but it was obvious I was losing the battle. There was no doubt I would need stitches.

My wife, Marie, was at work, so I telephoned her while the towel wrapped finger dripped on the floor. She is a fine woman who has shared many experiences with me. This was the first time I had ever telephoned her because of an annoyance to my anatomy. I had no other choice. No one else was around and I wasn't about to call the fire department or an ambulance. I've been told from time-to-time that my middle name is Mule. I told Marie there was no problem, but I needed a ride to the doctor's office to get some stitches. When I told her "digiti" whatever number was cut, she said she would be right home.

Marie checked out of work, engaged the wings on the car, and flew home. I was standing outside waiting for her when she pulled into the driveway. She got out and opened the door for me and connected my seat belt, and we were off down the road. Our first stop was at our clinic, where we received the joyous news that we would have to go to the hospital in Vallejo.

Within three-point-two-five seconds, we were in the car again heading down the freeway to Vallejo. I thought it was a fun ride, except for having to squeeze my finger.

Marie's car was one of those two-seater, sporty models, which corner as the saying goes, like they are on rails. Part of what made the ride fun for me was seeing Marie's face, when we cornered, running two red lights in a row. When I told her what had happened, she didn't miss a beat in her driving. She said she didn't see them because she was concentrating on her driving, which she was. It would be good, if more people concentrated on what they did the way Marie did on that drive to the hospital. The woman was definitely concentrating. Her man was "injured" and she was going to get him to help as quickly as she could.

We walked into emergency and the woman at the counter helped us with barely speaking a word. She walked us to a room and told me to sit on a table and said Marie could wait in the room if she wanted. She wanted to and sat in a chair by a wall.

A doctor came in the room with a nurse. They removed the towel from my hand and the doctor told the nurse some things he needed. A couple of minutes later he was sewing up my finger. It was interesting to watch. That needle had to be the sharpest point produced by mankind. It penetrated my fingernail like it wasn't there.

That is the basic story of the great red light-running trip. What can't be shown on this paper is the love my love showed for me in her care and dedication. She was a good trooper in time of need, as she has always been. Marie drove us home at

the correct posted speed limit. We didn't run anymore red lights. When we got inside the house, she told me how worried she had been for and about me. She told me she loved me, as she's told me more than once every day for close to forty years. I told her I loved her, as I have for close to forty years.
Mike

Letter 78

Kathy's Voice

Mr. Garrett,

It relaxes me to hear Kathy sing. I think having a woman be able to relax a man is a showing of love.

I've carried Kathy's voice in my head and on tape across half the planet. I've heard it on ships, planes, and buses. I've heard it early in the morning, mid-day and late at night. At times I was only able to hear it in my head, at other times the recordings were the actual sounds of peaceful reminders of our home in Benicia.

Kathy's voice is soft. It is tender and caresses like a breath, which surrounds me like a clear velvet fog. It clings, yet moves. It holds, yet frees.

The first time I heard Kathy sing was at an assembly at Benicia High School. She always had a secure shyness about her. When she walked out onto the gym floor and picked up the microphone, I was amazed. My eyes were on her for being the good looking girl, who walked out there, to being that, and more, as she walked back to the bleachers.

Her voice was great. She sang a song titled something like, "Can't Help Loving That Man of Mine" from the musical "Showboat". When she was singing, she moved her eyes around the audience. They seemed repeatedly to come back to meet mine.

For the remainder of the assembly I kept looking at her.

When she first sat down, the people around her congratulated her. After a few minutes she turned to look at me. She smiled.

We were sitting about forty feet away from each other. I wanted to tell her how well she had sung, and how surprised I was by her talent because I had no idea she could sing. All I could think of doing was to give her the "thumbs-up" signal. When I did that, she gave me the biggest smile I had ever seen shine on her face. She mouthed the words, "Thank you", looked at me for a few seconds and then turned to watch what was happening on the gym floor.

We had class together the next period after the assembly. There were no assigned seats in the class. I made it a point to watch for her coming to the room. When she got there, I told her she had sung very well and she thanked me. Then I opened the door for her and we walked into the classroom. I guarantee you I looked for the opportunity to sit behind her and got that chance.

I think we had a test in that class that day, but I don't think I passed it. I couldn't get my mind off the girl sitting in front of me and the sound of her voice when she sang and when she talked with me. Later, I learned she had sung at that assembly just for me. She said she tried to say with the song, her tone, and the look in her eyes, when she locked her gaze on me at the assembly, that she had sung just for me.

Kathy and I started dating. We've been dating ever since. The time after high school took us in different directions to earn our degrees. In that time we stayed connected. At times I would ask her to sing during our telephone talks. She sent me a ninety minute tape of songs with which she had fallen in love.

One Christmas, on a walk along First Street, she said she had fallen in love with me. I told her I had fallen in love with her. For her it had started long before I understood. For me, it all started with a song.

Bob

Letter 79

The Locket

Mr. Garrett,

There is a locket I always wear. The only times I've taken it off since first putting it around my neck are when I have to go through a metal detector. It is a simple silver locket attached to a silver chain. Both are strong but not gaudy, masculine, but not pretentious.

The locket holds a lock of the hair of my love, the hair of my Sandra. The hair is curled tightly in its home and fills the locket, but has never sprung the clasp. I think the locket knows the lock of hair is precious to me and wishes to hold it as dear as I hold it.

I know the scent of my love's hair as a mother knows the scent of her child. I rarely open the locket, and probably the lock of hair would have no scent remaining. The thought of the hair is all I need to remind me of my love and to keep her close to me.

There have been trying times in my life, since being blessed with my love, where I have touched the locket or the shirt material covering it, and thought of my love. The strength it has given me in those times is monumental. I think that in some of those times, it is all that has gotten me through those times. The thought of my love at those times was as sustaining as water in times of thirst. It sustains me always.

My Sandra's hair grows with thin lines of gray now. They

are the same lines which match mine. She says it is from sleeping with her head on a shared pillow for these many past years.

One day the hair of both of us will be gray. We will still lay our heads side-by-side on the same pillow. When time comes for eternity, we will also share that side-by-side.

With respect,
Clint

Letter 80

Holding Hands

Mr. Garrett,

"Holding hands in the picture show, when all the lights are low, may not be new, but I like it, how about you?" is, to the best of my memory, part of a song. I think "may be old fashioned" are some other words in that song.

Holding hands doesn't go out of fashion, if you love the one whose hands you have been chosen to hold. The hands I held in youth are held as firmly now as they were then. As I get feebler, holding Roberta's hand on our walks also helps keep me from tripping and falling down. I have been blessed with the challenge of some muscles in my left leg not functioning as they once did. Holding my love's hand, as we walk, gives me the assurance, which only holding the hand of my love can give.

We hold hands two to four hours a day, at least. When we watch television in the evening, go for rides or walks, or watch a movie at a theater, we hold hands. I admit, while at the theater, we eat popcorn first.

I've now known the touch of my love's hands for over forty years. The touch of her caress on my face, the hands holding my back in a hug, retains the gentleness and strength I've always seemed to know.

Her hands have felt my forehead to check for fever. They've given my hands a pat, or a squeeze, at moments common or special. They give love without a word.

My love's hands are the long, smooth providers for what her mind gives. Her skills are amazing. Her hands bring what the hands of no one else has ever brought me, or ever could, or ever will.

At times I joke with her about not being able to describe something while keeping her hands at her side, because she is so expressive with them. I tell her the hand movement comes from her Italian heritage.

She often automatically brings her hands to her face when humor finds her eyes. The same hands project the poise of composure when joy, or sadness, brings a drop to an eye or a trickle to her nose.

One April evening, when my hair was brown, she privileged me by allowing me to place a gold band on a finger of her left hand.

My hair is gray now. The hair of my love holds whispers of the same. The hands of my love cut what remains of my once brown hair.

The same hands give me guidance, correction in writing, treasures for our home, life growing in the garden, wonderful meals, and the comfort of their touch.

What Roberta's hands give most is the present of her presence, her very being, her soul, her love.

James

Letter 81

Life is Simple

Mr. Garrett,

It takes two to make a child, but it starts with the love of the two. One can't make three without the other one of the two. To truly produce a child, and not simply another producer of fertilizer, isn't simple biology. Pigs mate. I don't think they have a feeling of love between them. To produce a child can only be done by the feelings of love.

I couldn't have found love, if it wasn't for Barbara. I couldn't have kept love, if it wasn't for Barbara.

After thirty years I retired from Mare Island. I could have kept going, but it would have meant a transfer which would change our home from Benicia to another site. That wasn't going to happen.

Barbara and I had only one child, Ken. The Lord wanted it that way, so that is how it was. He has been such a blessing to us. Watching his family grow is much like watching a similar period in the lives of Barbara and me.

Ken has more than one child, but all are raised with the same loving care I think Barbara and I gave him.

He and Karen get up together whether it is a work day or the weekend. On workdays Ken leaves their home about an hour and a half later. Over the years he's had to leave earlier and earlier because of the traffic. He still does it and doesn't complain, but he does show some exasperation at times.

Karen takes care of what she needs to do during the work days. On the weekends they are hardly ever seen without being in the company of their families. It is a wonderful sight and feeling. I'm happy for them.

Ken says what makes it all worthwhile is the knowledge he has Karen in his life and through her their children. It may sound simple, but life really is simple. Have someone to love and pass that love along.

Charlie

Letter 82

The Golden Rule

Mr. Garrett,

Until someone has a child of their own they can never understand what it means to be a parent. There are responsibilities for the child in a parent's care. They may not know nor understand until after they have been parents for a few years.

Dawn and I read all the books we could on parenting before our first child was born. In most of the books I think someone sold a lot of paper without saying much.

The Golden Rule is a good primer for parenting. Treat others like you would want to be treated. Treat another child as you would want others to treat yours.

It doesn't require being a genius-level academician. It means holding them whether they think they need it or not, being there whether they think they need you there or not, giving them food and shelter, taking their hand step-by-step as you prepare them to accept the challenges of life, and finally letting them go out into the world. You didn't raise them to keep them in your nest.

Our children were never hungry. When their clothes were supposed to be clean, they were. They had a safe home environment, whether the boogey man came to visit them in their dreams or not. They were all praised by neighbors and others for their manners. They were good students. They were all of those things because they are good people raised with love.

It all started with our first son. He taught us of stroller trips down First Street, catching him at the bottom of the slide at Mill's Elementary, and graduation at Drolette Stadium.

Hopefully Dawn and I got better at parenting with each following child. It takes practice and experience, and mistakes will still be made while trying to be a good parent. If parenting is done with the love of your partner, and the love the two of them produce, things will work out. Love isn't biology, and biology isn't love.

Art

Letter 83

A Child Overcomes Illness

Mr. Garrett,

Sometimes it takes your child being ill to reinforce how much you love them. When your child is ill, or sick, it gets to be like something is attacking your body because of what you feel for your child.

Our son, Mike, was born premature. God gave him some competition to defeat, but he did it. It is amazing to think of him being that tiny bundle in the incubator and seeing the tough, good young man he has become.

His mother, Jennifer, definitely gave him his intelligence. I'll always brag that I gave him his physical strength and helped develop some courage and stubbornness.

With his early arrival on the planet, and the weakness it gave him, the three of us had more than the normal number of trips to the hospital in general and the emergency ward in particular. In going to the emergency ward there were two times we wouldn't have made it in time if that wasn't what God had wanted.

A doctor gave him a breathing test which I hoped would have come out better.

I thought part of his problem, as he was growing, was he was weaker than he should have been. It may have been clumsy, but in my own way I tried to make him stronger. As a teenager he ran three miles in less than sixteen minutes and bench pressed 300 pounds.

On the return trip to the doctor she said, "I don't know what you've been doing, but keep it up."

Along the way Mike twice said he hated me. If it had to be done all over again, I would do it. I would hope I learned from my mistakes. The runs downtown, to the state park, and up the hills and the hours lifting weights were bonding times I miss. Maybe it was for pride or responsibility. It was also love.
Dan

Letter 84

Flowers for My Love

Mr. Garrett,

At times, I deliver flowers to my love. At other times I have them sent. I enjoy seeing the look on my love's face when I present the flowers, or when she opens the door and they are delivered, or when I see her after I have the flowers arrive before I get home from work.

The flowers don't come at what society states are the designated subjects, times, and days, for flowers. They come for no special occasion, on no special day, except to show my love I was thinking of her, as I do every day.

My Margaret has favorite types of flowers, and favorite types of arrangements, and I try to show my understanding of her favorites by getting them for her as often as possible. At times the favorites aren't available. At other times something new to me catches my eye and I purchase it. She treats each gift as the gift of a king to his queen. It makes me feel good, so maybe my giving the flowers is selfish gratification. I heard some instructor talking about that one day in a psychology class in college. I think he missed the point. It makes me feel good to make Margaret feel good.

Some of the flower shops I've used in the past are only business memories now. The one remaining in town gets my business now. Fifty years ago the spot, which is now a flower shop, was a shoe store with a market on one side and a Chinese restaurant on the other.

When the flowers fade, leaves wilt, and petals fall they are taken outside to rest in our garden as compost. They help bring to life the May flowers and sustain the perennials. Their cycle of beauty is added to the beauty of the flowers Margaret nurtures in our yard.

Margaret and I enjoy flowers. We've each lain in the midst of California golden poppies in what were once empty fields around Benicia and now have blossomed into homes. The first flower I gave Margaret was a single red rose. I loved her then and love her now.

Keith

Letter 85

If You Love Someone, Tell Them

Mr. Garrett,

Others have said it long before me, and others will say it long after me. Life is simple when you stop to think about it. Try to be a good person. Along the way tell those you love that you love them. Don't let the chance to tell them pass you by. Tomorrow is a dream, a thought, an illusion. What you have is now.

There were those I now know I loved, when I was a younger person, but I didn't tell them. I didn't know I loved them then, and now, for what they did and who they were.

A part of each of them rubbed off onto me without me realizing it until they were all gone. Mother and father, mother-in-law and father-in-law, sisters and brothers, teachers, coaches, the woman around the corner, and some people with whom I worked were all part of the rubbing process.

It is only my wife and I now. We no longer go to visit on Military East. It was called East "M" Street then. We no longer go to visit on East "G" Street. The houses are empty to us now, though they have other families long in residence.

On walks my wife, Jackie, and I often pass houses which to us will always be known as the homes of people long forgotten by most in Benicia.

I tell Jackie a number of times each day that I love her. It bothers me that it took me so long to realize what little of the concept of love I do know. I try to insure that Jackie knows I love her.

One day others will walk by the home where I sit now and write this. Some will say it was our home. I hope they know there was love here. I also hope they will see, far earlier than I, the need to tell those you love that you do love them. Perhaps they will understand, and perhaps they won't, but at least the ones expressing love will have tried. That's all any of us can do, try.

Anthony

Letter 86

It Wouldn't Have Happened Without Frances

Mr. Garrett,

For years I imagined what the first home my Frances and I lived in would look like. It would be located on one of the hills where Southampton homes are now.

I've been good with my hands, and making things, all my life. There have been some people who told me I could make, or repair, anything. Some people have asked me to work for them. I took my own course for my life's work, but I enjoy building things.

I think I have about every tool needed to do anything from building a home from the ground up to repairing anything in one. Those tools were used in building a house, landscaping around it, and maintaining the property for a lot of years. Most of those tools sit idle now. There is the occasional small project, but no more deck building, or retaining wall erecting, or roofing will ever be in my future.

That house we built isn't where I thought it would be, and it isn't totally as I imagined. Much has changed in Benicia over the years. When I had the youth and the strength, I didn't have the money or the time. Now it is just the opposite.

I had great plans for the home I would build for my wife

and me. Every moment possible she would be alongside me helping out.

Our plans would be made in the evening after dinner as we sat in the kitchen of our ground floor flat. That space was all we could afford because we wanted to save enough money to build our first home. We planned for children, and planned the home with them in mind. The laughter to be heard in the home, and the sights to be placed in our memories, filled our imaginations.

Our home is a joy to each of us. The nest is empty, but the memories of the times with sons and daughters will linger forever. It wouldn't have happened without Frances.

Lewis

Letter 87

We Grew Up in Benicia

Mr. Garrett,

Virginia and I came to Benicia for a day trip last week and saw your advertisement in the Benicia Herald. It brought back many good memories for both Virginia and me.

We ate lunch at Captain Blyther's. When we grew up in Benicia, that site was definitely not the location for a restaurant. It is good to see the old building is still in use. I often wonder how many of the people are still alive who remember some of the things that went on down in that part of town in the 1950's and 1960's.

After lunch, Virginia and I walked past our first home. It is one half of a small, but comfortable for two and later three people, duplex a block off the east side of First Street.

I hadn't been discharged for long when I took a government test. I passed it and was offered a good paying job which would provide security for my family.

We had no choice except to move, because of the career opportunities the job offered, though we wanted to live in Benicia. Back in those days there weren't a lot of job possibilities in town for a young man starting a family.

As the years passed we moved three times. I kept moving up the ladder and couldn't take the chance of giving up my job to try something which would allow us to return to Benicia. I was responsible for my wife and four children and had invested too much time in my job to do otherwise. Beside, there was no call for my vocational skills in Benicia.

During our trip Virginia and I were almost overwhelmed with the thoughts, memories, and stories of what we had shared in Benicia in our youth. It was a fondness, not a nostalgic longing.

Virginia and I are going to move back here when I retire. We know a realtor in town. We have asked her to be on the watch for a nice property for a retired couple returning home, home to Benicia.

Dennis

Letter 88

Connections

Mr. Garrett,

I so often wonder what I did to lose the connection with those I have loved and love still. Those loved, who used to come over often, but no longer do. I wonder, but I understand.

There were dozens of them. They were our children, and they were the children of others. We saw them ride their tricycles and drive their first car up to the curb in front of our home. They went on their first date, and they went to the prom. There were birthday parties and Christmas parties. There were familiar routines and planned surprises. There were cookies and milk, and there were dinners. There were times of laughter, solemn occasions, and times of tears.

I sat on bleachers for hours at a time watching them play for pride and glory. By my side was Eileen, my love, my wife, my life. It didn't matter if it was their first competitive teams at young ages or, for some, college games.

There were some cold nights at Drolette Stadium for football and soccer. There was warmth, but almost empty bleachers, in the gym for basketball and volleyball; the same in the cafeteria for wrestling. There was many a windy day on the baseball and softball diamonds, at the track, and at the pool. They said they wanted us there, so we were, as often as we could.

Some of those young people we watched used to come by after the games and ask what we thought of the contests. They asked advice and thanked us for attending their games.

Nothing stops the movement of time, and it shouldn't be stopped. The young move on. Connections are held for a length of briefness which varies with the person. Finally separation occurs. Youth moves on and creates more youth in a beautiful and never ending cycle of growth.

I miss them and hope they miss me. Dust on the handle of a door is erased with the touch of movement.
Tom

Letter 89

She Wasn't a Bad Girl

Mr. Garrett,

I loved a girl once, the fool that I was. She was a real beauty, but she had the heart of a whore. Being stupid, I guess I was one of the last to know.

Anyway, at least I thought I had found love. It wasn't real. Maybe love isn't real, or I'll never find it if it is real.

Man, I thought that girl loved me! I think some of the guys got whiplash when they saw her. Going to a dance after a game meant I almost had to use a club. It was amazing how much friendlier my friends were when Irene was with me. Stupid of me again, I didn't know then that some of them had been very friendly with her. Love is blind, and I must have had my eyelids sewn shut with it.

God knows that girl was affectionate. There were times when she was on me and me on her, tighter than paint on a wall. It was often, and it was intense, and I didn't mind at all.

She wasn't a bad girl. She was friendly, intelligent, warm, and a good dancer. She was a fun date no matter what we did. I think a guy could be comfortable with her in a minute, she had that type personality. I guess she still does.

We broke up after the Prom our senior year. Like the rest of our friends, we had rooms at the hotel. There is some song where the guy leaves his love for awhile to take care of something. When he gets back, she is taking care of some business of her own. That's what happened between us. I'm a little slow I guess, but my thought process with her sped up at that moment.

She and her husband live in town. I think she experienced life, and more power to her, and then decided it was time to get serious with one guy. If there is a paragon of virtue, you can look at her now and see it.

It took me a long time to get over her. A girl like that can make a strong impression on any guy. Thinking of it now, maybe I did love her just a little.
Stephen

Letter 90

My Father Came to My Rescue

Dear Mr. Garrett,

Jason and I grew up in Benicia, but moved and later got married. My Dad said, many times, what he would do if the man in my life ever hit me. He said there would be no hello-goodbye, questioning of what happened, or kiss his ass. He said the first thing the guy would see when he opened the door was Dad's fist heading for his face.

My husband started hitting me less than a year after we were married. Finally I called Dad, and told him what had been happening. For a few moments Dad was silent. When he spoke, I could almost hear his teeth grinding. His voice was scary. I had never heard that tone in his voice before. It was seven at night when I phoned, and we lived about a ninety minute drive from Benicia. Dad said he would leave right then, and drive to our home.

Jason was surprised when I told him I called Dad. I had told Jason I would call Dad some day, if he kept hitting me, but he didn't believe me. I was too ignorant, fearful, and hoping for love to have told Dad the first time Jason hit me. I let things build, and they only got worse.

Jason told me to not say anything about his hitting me when Dad got there. He said to just say we had gotten into an argument, and I had fallen, and I was sorry I had phoned. There was no way that was going to happen. I had finally understood Jason and how our marriage was going. Dad had always been my salvation and I knew he would solve this situation.

Dad is slightly over six feet tall and a little over 200 pounds. Jason is taller and heavier, but he's a bully and a coward. He always talked so bad when he and I were alone, or when we were with his friends. He liked to brag about how he could kick my Dad's ass. When he was with Dad, he called him "Sir".

Mom told me, when I was in high school, that Dad has a mean streak in him, which he tries to control. But if someone messes with his family, or what is his, it is released.

She told me she had seen it once when a guy said something about Dad's sister at the high school after a game against Vallejo. She said he walked up to the guy and asked him if he had said what Dad had been told. The guy laughed and said he had and Dad hit him. Dad and the other guy had to leave the dance, but nothing else happened. It was the only time Mom had seen Dad like that for herself. She did tell me of two times of which she had been told, by Dad's friends, where similar situations had occurred.

I had a good idea of what to expect from Dad when he arrived. I was right, but it was more severe than I imagined it would be.

From a front room window, Jason saw Dad get out of the car and walk towards the front door of the duplex where we lived. He waited until the doorbell rang before opening the door.

Dad took one step to move inside our house and, as he was doing that, hit Jason with his right fist square on his nose. The hit knocked Jason back. He stumbled and landed on the floor. Dad hit Jason so hard I thought he might have killed him. I had never seen anyone get hit that hard before in my life.

Then Dad straddled Jason, and beat him worse than Jason had ever beaten me. His nose ran red and his eyes were swollen when Dad got off him.

In seeing what happened part of me felt a joy I had never known. It was like I was an up-close-and-personal observer at some kind of event where my favorite team was going for the championship, and they were dominating.

Part of me felt shock, and regret, for what had happened to Jason. We had lived together and then gotten married. We had been a couple for almost seven years from when we met in Algebra class. He took my virginity, because I thought I loved him and he loved me. Another part of what I felt was fear for what legal problems my Dad could face for beating up Jason. Another part of what I felt was simple revenge on Jason for having hit me even once.

There was no fair fight about what happened that night between Jason and Dad. Dad told me what he would do if any man in my life ever hit me and he did it.

I was proud of him, but a little fearful of him too. It wasn't a fear for my safety. It was a fear for what might happen to him someday. Dad would try to walk away from a situation if he could. I had seen that with a drunk and another man who was being a complete idiot with Dad. I could not imagine Dad backing down from protecting his own. I don't think he could if he wanted to.

There was no police report filed. Jason and I got a divorce as soon after that night as we could. He was glad to be rid of me and I felt the same. I haven't seen him since we went through what we had to go through for the divorce. Jason and I didn't even as much as shake hands in the time between Dad's arrival that night and the divorce.

I never heard Jason speak badly about Dad after that night. For all I know he is talking behind my back, but that is on him.

Many times when I was growing up Dad told me the same things. There was a consistency in his words. He was like a rock to which I could cling. Anyone close to him knew where he stood in what he believed.

He told me that certain things in life would happen, and they did. It was like he had a crystal ball. That night when he confronted Jason was one of those things which came true.

No matter what happened, where I lived, who I dated, or who I married, I would always be his little girl. He would be there for me, and defend me, whenever it was needed. He did, and he was. I think few people keep their word these days.

My Dad was a man of his word. What love I have for him for that, and all the things he taught me, when he may have thought I wasn't listening. He was my knight that time at my home, as before in my life, and has remained one.

As soon as I could, I moved back to Benicia and rented an apartment. For awhile I worked as a waitress at a restaurant on First Street. It was more of a time of getting my mind back in the right place than for anything else.

As should happen, one night at the restaurant I met a great guy. Carl was a gentleman. One thing led to another. Along the way I told him I had been married. I told him about Jason and what Dad had done. Anger came to Carl's voice when I told him about Jason. He wanted to hit Jason right then. When I told him what Dad had always told me, and what his reaction to Jason's actions had been, I swear Carl said, "Way to go, Dad!" Then he said he totally agreed with Dad, and would do the same for me. I opened to Carl more.

We had been dating for about a year, when he told me he wasn't getting any younger. I told him that neither of us was. I think he knew that if he asked me to marry him the answer would be "Yes".

We had been sitting on a bench looking at the boats in the marina. He knelt in front of me and told me he loved me. Then he gave me an engagement ring. Then the love of my life asked me to marry him. "Yes, yes, yes", was all I could answer.

Six months later we were married at the marina in the warmth of sunlight as a cool breeze blew off the water. My first knight gave my hand in marriage. My second knight placed a ring on my finger. Because of my knights, my life has gone from darkness to sunlight.
Tami

Letter 91

A Bottle Buried in the Sand

Mr. Garrett,

Our parents took us for our first walk on the Ninth Street beach. It was a special Sunday excursion in those days. Most in Benicia stayed local for their growth, pleasures, and memories. I fell in love with Richie on that first walk on the beach. We were almost kindergarten age. I think he also fell in love with me then.

As teenagers we sat around small fires in the evening on that beach. Sometimes it was just the two of us, and sometimes we were with other friends of ours. Things were so different in those days. We probably couldn't do today, what we did then, without someone calling the police, or without fearing for our safety.

The beach was much different in those days, in terms of cleanliness. A drain pipe dropped its offerings near the middle of the beach, an old car had gone over the side by the point, and people had dumped trash where ever they felt like doing so. It was still our beach and the only one we had. It is nice to see it much cleaner now, with the grass and play areas on the level above.

One day Richie and I tossed message filled bottles from the point by the beach. That point has a name now, but then it was just the point at the beach. Days later we found two of those bottles washed up on the beach. What happened to all of the bottles is what happens to people. Some moved down the straits, and perhaps out to sea. There might have been some bottles the water started taking that way, and then the tide might have changed and pushed them farther east. Perhaps someone found one in Rio Vista. Perhaps none of them got farther than the ferry slip at the end of Fifth Street. Some, undoubtedly, sank.

Another day Richie and I decided to have a picnic lunch at the beach. We had done that a number of times in the past, but Richie had something special in mind. He surprised me with what he wanted, when we got to the beach.

There was no sound on the beach, except for the occasional call of three seagulls making their cry for donations of food. I could say they must have known us well, as they waited for us to eat and leave scraps for them when we left, but they were just being seagulls.

We placed our blanket on the sand. Then we got our food out of the basket he had carried, and ate our lunch. When we were finished, I asked Richie what it was he wanted to do that was so special.

Richie smiled. In truth he had a lecherous, and almost a humorously evil grin, at times. That was one of those times. We had never done anything more than hug each other and kiss.

Then Richie took a bottle, two pads of paper, and two ball point pens from a small bag he had brought along but hadn't opened yet. He said he wanted each of us to write our feelings about the other, read them to each other, seal them in the bottle, and bury them next to where we sat. I thought that was the sweetest thing ever.

Richie and I leaned back-to-back and wrote. We had sat the same way before, on the same beach, writing the rough draft of papers for Mr. Simons' English class. I felt more pressure on me then than I had ever felt for a class assignment.

When Richie finished, he told me he was done writing. It seemed he had written in an instant. I kept thinking and thinking, searching for the best words to tell him what I felt.

Finally I started to write. I must have finished in about the same time it took Richie to write his words.

I sat there wondering what to do next, and wondering if what I had written would be good enough. Then I told Richie I was finished.

We turned to sit with shoulders touching and he said, "Ladies first." He was always so polite. I told him he might not like what I wrote, but that it was all I could think of. Then I read, "I love you, Richie." I told him he was probably disappointed in me for my effort, but it was the best I could do.

Richie said he thought what I had written was wonderful. Then he read, "I love you, Alice." When he finished, he held the piece of paper so I could see his words. Then I did the same for him with my piece of paper.

We each had only written the words that we loved each other, but the words were so precious to each of us. The age at which love is found makes no difference. When it is found, it is found, and it lasts.

We had found our love on that first walk on the beach, though we didn't know it at the time. It had been nurtured through the years with the ups and downs relationships have, as a boy and girl in a small town grow to know each other.

Richie had girlfriends along the way, and I had boyfriends. That time, that distance, and that separation, had actually drawn us closer without our knowing it. The spark, which had come to both of us on that first walk, had grown to a flame which will never be extinguished.

We used the metal cups from our picnic lunch to scoop out the sand to make the hole in which to bury the bottle. I can take you to the exact spot where we buried the bottle this very second.

Richie and I had a good life together. Part of that good life was the memories we made. At times we would ask the other about the bottle, and wonder if it was still there. We would take drives around town and sometimes stop at the parking lot on Ninth Street and look at the water. A few times we walked down to the beach and stood over the spot where we had buried the bottle.

After Richie's funeral, people came to console me and offer their prayers and good thoughts. I thank them all so much for all they did. They helped me bury my love, but the love of my love can never be buried.

One day something strongly drew me to our times at the beach at Ninth Street. I understood what was drawing me. It was the bottle which held our notes of love. I took a garden trowel from the planting shed Richie had built and drove out to the beach.

I was drawn to the spot where we had buried the bottle as easily as light comes to a darkened room when the switch is flipped.

Four scoops of the trowel straight down and the bottle was in sunlight once again. When I brought the bottle to my hands, it was like Richie was standing beside me smiling.

Time erodes all things that nature has given us, or which man has made. The papers in that bottle, on which we placed our words of love, had long been history. In our youthful ignorance, we didn't seal the bottle very well.

When I saw all that was left was the bottle, I cried. A kind young man saw me. He asked if there was anything wrong, and if he could help me.

I told him the story of the burying of the bottle and the loss of my Richie. That total stranger hugged me and then helped me push the sand back into the hole. It was almost like burying Richie all over again. Then the young man walked me back to my car and watched me drive away. He was so kind.

The bottle sits on the night stand next to my bed. Richie was my first, my one, and my only love. When he died, I thought I couldn't get through life without him. The bottle is a connection with our past, our youth, and our love.

It has been a very hard time for me without Richie. Night after night I stand looking out a window in the front of the house. I look at the water. The water is calming to me. Looking at the water makes me think of Richie even more.

Before I get too feeble, I will take the bottle from the night

stand and ask someone to drive me to Ninth Street. I will walk with that bottle along the sand Richie and I walked so many times. It was the first beach we walked. One day it will be the last beach we walk.
Alice

Letter 92

He Says... She Says

Dear Mr. Garrett,

He sees it one way, and I see it another. It just goes to show how two people can see the same scene from different viewpoints. In his mind it was fate. In my mind it was love which was meant to be.

He said I was just an attractive female and he was interested at the first look. I was looking to find my hero, and found him that day.

Asking me out, with no intention of a long term relationship, was all he had in mind. He knew the Air Force wouldn't keep him at Travis long. Accepting his invitation to go to dinner was what I knew was the first step in being with the only man I've ever loved.

When he took me home, he thanked me for my company and kissed me goodnight. I told him we would be seeing a lot more of each other in the future.

He said he was only in the area temporarily and would be flying out soon. When I told him I knew and understood that, but his heart had found a home in mine, he laughed. At that moment I think life was going a little too fast for him. I knew what I had found that day was what I had searched for all the past years.

In his youth he had read of daring deeds performed by heroic figures. In mine I had read of the image of my hero, the man I would someday marry.

The Air Force did take him away. I stayed in Benicia and waited. Letters came from far distant places. I sent letters in return. He wrote questions, I wrote answers.

He says the times he just happened to be able to come to Benicia were based on spur-of-the-moment decisions, and the luck of getting military transportation. I told him the decisions were well planned and the luck was made. He said our meeting was nothing more than chance. I said the love we had each been searching for, we found in each other that day.

He said the attraction was nothing but loneliness, and hormones. I told him there was a guiding light which led to our meeting each other that day.

Our meeting, he said, was based on his having some time off and coming to Benicia. The splitting of the plastic bag, which held my groceries, as I walked across the parking lot towards my car, was the result of a faulty bag. I said love guided him to be at that place with me at that time. He felt nervous walking me to my car, but emboldened enough to ask a pretty stranger for a date. I felt completely at ease. He was the one.

In his mind, I came to grow on him. In my mind, all my thoughts of the man I would eventually meet emerged in front of me that day in the parking lot. He still says our meeting was a chance encounter, which would never have occurred, if he had done any number of things differently in his life. I say each thought before we met, each movement, each decision led us to finally standing before each other.

He said asking me to marry him was just being practical. I said asking me to marry him had been part of the journey we had been on all our lives.

Our connection for life was shown to the world on our wedding day.

Joshua still talks of our meeting as being nothing more than a chance of fate and what has happened since then as being the

way things work out. I still tell him our love was meant to be, and I know he agrees. He just acts stubborn and plays with me about it. He knows I'm right.
Trina

Letter 93

Love Grows on a Paper Route

Dear Mr. Garrett,

My neighbor became my friend, my friend became my boyfriend, and my boyfriend became my husband because of a newspaper route.

Larry's family, and mine, lived three houses from each other. He and I were each just two of the kids in the neighborhood. We played together and went to school together.

One afternoon Larry passed by on his paper route and said hello. On an impulse I asked if I could go along with him, if my mother said it was OK. He said it was OK with him and my mother agreed, so off we went.

Before we were through with the route that day we were friends, and not just neighbors. I learned to fold papers as I walked and discovered homes I never knew existed. It was a real learning experience. That was probably my awakening to the "real world".

Whenever I could, I would go on Larry's route with him. Time and closeness do what they do. Larry and I were soon holding hands and kissing behind the bushes.

We lived in West Manor. The high school was downtown in those days. For the first three years we walked to school together. Then Larry was able to buy an old car. For awhile, he and I spent as much time fixing up that car as we had ever spent walking. It was fun time, because we were together.

We live in Southampton now, in a home with three garage spaces. Two of the spaces house classic muscle cars Larry couldn't afford when we were young. The other space is a workshop. In the driveway sits a great SUV.

Things couldn't be better for us. It all started because I saw a neighbor boy walking down the street doing his paper route. I read every edition of that paper, and so does Larry.
Gloria

Letter 94

Cowboys and Indians

Mr. Garrett,

We played Cowboys and Indians on the grass at the kindergarten on East Fifth Street. That building has seen some different uses since then. In the days before the political correctness we know now, the whiteman made friends with the redman, fought him, and married the redman's daughter.

It seemed I often was a buffalo in those heroic epics of our youth. Others had more, and better, words to say than I. Strong and silent, taciturn John Wayne or Gary Cooper had no edge on me.

Cindy was always the cattle queen, the school marm, or the Indian maiden, and, as the belle of the ball, always the one with whom the boys wanted to dance.

The dancing was the childish version of square dancing. In our minds the dancing was done in the barn in Dodge City depicted on television's "Gunsmoke", which all of us watched each week.

When we lay down for our rest period, we often pretended we were unrolling our blankets next to the chuck wagon for our night's rest along the trail. Cindy always had guardians lying on each side of her. I was quietly one of them.

Our drink containers were our coffee cups around the campfire. Cindy shared drinks from mine.

Even at that age, there were a couple of shoving matches,

and some bruised knees and scratched elbows in contests for her affections.

At one of those contests she was especially cute in her anger, when she stamped her foot, and told us not to fight over her. Young men weren't supposed to do that kind of thing, she said, they could get hurt. Anyway, they were supposed to bring flowers and say nice things instead.

When I played the role of the buffalo, I grazed at Cindy's feet. She petted my head, my first love.

Ralph

Letter 95

The "Old Man" Was My Mentor

Mr. Garrett,

I loved that "Old Man". I call him "Old", but he was only ten years older than me. He took me under his wing at a time when I definitely needed someone to do that.

I'll refer to him as, "Iani". He was of Italian heritage, so the suffix found on many Italian heritage surnames will be good for telling of him. My wish is to honor him, but not have anyone, who may disagree with some of the things he did, have the chance to degrade him. He was an honorable man.

There are a number of connections with Iani and Benicia. He grew up in another county, but played football against Benicia on Sanborn Field, basketball in what is now the Civic Center gym, but was built as the high school's gym, and baseball at Fitzgerald Field.

Along the way, through family connections, Iani met a Benicia girl, and married her. They were married in St. Dominic's Church, just as my wife and I were later.

After we had secured for the evening on the barracks ship we called home, when he and I were together, Iani showed me a photo of the wedding party. Iani's wife is of Portuguese ancestry. The photo was black and white, but I don't think there was a crop of blond hair in the bunch. Not that it matters, but it resembled a photo of a much earlier time when members of immigrant families from Mediterranean Europe married.

Circumstances meant Iani and his wife couldn't live together in Benicia. He went where the Navy sent him, and she followed when she could. When she couldn't, she lived with her parents. Eventually, three children also followed them to Navy housing here and abroad, before the family moved into Iani's parent's home up the coast after they died.

Iani and I met at Small Boat School. He was career Navy. I was just giving four years to the Navy and my country, while "seeing the world" and learning some skills. In conversation, while waiting for the order to travel over the water at night once again, he asked where I called home.

When I told him home for me had always been Benicia, his face lit up. He said he knew the town well. Part of Iani's knowledge came from playing against Benicia teams when he was in high school. As we talked that night, he spoke the names of some of those against whom he had played.

Iani had special praise for one of Benicia's high school legends in particular. He said, "That guy was one tough competitor." Since those words were spoken by "One tough competitor", they were words of high praise. I knew the man of whom he spoke, and Iani was absolutely correct in his evaluation.

Iani was a "boat driver". He had three stripes below the bird, the crow, on his insignia. I had one stripe. He had the opportunity to choose me to be part of his boat crew. It was an honor to be chosen by him. He joked that he had done it so we could tell each other "tales of Benicia", and "sea stories", and so he could lie to me of all the things he had done in his life. I think part of it was his desire to remember some good memories from his youth, to share those times, and to just talk of something which didn't involve "getting the job done". I think he also saw a little of him in me. If so, I gladly accept what would be high praise.

Another night he said he guessed I had a girlfriend back home in Benicia. I can still see his smile when he said a big, good-looking guy like me must have lots of girlfriends. I told him there was a girl, of whom I was very fond, but I didn't think she was my girlfriend.

Iani told me I should get her to be my girlfriend, and make sure I married her when I got out of the Navy. He said I should think of her as the reason to go back home, as he thought of his family.

We served well together. He was the description of "shipmate" to me, and the others in the crew. I hope I came, at least close, to being that for him. He was my Navy mentor, my big brother, and my guiding light.

I thought on what Iani had said about the girl I knew back in Benicia. A few months after I returned from that third, and last, tour of Vietnam waters I was discharged.

I took Iani's words to heart, and married that Benicia girl. She was the reason I came back. If not for her, I would have become career Navy, like Iani, or died over there, or in some other exotic spot on the planet. There was no goal; there was no end, except Betty.

Iani became ill after giving the Navy and our country 22 years of service, the equal of any sailor, and better than most. We had as much time together over the years as we could when he was in the Navy and later. Letters from him were like Christmas packages to me. I don't think mine lived up to what he wrote, but I tried. Just keeping contact was the important thing.

That good man died of cancer. Possibly it was caused by Agent Orange. I will forever believe that the birth defect of his oldest child happened because Iani and I served on the boats, and traveled waters poisoned by that product. Iani believed that, too.

Iani and his wife had good memories of Benicia. He wanted his ashes placed on the waters of the Carquinez Straits, off the end of First Street. That wish was completed when Angelina, his wife, my Betty, and I stood on the deck of a small boat. It was the civilian version of the Navy boat on which Iani and I once rode together.

Bravo Zulu is the United States Navy signal for, "Well Done". It is a high honor in the Navy for an individual, or crew, to receive that signal. Iani received that signal when we were on our way back from a ride one night, and proudly acknowledged it. When we tied up at the dock, Iani turned to those of us in his crew and said, "You all helped us get that signal. Bravo Zulu, men."

The President of the United States couldn't have given us praise as high. The President was an almost imaginary figure. Iani stood in front of us. I loved that "Old Man".
Johnny

Letter 96

The Girl Brought Her Dog to School

Mr. Garrett,

The girl brought her dog to civics class at school for a demonstration of obedience training. I tell you truly, by the end of her showing of her dog, I had fallen in love by just watching her. We were just idiot kids, I guess, but I had an attraction for the girl, when I saw her the first day of class, and it has continued.

Puberty was just hitting its flying run at life at that time. There had been hints before, but now was for real.

The dog was good looking. The girl stood in front of the class, and commanded the dog to sit, lie down, and stay. She had spent some time with that animal.

Somewhere in its olfactory senses, the aroma of some bitch-in-heat must have come to the dog's nostrils. He started getting an erection. Things happen.

The teacher didn't know up from down about dogs, and maybe not much more about life. Anyway, she wasn't much help to the girl. The girl was so darn cute! She knew exactly what was going on. She tried to slyly tap the dog to get its attention off matrimony, but it didn't work.

Finally the teacher got a hint on life and told the girl she thought the dog needed to go outside for awhile. The girl responded like the A+ student she had always been, and took the dog outside. They came back about ten minutes later. The dog was panting, but it wasn't from affection for another of its kind. The football field was near the classroom, and the girl had taken advantage of it.

It would embarrass the heck out of my wife, if I told you our names. It was love in Benicia, pal, and that's what you said you wanted.

That afternoon class at the old B.H.S. campus with the woman, who became my wife, is one of the joys of my life. (Unsigned)

Letter 97

Coach Died the Other Night

Mr. Garrett,

Coach died. I telephoned and emailed a lot the next couple of days, letting some people know, who might not have gotten the word. Some of the people who came for the services stayed at our home for a night, or two. I hadn't seen some of them in over twenty years, but the common bond was Coach.

A lot of "Coach Stories" were told over a few days. The funeral services, and the time at Coach's home later, were almost like reunions. Scenes like those are coming more rapidly. We are all losing parts of our youth, with the passing of the people, people like Coach.

One day at practice, when we had done something Coach didn't like, which has since been lost in the annals of time, he got angry. Coach told us to gather around him and "take a knee". He vented for a minute and told us what we had done wrong. Some guys took it personally, but he was angry at players, not people.

Then he let us all go to the single spigot water fountain Sanborn Field possessed and get a drink of water. We hustled to the water, gulped a mouthful or two, and hustled back to where the coaches stood. We had been forgetting the little things and we were forgetting to play like champions. That was what had upset him. The man was Coach, and we all wanted to please him. We dutifully carried on the best we could.

Practice got over a little early that afternoon. I don't know if Coach had an appointment, whether he thought we needed a break from practice time, or just wanted to go home early. In the locker room some of the guys congratulated themselves on doing so well at practice that Coach let us go home early. I would have rather stayed. I enjoyed the practices.

I had observed Coach in classes and in athletics for over three years. Being seventeen years old at that moment in the locker room I thought I had a pretty good understanding of him. In some ways I did. It was so much later that I came to understand so much of the things Coach had said in my youth. I don't think I could ever understand all of them, the man was deep.

All along at the practices and games he was telling us to do our best, to look out for the other guy, to be good people, to have honor and pride, to show love, to be accountable for our actions, and to never let ourselves, or others, down. He was doing as our parents did only he did it on the football field.

I've tried to pass those lessons of my youth along to others. Some probably think I'm pushy, or that I'm preaching. I've merely been passing the torch, as I think we all should do, when able. As with Coach, if those to whom I make the offer see it now, later, or never is on them. I do my best, as did he.

Coach's wife immediately recognized me and said "Hello" when we met before the services. It is an honor I accept with great respect.

I've been told Coach and I had a special relationship. Again, I am honored.

The time at the services was hard. Some of the time later was also. What makes his passing good, if that can be said, is the love for the man for what he gave us. I'll bet he had no plan or vision for what he did in the way it affected so many of his students and players. He was simply fulfilling his role as a human, a teacher, and a football coach in the time he spent with us.

I'd like to run around that field for Coach again, just one more time.

Ted

Letter 98

Chuck Set Me Up With a Blind Date

Mr. Garrett,

My friend, Chuck, was feeling sorry for me because he thought I was moping around, so he set me up on a blind date. I think he also wanted to double date and be in the back seat with his current flame.

There was no special girl in my life then. The only girl I wanted to date always looked like she was booked solid. I was naturally curious, but not excited. The only girl I really wanted to date would probably be dating someone else that night. I didn't think she would go out with me anyway.

The first thing I did that evening was pick up Chuck. After we picked up his date, Chuck told me where to drive to get to the home of my blind date.

We turned left on Hillcrest, off of East Fifth Street, and my mind really started working. Believe me, like many boys that age in Benicia I knew the residence of every girl of high school age in town. Benicia was a lot smaller then than it is today. There were less than five hundred kids attending Benicia High School. It wasn't genius level knowledge or observation.

I thought Chuck must have met someone, who had just moved into town, and hadn't signed up for school yet, or someone who was visiting someone we both knew. He is a lot more gregarious than I am.

When he told me to stop, I did. Then I told him if what he had planned was a joke, I wasn't going to be a very happy camper. Chuck said he was serious. He said the girl, who was my blind date for the evening, lived in the house in front of which we were parked. I still didn't believe him. I knew who lived at the address.

Chuck told me I had to go to the front door of the house and ring the doorbell. Then I had to tell the girl, who would answer it, that I was her blind date. He said it was all worked out the way the girl wanted it done. I did it. My manhood was in question, and I wasn't going to put up with Chuck ribbing me for the next month about not having the courage to do it.

I guess it is pretty obvious, by reading this far, that the girl who was to be my blind date for the night was the girl I had always wanted to date. Her name is Eileen.

When Eileen opened the door, I said hello and then spoke the line I was supposed to speak. She replied with a smile, said hello to me, and invited me into her home. It was the first time I had ever been inside her home, or even on her property for that matter.

Most of the times, when I rode around Benicia, I made sure I went by her house at least once. If it was around the time guys picked up their dates, for that Friday or Saturday night, there was usually the car of one of my friends in front of her home. If it was later, when I brought a date home, or after I had done so, those same cars were there.

When Eileen closed the door, I felt very uncomfortable. I told her that, if what was going on was meant as a joke, I didn't enjoy it and it needed to be ended then. Eileen said there was no joke. She said she had given up on waiting for me to ask her out and thought of the plan to get me to go out with her.

"I've wanted you to ask me for a date since we were sophomores", were the first words I ever felt Eileen spoke directly to me. All the other words we had shared had seemed to be simply social conversation. I will never forget those words. When she said them, her eyes showed more moisture than they had moments before.

I was surprised, but very, very pleased. I told her I didn't know she had wanted to go out with me. She said she had started planning to bump into me, and had practically run me down, in the hallway every time she could. It was funny when she said how she had it planned.

It would have been easier for her to get to her classes by taking different routes than what she did. Instead, she found out my class schedule and put her strategy into effect. Eileen was a planner all along, to get us together. She had two of her girlfriends working in compliance. It seemed I was being crowded near Eileen in a hallway every school day. She would say something to me each of those times, and I enjoyed it. I may be a little slow on the uptake, but I thought it was just the flow of the traffic, or that she was going to see someone. To me, that someone could only be another guy.

We were having good, warm October weather then, like we so often do here in Benicia. She, and her friends, started sitting near where Chuck and I, and some of our other friends, sat in the quad at lunch. I enjoyed being by her. She seemed to talk with the other guys as much as she talked with me. I didn't see any kind of close or strong connection between us from her. I certainly wasn't going to show it. It must have been that old caveman thing, of not wanting to seem weak to his male friends.

When we got in the car, Chuck and his date were laughing. He said everyone knew Eileen wanted to go out with me, except me.

We went to see a movie at the El Rey Theater in Vallejo that night. When I sat down, I put my right arm on the armrest between Eileen and me. During the opening credits Eileen placed her hand on mine. I automatically spread my fingers, and she interlaced her fingers with mine. I thought I had died and was in heaven. What had happened couldn't have happened.

We sat like that the entire time. Chuck was busy taking care of romantic business with his date. I didn't think he had noticed Eileen holding hands with me.

After the movie we drove down Tennessee Street to Patches, to get something to eat. Dating wasn't as expensive a proposition in those days as it is now, even with inflation. For less than ten dollars two people could have a good evening, but sometimes it was a challenge to come up with the ten dollars.

Just before we left to come back to Benicia, I told Chuck I was going to drop his date and then him off and then take Eileen home. When Chuck said that I had it bad with Eileen, I told him I did. He laughed, and told me to drive around the block real slow after I let him and his date off at her house. He wasn't quite through romancing yet.

On the way to the movie, Eileen sat about halfway between the passenger's door and me. On the way back we sat with our bodies touching each other. She leaned into me and held my right biceps with her right hand. Once she put her head on my shoulder for a few moments.

I dropped Chuck and his date off and started to drive away. When I did, Eileen asked how Chuck was going to get home. I told her what I had told him. When she asked why I had done that, I told her I wanted to be alone with her. She snuggled even closer to me.

We picked Chuck up and drove him home. Then I drove Eileen home. We sat in front of her home talking until the lights on her front porch started blinking off and on. There was no electrical problem. It was time for our evening to come to an end.

Eileen and I kissed for the first time sitting in my car in front of her home that night. We have kissed many times since then. Eileen became my girlfriend, and later, my wife.

Eileen and I still go to the movies in Vallejo, but it is at the complex. Sometimes we drive on Lake Herman Road to get there. We always hold hands in the movies.

A hint guys: take the chance of asking that special girl for a date. Girls, if that doesn't happen, it doesn't hurt to have a plan. Things could work out. They did for me.
Ben

Letter 99

Maureen Is My Everything

Mr. Garrett,

Maureen is my everything.

We aren't a couple depicted on screen by Hollywood, or lovers sung of by balladeers or singers of rap. We shop at Safeway, buy gas at the local stations, our children attended Benicia High School, and our music is our own for each other.

We spend as much time together as we can. We know each other about as well as any man and woman can know each other. Along with knowledge of each other we have an understanding of each other. It isn't perfect between us. We have our misunderstandings, confusion, and upset. I wouldn't change what we have.

I don't know love. I don't know what it is, how to describe it, what it looks like, how it sounds, or anything else about it. There are things I know and understand about connections between people. For example, if they honor and respect each other things will work out better between them. There will always be arguments between people, but that is as much a part of life as is the need to love and be loved.

If people stand their duty, in all they do and are as humans, others tend to think well of them. Be polite to all and especially that one in your life who means so much to you.

Watch people in their daily lives and they will reveal themselves. Be a gentleman and be a lady. If the lady wants a gentleman, she acts like a lady. If a gentleman wants to be with a lady, he will find her, if he is a gentleman. He can speak all he wants of how much he loves his lady, but does he open the door for her when they exit the restaurant on First Street? Consistency, as everything else, is a way of life.

She can express her love in words of no feeling or passion. Does she gaze into his eyes as he speaks, and honor his words as treasures, or are his words background noise?

When people give, they receive, the same as when they share, whether they know it at the time or not. It would be foolish to say I expect nothing in return when I give something to Maureen. People always expect some kind of return in life for what we give, or are willing to share. I'm no different. Maureen's return for what I offer is not measured in dollars or a function performed. It comes in her "Thank You". Those words are a bond between us.

I've longed for Maureen, ached at being apart from her, felt the anticipation of meeting with her, and the fear of losing her.

I understand being there for Maureen in anything she needs, or desires, as she is for me. We fold clothes by the dryer together. We both cook. We garden.

Her hands are my hands, and my hands are hers. What she does better than me, she does. What I do better than her, I do. What we can only do together, or do better together, we do.

I know forever in numbers, space, and the commitment to care for someone by giving your word. I know people say they will love forever. I wonder what they mean. I wonder the length of that forever.

I know the vow of people willing to die for another. I would die for Maureen.

Love is. It isn't definable.

I try with my Maureen, the love of my life, to give her the love of my life and the life of my love. I give all I have. If that is love, then that is love.

Confusing, isn't it?

Gabe

Letter 100

Seeds Are Planted—Love Is Blooming

Mr. Garrett,

The seeds of love between Jennifer and me were planted long ago.

I freely admit that my thoughts, when I saw Jennifer, were not about love. Hot, young blood was boiling in my veins, and the initial thought was pure lust. She was a good looking girl.

I was nothing but physical and still am. Brain power isn't my strength. When the physical leaves me, I'll be a hard guy to live with. The physical is where the lust part comes in, I guess. Gosh, she was good looking.

Just getting together with her was about the hardest challenge I've ever had. First she politely ignored me, then she acknowledged my existence, and finally she accepted me into her circle of life.

She must have been attracted to something in me. Maybe it was pity, at the start, for how stupid I was. Maybe I was the stray she was fated to take into her life.

Believe it or not, our first date, if you can call it that, was fishing off the pier on the spit on First Street with her father. It was really a kick. He stood between us when we fished.

The day before, Jennifer had been down by the train depot with her paint and easel. I saw her by herself and thought there was no reason why I couldn't go over and talk with her.

She was friendly from the start, but she was also almost

wary. I've seen dogs like that when they don't know right away if they should trust the person they see.

I made a point of staying with her until she had to leave. During that time I asked her if she liked to fish. She said she didn't, but that her father did. I thought, "What the heck", I'll ask her if she and her father would like to go fishing with me the next day. She said she was sure her father would.

I didn't have "clue one" about fishing. Standing next to the water trying to beat holes in it with a piece of lead seemed like a real slow way to pass time. I definitely wanted to make time with Jennifer so, as soon as she drove away that day, I went to a sporting goods store and begged for help. I was awake most of the night wondering what was going to happen the next day.

It was a beautiful day when we went fishing. It was like an awakening of the world.

We stood out in the sun and the breeze for hours that seemed like minutes. All of a sudden Jennifer's father stepped from between us and said he was done fishing for that day.

Then, in one of the shocks of my life, he said he was going home and that he was sure I would be able to take care of Jennifer and take her home. Jennifer's father had been testing me. As time has gone on, I've grown to know he tests people all the time to see who they are. I am happy, and honored, that I passed his test with his daughter.

After spending over an hour alone with Jennifer, I took her home. When we got to her house, I asked her if she would have dinner with me at Captain Blyther's the next night. She said "Yes". It was the best answer I've ever received to a question in my life.

We were seated at a table looking out over the water. I hope I paid enough, and gave a big enough tip, for the time we spent there. I would have paid all that I had for that time with Jennifer. We sat and talked, that was all. I didn't touch her hand. I didn't say anything inappropriate. Knowing her, even as little as I did then, I know she would have told me, if I had done anything wrong.

After we had dated a few times she definitely told me when

I had done something wrong. "You can't do that" seemed to be coming out of Jennifer's mouth every other sentence one night. I'm sorry for the actions and words I often did and said, but they were all I knew. I hadn't led the life she had led.

She was so good looking. I knew I had to at least adjust, if not totally change some things, or I wouldn't have had any more of a chance with her. That was obvious. I had been too blunt and straight forward. I had a goal, but it was a foolish goal. The lust was in my head, and she saw it.

Jennifer lives alone in an apartment by the Raley's shopping center. She is a college graduate and is employed in the medical profession. She has long been an independent woman. We walked to her home after our dinner. I later checked the distance on the odometer in my car. It was almost four miles! She was testing me, as her father had tested me. I passed.

I didn't feel the walk back to my car, which was parked on First Street. My mind was almost completely filled with Jennifer.

Jennifer gave me her telephone number that night. I've telephoned her every day since. When I told her I hoped it wasn't an annoyance, I was testing her. She answered as I hoped she would.

I love that woman. It isn't the initial attraction of how good she looks. That was the initial lure, but the hook was set in discovering who she is as a person.

People call us a couple now. We are invited as a twosome to the homes of friends who were once hers or mine and are now ours. It is a nice feeling.

Last night I asked Jennifer to marry me, and she said she would.

Our love is blooming.

Dean

Letter 101

The Photograph

Mr. Garrett,

From what I've heard, you once served in the military. Maybe that will make it easier for you to understand how I feel about my wife, and how important a photograph of her has been to me.

The time of Vietnam was a very divisive time in the life of our country. Benicia wasn't excluded in that divisiveness.

Some of us younger guys at that time remembered the stories our fathers, uncles, older brothers, brothers-in-law, and neighbors had told us. Many of those stories dealt with serving our country during World War II, and the Korean War. Those stories took root in the minds of many of us, including me.

When the Vietnam War increased in scale for the United States, many of the young men, who had listened to those stories in their earlier days, volunteered to serve our country. We felt the torch had been passed to us, and it was our duty. We believed in the need to stop communism, and to help free people from oppression. That might read weakly now, but it was how some of us felt. My father and big brother had done their part when the country was in need. I felt the same call. I felt it was my time.

The hardest part wasn't going. In honesty, going and doing the job was something of an adventure. I was sent more than once. That was enough, and I wouldn't like to do it again.

However, like the old saying states, we were, "in for a penny, in for a pound". We signed up and did our duty. We held the line the best we could in whatever we were called on to do.

The hardest thing for me was being away from Lisa. We hadn't made any kind of commitment to each other when I left the first time. She was my girl the last two years at Benicia High School. When we graduated I went to Southern California for training, and she went to college.

I guess every guy has their last night with the girl they will be leaving behind, if they can. Lisa and I had ours. Most of the evening was spent on the couch in front of the television.

Lisa's parents went to bed early. I know, because I had spent many hours at Lisa's home. It was very nice of them to give Lisa and me the time alone.

I told Lisa I would have to leave at midnight. She said she understood, and knew I had to go about then. She also said she knew I had to do what I was going to do, and believed in my commitment. She said I wouldn't be me if I didn't go.

At midnight the camel-hump clock chimed the notes neither of us wanted to hear, but knew were coming, and which I had to obey. That was when Lisa reached for an envelope which lay on a side table. She told me to open it and remove what was inside.

What the envelope held was a photograph of a pretty young lady leaning against my car. The photo was sealed in flexible plastic. There was no writing on either side of the photo.

Lisa told me she thought the plastic would keep the photo from being damaged. She said she didn't write her name, or that she loved me, on the photo on purpose. It wasn't that she had forgotten. She said she wanted me to think of the person in the photo when I was gone.

At that moment the car in the picture was parked by the sidewalk in front of Lisa's home. I had a surprise for her, also. I reached into my pocket and pulled out the set of keys to the car I always used and handed them to Lisa.

She asked why I had done that, and I told her I wanted her to have the car while I was gone. She didn't have a car of her own, the car would need to be run, and there was no one else I would want to have it while I was gone.

When she asked if I wanted her to drive me home, I told her I had planned to walk. I knew I would need some composure time before I got home, and the walking would accomplish that.

I kept the picture squirreled away where I could for the next four years. At times I could have it with me in my wallet. At other times, situations made it such that I had to leave it behind as I fulfilled what I was ordered to do.

Whenever I could, I came back to Benicia. I was granted leave twice. Three times during training in Southern California, between tours, I managed to fly to San Francisco and take a bus to Vallejo.

At the bus depot I phoned Lisa and she picked me up and I drove us to Benicia. When I had to leave, she drove me back to the bus depot and waited until the bus departed.

The last of those times home, I told Lisa I loved her and she said she loved me. When I told her where I would be going again, she teared up a little. She had shown the willingness to wait for me with her words, actions, letters, and packages all the times before. Now I was going again.

I had to be honest with her in another way. I had to tell her that she had waited a long time already, and that I didn't know how much longer she would have to wait. Her waiting may have been in vain. There were more bad times ahead for a lot of guys. They could only try their best, hope, and pray that things would work out.

Lisa knew what I meant. She took my words with calmness, and a firmness and conviction I had only seen in men with whom I served. She knew the risks of our fully giving our thoughts and emotions to each other. When I told her I would like her to keep waiting for me, she said she would wait for me as long as it took.

Lisa waited for me. The photo of the pretty young woman leaning against my car is in a stand on a bookcase in our living room. I look at it every day and in my mind thank Lisa for giving it to me and God for letting things happen as they have.

Lisa has told me many times that I wouldn't be who I am without the experiences I've had, including the time serving our country. She is correct. I also never could be who I am, if it wasn't for Lisa.

Glen

Letter 102

I Met My Love in Church

Mr. Garrett,

"I love you, and I pray God takes care of you," are words I've said many times over the years to my wife and our children. I've probably thought the words more times than I've ever said them.

Lois and I met at the old First Baptist Church in Benicia. It was located on the northwest corner of the Military East and East Second Street intersection. A little shopping center does business there now. We've eaten Baskin Robbins ice cream and Nation's hamburgers at that location. The ice cream shop is where grass grew and a small parking lot was located. The place where we've eaten hamburgers is in the area where some rooms were attached to the right of the main church building.

My first few times at the church had been when I had gone almost kicking and screaming in the company of my mother. Lois was the reason I kept going to the church as I got a little older.

The company for which I worked for over thirty years sent us over most of the western United States. If I wanted to move up the ladder, I had no other choice but to accept the positions and go. If things had worked out differently we would have wound up in Benicia, where we started. Fate takes us where it will.

The love for my Lois started in the First Baptist Church. The love for our children followed because of the love for Lois.

Lois and I drive down to Benicia every couple of months from our place in Mendocino. We talk with some friends and have lunch.

Benicia has really changed over the years, but if you think you are lost, all you have to do is head for the water. That has always been there, and always will be. It is the same with love.
Ian

Letter 103

Ed Never Knew His Father

Dear Mr. Garrett,

Ed never knew his father, but I think they would have loved each other. They were so much alike in their youth. As Ed has aged past the number of years his father lived, I have often wondered if they would have stayed similar.

Each had a bit of the need for adventure in them. Ed's has toned down quite a bit as he's gotten older, and especially since he got married.

I never married Ed's father. When we could have gotten married, and should have, we were both a little too free-spirited. We had gone in search of fame and fortune in San Francisco through music. We came to know the Haight-Ashbury district like we knew our way around Benicia.

Money was really tight, but we loved each other and thought things would work out, if we just kept trying.

To this day I can't remember what we argued about that last time. I didn't want to lose Ed's father by having him think he was chained down. I really thought that when he found just what he was looking for he would settle down. Regardless, I would have gone with him anywhere he wanted to go, like I had in going with him to San Francisco.

What I wanted for both of us was a child, but I think he would have felt his lifestyle would be threatened. The day came when there was no doubt in my mind I was pregnant. It was the same day we had our last argument.

He went out the door and down the hallway like he was trying to pound holes in the flooring with his feet. The slamming of the door in my face stunned me.

I wish I knew what had made him so angry at that moment. I don't want to believe it was something I did, or said, but perhaps it was. If so, I regret whatever it was so much.

I think he was feeling frustrated in not being able to provide me with things he said he would. His expectations were the expectations of many youth. He thought things would come sooner and easier than they were. I kept telling him things would work out and get better. I was happy with him and would be regardless of the circumstances.

Before, when he had gotten angry, he usually calmed down after a few minutes. He had never acted as he had then.

We lived on the second floor of a converted Victorian. A few seconds after he slammed the door I went to the bay window and looked down at the street hoping to see him. I hoped he would turn and look back at me. I was going to motion for him to come back if he did turn to look.

It was a rainy late afternoon. The streets were slick and I'm sure people were having a little bit of a hard time driving, though some of them were definitely speeding.

Ed's father stepped out into the street from between two parked cars. He hesitated for a moment, turned, and looked up at me.

When he saw me smiling down at him, he smiled back. I motioned for him to come back. He took one glance to his right and saw a car almost upon him. He had just started to take a step when the car hit him.

Ed's father was dead before I could reach him. He never knew he would have a son in just a few more months.

Some nice people helped me out along the way. I try to give back for that help by doing the same for others through a clinic I run. It was hard going to San Francisco State to earn my degree for the work, but the work is so rewarding.

I don't live in Benicia, neither does Ed, but my love for his father started there. From that came my love for Ed. I don't want Ed to hear expressed what some people may think of him, or his father, or his mother. We stay away.

I've explained to Ed the relationship his father and I had, and how he died. He accepted it all long ago. I always tell Ed I loved his father. I still love him.

For my name, think of a wine. You know who I am.

(Unsigned)

Letter 104

Does He Feel the Same?

Dear Mr. Garrett,

There is someone I love as I've never loved before, but I wonder if he loves me. I wonder what he would do to show his love for me. I wonder if he has shown it in his own way, but I have not been aware. I wonder if my chance with him has passed me by through my lack of awareness of the subtleties of his words and actions.

We live across a parking lot from each other in the condominiums by the marina. We talk almost every day, but we have never dated. If the vapor of the curtain, which seems to separate us, ever vanished, life would be so different.

If he asked me for anything I could do, I can't imagine anything I wouldn't do. Does he feel the same?

When life is happy or challenging I want the touch of his caress, and the warmth of his arms. I would give him my warmth, and the touch of my lips.

If things go bad, I want him to hold me close in the strength of those arms, and tell me everything will be alright. I would comfort him with all the care I could provide.

I hope he would wait, no matter how long it took, for us to be together at a coffee shop on First Street. I would wait for him.

I pray he will love me forever. I would love him for the equal eternity.

Gray hair gains dominance on my head each day. Perhaps he looks for someone much younger.

Perhaps he has someone in his heart whom he seeks or whom he has lost. If so, I would never try to take their place. I would hope only to gain a little place in his heart.

Today he asked if I enjoy boating. I said yes. I see the vapor fading in the warmth of his words.
Charlene

Letter 105

Dan's Life in a Box

Dear Mr. Garrett,

Yesterday I opened a box. It has been stored in the back of the walk-in closet of the master bedroom of what has been my home for many years. The house is too big for just me, though I've wandered around inside it all these years. I'll be moving to a much smaller place, so I had to go through things.

I think it was finally the right time to open the box. I had gone through everything else in the house. I had discarded what needed to be discarded and gave away what would be useful to someone else, but which no longer had a place in my life.

I miss Dan just as much now as when he died, but we all have to do things in life. Opening the box was one of those things for me. Opening that box was the duty I put off until the last. It was the last act on the last day I would be in the home Dan and I knew as ours for so many years. It was raining, and I sat on the floor leaning against a wall, while I went through the contents. The tissue box next to me became emptier as time passed.

Heidi, our dog, lay with her head on my lap, as I sat on the floor. I think she knew what was happening. Heidi has seen her new home, and knows Dan won't be there with us.

She misses Dan, also. Part of what she misses is the play time where they would roll around on the grass, or our carpet, or play throw and retrieve with ball or stick. She is getting much slower in her movements now. I play tug with her still, but her time is approaching as it does with every living thing. She is such a good dog. She has been companion and protector and a loyal friend.

When Dan and I met, the attraction between us was instantaneous. He was such a gentleman. He actually cared for me as a person from the moment we saw each other.

He complimented me so many times over the years by saying I was attractive, or I was a good looking woman, but it was deeper than that. Other men had told me the same things, and more, but with Dan I felt he was reading my soul. He saw inside me, no matter what barriers life may have prepared me with to resist opening myself to a man.

We started dating, and became closer and closer. I didn't know for sure where things were leading, and maybe he didn't either. I did know I very much enjoyed being with him.

An example of his honesty was when he said he didn't want me to waste my youth on him. Dan spoke of that when he talked with me of marriage. Dan was older than me. That conversation started out mildly, got rather heated, and then calmed again.

Dan asked me to move into his house with him. He said we spent so much time there that it seemed like the obvious thing to do. He told me that, if I accepted, I was free to leave any time I wanted. He said he would understand. There would be no questions asked, and he would help set me up somewhere else and pay for everything.

I very much wanted to live with him in any way I could. I truly didn't care if it would be as his friend, his lover, or his wife. I became all three of those and more.

He was just making sure I understood how the cards had fallen between us, in his opinion. Life had left its lines on his face, and in his heart. He didn't want me to hold lines such as he held.

He said my being in the house made a home of the place where he had been living alone. I'm very happy about that. I think I added a female presence the house needed. Dan said he could do everything around a home except have the babies, but he could get the babies started. I miss his humor.

We had lived together for a year to the day from the day I entered his house to live with him, when Dan proposed to me. I think he had given me time to see him in all his facets so I could leave, if I had wanted. I had no desire to leave.

In that year together, we had made the house a home. I was as much of a wife to Dan in that time, as I would have been if we had stood at the altar a year previous. I told Dan it would be a privilege and an honor to be his wife.

Dan and I never had children. He said he was too old, and if we did have children he would be like a grandfather to them. He wanted any children he had to see him young and strong. Age does get us all, if we live long enough, but Dan was strong to the last. He handled everything life had to give him with his strength. He was a man.

Dan wasn't secretive with me in anything. That may sound strange. I think he didn't tell me some things, or explain some other things in detail, because he didn't want to take the chance of hurting me in any way.

A couple of times Dan let something from his past slip in when we talked. Some of those times were when he talked of Rupert and Andy. He always immediately covered those slips with a laugh, self deprecating humor, or by telling me he had been lying, or had merely made up a story. When he slipped in his comments in front of others, he would turn to me and say he knew he had never told me that story before, and make a joke and laugh.

Sometimes the laughter quickly passed. At other times he laughed so hard everyone else laughed as hard, and Dan had to wipe his eyes. You could read the truth of the stories he told in his eyes.

One thing about Dan, which I saw at the outset, and others told me they had realized shortly after Dan had let them into his circle, was the fact he spoke his mind. It was so refreshing. The man said what he meant and meant what he said. If he liked you, he liked you. It didn't matter what anyone else may have thought of you in any way. If you were accepted by him, you were accepted in totality.

It was such a nice feeling to have that acceptance. That isn't to say he and I, or others he accepted, didn't have moments of disagreement. Believe me, we all did. He might erupt like a solar flare, but, if you had been honest with him, things worked out. If you hadn't been honest with him, there was a problem. He gave everyone one lie. Any more than that, and he cut the person off from his life as much as he could. I never lied to Dan, and he knew that. He respected me so much for that. He didn't always agree with what I said, but he respected it.

What memories the box held. Decades of attachment were enclosed within it. I think he saved every word I ever wrote him. There were Valentines, Christmas and birthday cards, and even two notes asking him to pick up things at the store. There was a paper he had written in school of which he was very proud, though the grade was B. He was like that.

Included in the box were his high school senior yearbook, his boot camp graduation book, and a form showing his marksmanship ability, a laminated copy of our wedding announcement, and a cork from a bottle of our favorite wine.

There was nothing connecting him with college. I think he felt college was just something he had to do in his life, so he did it. I don't think he enjoyed the experience.

Small things intrigued me as much as the larger objects. Why the faded flower? Why the ticket stub to a theater long since closed? Why the post card depicting a place I never knew he had been?

Looking at what was inside the box helped me to understand Dan still more. There were things he couldn't and wouldn't have talked of when he was alive. He wanted me to know how much they meant to him, and how they had helped form him, though he would speak little of them, if at all.

His old baseball glove and the pair of football cleats he wore in the last game he played were wrapped in plastic as was his Benicia High School letterman's sweater. There is something in the bible about giving up childish things. I think Dan did that the best he could, but he still had much of the child in him.

The box held Dan's military decorations and papers. He had shown them to me only once. The box also held three photos. One photo showed Dan and Rupert. Another photo showed Dan and Andy. The third photo showed all three.

I never met Rupert and Andy, but Dan had told me some things about them. I never asked Dan if I would ever meet them, but I think I would never have the chance to meet them. It had been forty years since Dan had seen Rupert and Andy, but he still held them in his heart. In his heart, they were as young and strong as they were in the photos.

At times, while watching television or after going to a movie, Dan would tell me things about the military. In time, I came to ask him about certain things and to explain certain things.

Dan would usually say he didn't know what he was talking about, and just made things up. Then he would give me his opinion on what we had seen, or the question I had asked.

Dan knew too much about the military in a broad range, and too much about it in detail in some specifics, for him to not have had, at least, a good working knowledge of the things of which he spoke. I know, in my heart, that Rupert and Andy were part of those times and events.

I hadn't always understood some of the things Dan told me through the years concerning the military, either in part or in whole. His experiences gave him a language with which I was unfamiliar at times.

The few times certain others, who visited over the years, and who had served in the military, would sit and talk with us, I learned more. It was obvious Dan and they spoke the same language and knew and understood those things they all said when they talked.

At times Dan would explain to me what he talked about, when the feeling came to him to speak of them. At other times he merely stated what he had said wasn't important and changed the subject. There were rare times when I could see just how important the words he spoke were to him. I knew that because, after saying them, he would leave the room. When he came back, his eyes were red and he sometimes sniffled. His face still held a watery shine from washing away the tears the memories had brought.

There are other things in the box he had shown me. Twice, when he did that, he told me there were 10% of parts of his life I would never know. I think that is still true. Going through the papers in the box, and looking at the photos, I understand more now.

I held Dan's hand at his bedside when he died. He had been in the hospital for a few days. When he knew the time was near for him to go ahead to wait for me, he told me he wanted to go home and to die in a bed in one of our spare bedrooms.

Some wonderful people helped me in that time, and have stood by me since. I didn't realize Dan knew so many people. He knew people all around the world. Many were people he had never spoken of, or had mentioned casually, or had told me of when telling me a story.

Dan's funeral services were held at St. Dominic's, where we had been married. He often stated the life someone led would be shown by who attended their funeral services. Dan wouldn't have been disappointed.

The opening music selection played was "Amazing Grace". I knew the words of the song meant much to him. He had talked to me about how he thought he had sinned earlier in his life. Because of that, he wished he had done more than enough good to counter any bad held resting on the scales of his life. I know he had far exceeded his wish.

Many of Dan's favorite pieces of music were played at the service. I think some people were surprised by some of the selections. The pieces were important to Dan, and the life we had shared together.

When I stood to walk out of the church the words of "Danny Boy" filled every part of the building. They were sung by a young woman with a charming, sensitive voice. I saw men, who were very tough and strong individuals, have streams of tears run down their cheeks. Some of them were also smiling as the tears fell from their eyes. Through their tears, there were smiles. It was so nice to see the sorrow, and the joy, at the same time.

I didn't waste a second of the part of my life I spent with Dan. I only had that period of my life, and the years since, made better by being with him. I grew, and gained strength, by being with him. He is my one and only.

The box, which holds so much of who Dan was, now sits on an oak table in my bedroom. I can see it when I am lying in bed. It brings me comfort to see the box, and think of the memories of treasures it holds.

At times I will open the box, and hold close to me things Dan held dear. Some of those times will be anniversaries of special moments in our lives, which hold no meaning to others. The times such as Christmas, which others share with their loved ones, I will share with Dan by opening the box. At times I'll be able to open the box to be near Dan. I would never part from any of the items in the box. I love Dan.
Priscilla

Letter 106

She Was My Best Friend

Dear Mr. Garrett,

She was my best friend. I didn't mean to have an affair with her boyfriend.

Both of them are gone from my life now, and gone from the lives of each other.

I don't even really know how it got started between him and me. One day we were shaking hands, and the next day we were in bed. My head swims with a kaleidoscope of images of what happened.

Where he and I worked, we both sometimes put in extra hours. Much of that time we were alone with each other.

I think I loved him then. He said he loved me, but he said that to my best friend, also. I was foolish in not seeing that at the time.

When my best friend found out what had been going on, she told him that if he wanted me, he could have me. She said he was out of her life.

I tried to explain, to my best friend, what had happened, and that I hadn't meant for it to happen. She said that all I had to do was talk to her when I first started having the feelings towards him I had. She said she would have solved the problem.

I don't know what she meant by solving the problem, but I so wish I had talked with her.

Benicia is very lonely for me now. I don't think I can stay here anymore. There are too many thoughts, which come to my mind every day, I don't like. I've lost my best friend, who I loved, and a man I thought, for a short time, that I loved.
K.

Letter 107

She Didn't Wait

Mr. Garrett,

You stimulated a lot of memories in me with your advertisement. You also probably did with a lot of other people.

I think a lot of the memories we all have are memories of love in our youth. Those loves help make us who we are, and provide a basis, with most of us, for choosing the person who becomes our true love.

Don't get me wrong, I believe in love at first sight. I also believe that love can be found from kindergarten on, and it can, and does, last.

Most of us have what we might call love experience as teenagers, or when we're in our early twenties. I think that's the nature of the beast, so to speak. That's what happened with me.

In my case it was a young woman, who said she would wait for me forever. Forever didn't last too long with her. It was my fault.

The time we had was a good time, but I came to understand later that it was veneer. There wasn't much depth or basis to it.

There were things I had to get done in my life, before I could settle down. Maybe it can be called having a time to find myself. While finding myself, I lost Valerie.

I can't blame her for not waiting. I shouldn't have expected her to wait. If we had set a target date, for me to fulfill what I felt I needed to do, it might have worked out differently. I don't really think so.

Valerie married well, by any definition of the term. She travels the world with her husband. I work here in town.
Bob

Letter 108

God Wanted a Good Boy by His Side

Dear Mr. Garrett,

Barry and I loved our son very much. We didn't have him long, only until the seventh grade. Then, God took him. God wanted a good boy to be by his side.

Will gave us so much goodness in his short time with us. There was joy in his eyes and his voice. He shared so much with us and with the others in his life.

Barry accepted the loss of the only son he would ever have sooner than I, but he took it just as hard. He handles stress and emotion differently than I, but I've know him long enough to understand what he feels most of the time. There is no doubt what he feels for his son.

It took me nine years to finally accept his loss. I kept thinking how his life would have gone. He would have played sports for the Panthers of Benicia High. He would have dated the girl down the block. Barry would have shown him how to do maintenance on a car. I would have taught him how to cook for that time in his life when he might be an eligible bachelor.

Part of the acceptance of Will's loss came when I finally forgave the drunk whose driving killed him.

We visit Will's gravesite in the city cemetery from time-to-time, and never miss being there on his birth date. Barry and I visited his grave on what would have been Will's twenty-first birthday. With Barry and I on that graveside visit was the man whose driving killed our son. He had previously spent some time in a penitentiary atoning for his mistake.

There is a love which exceeds time and distance.

There is also a kind and forgiving love. I came to understand that.

Maryann

Letter 109

A Question Unasked

Mr. Garrett,

A young lady and I had been seeing a lot of each other for about a year. My feelings for her were very strong.

One afternoon, we were sitting on a park bench by the marina. I asked her something about people getting married and growing old with each other. That's when she told me she was glad we were good friends, because we could talk about anything, and she could tell me anything.

I thanked her for that, but knew right then that I was shot down before opening my mouth about what I wanted to say. I was going to propose to her the first chance I got that looked romantic. That time and place had looked romantic to me.

Then she told me of things she wanted to have happen in her future and how she was working on them then, and would continue to work on them. She used the contraction "I'm" many times. She didn't say "we" or "us" once.

I had the engagement ring in my left front pants pocket wrapped in a piece of red velvet tied with a gold cord. I thought that would be a nice touch. I would get on my knees, take her hands in mine, and ask her to be my bride.

I hadn't planned what I was going to say, other than that, or where I was going to propose. Things seemed right then. Since I didn't go through with what I thought I was going to do, I guess everything turned out fine. When I look out my window,

I can see the bench where we sat. I have good memories about it. No harm no foul, as is sometimes said in basketball.

Maybe she guessed what I was going to say some day and wanted to keep from hurting my feelings by avoiding a situation where she would say no.

I loved that young lady enough to ask her to marry me, but she didn't feel the same. Things work out for all of us as they are designed to work out. We're still friends, but we've pulled away a little from each other.

Scott

Letter 110

A Rain Storm Brought Love

Mr. Garrett,

The first words I heard Ashley say that day were: "Why are you laughing at me like that?" I couldn't help it. She looked like a wet puppy. She could have just stepped out of a shower, and she couldn't have been wetter. Her hair was dripping like bundles of stalactites gone wild.

I had been about to enter a store, but stopped just outside the doors of the store because the day had suddenly gotten much darker. That was when I saw her running across the parking lot. She had run towards the front of a store in Raley's shopping plaza, where I was standing, to get out of the rain and the wind.

When I asked why she hadn't gone back to her car for a coat, she said she was halfway between the store and the car and didn't want to turn back. She gambled she could make it from her car to the store without getting wet, but a deluge hit and she got soaked. She laughed all the time she was speaking. She has a good laugh. It's hearty, and healthy, and strong.

I asked if she thought it would be raining when she went back to her car. She said she bet that it wouldn't. She lost the bet with herself.

I was wearing a hooded, insulated jacket over a long-sleeved wool shirt. I took the jacket off and offered it to her to warm her up. She hesitated for about a millisecond. Then cold and logic took over and she did the prudent thing. She thanked me, and accepted the offer.

We entered the store and walked around in it. As we walked, we shared words about others whom we knew. After we had selected from the shelves what we each wanted, we paid for our purchases and walked towards the doors.

She thanked me for the loan of the jacket. When she started to take it off, I told her there was no reason to get wetter and cold again on her way to her car. I told her I'd carry some of her bags, and she could give me the jacket then when she put on her own.

I had never seen Ashley before that day and she had never seen me. We were two people who came together in the rain. I liked her look and her laugh. I liked talking with her. She accepted what I gave as the friendliness of one person to another. At first that was what I saw. Later we came to see things differently. We came to see things in a stronger connection.

When Ashley said she needed to do something to repay my kindness, I told her there was no need, and that I was glad I was there then. She insisted, but I think she was unsure of what to say. Finally she said she could buy me a pizza that night. I was happily surprised, and told her I would like to eat pizza with her.

She said she had to go home and change, but she would meet me at the pizza parlor near where we stood later.

It was about 4:30 in the afternoon. At 6:00 I opened the door to the pizza parlor for her. She said she was glad to see me again, and I told her I was glad to see her again.

We sat down and ordered a pizza. It was a combo. Ashley and I have become a combo since that day.

What happened occurred because of events during a rainstorm, but I think Ashley and I had been led to that meeting all our lives. Soul mates can travel for a long time on separate paths, until fate makes those paths join. The merging of the paths of two forms a path for two on their journey through life.

We've been married for almost three years.

Tony

Letter 111

I Hope She Married a Good Man

Mr. Garrett,

I'm sitting here now in a far distant land, and I don't like it. I have to be here now, though, so here I am. It all comes with carrying the gear I carry.

At mail call today I received my backlog of correspondence. Included in that was a clipping of your advertisement. It was the only thing in the envelope. There was no return address on the envelope, and my address was typed. I guess someone is trying to give me a message.

The only girl I've ever loved lives in Benicia. If she would have married me, we could have lived in government housing on base, until I was deployed again. She could have waited there until I got back. She didn't want to come with me, though I told her things would work out.

She said she couldn't take a chance on me, because of my chosen profession and lifestyle. Looking back at it, she must have known she was pregnant and was looking for security. I don't understand why else she wouldn't have gone with me.

I'll be here a while longer, and then be rotated back, trained, and sent back here, or off to somewhere else. There is no need for me to go back to Benicia anymore. I have everything I need.

In my ex-girlfriend's last letter she told me she was going to get married. I hope the man she married is a good man.

A friend wrote me and told me my ex-girlfriend was married and had a baby. I hadn't known she was pregnant at the time I left, but she must have been. If not, the child was born very early. The boy must be my son. I'll never know him.
Eric

Letter 112

The Flames Were Strong

Mr. Garrett,

I don't know how others write to you about these things, and I won't know until I read your collection. In every case others may use the names of those they've loved and give their own name as well. I think there will be some letters where no names will be revealed. The person writing the letter will still want to tell you of their love. Anyway, that's how I am.

At first, and for months after, the flames were strong. They turned to warm coals, but the love was still there. Then there was no warmth. There was still love, but not what we had known.

At the start, I didn't know how lucky I was. I let it all slip away. There were signs and warnings I was too oblivious to see. All I have left is the memory of that love which once was mine.

I fell for the woman I would marry in an instant. After we got married, I thought everything was fine and would continue to be fine. I had my career, she had her career, and we had the house and eventually the kids.

I thought I was doing what was needed to make a successful career and make life better for us. All I was doing was making things worse. She kept telling me we didn't need the boat and other things I kept working to get us. I, foolishly, didn't see what she saw.

Now she has the house in Benicia, I have the kids every other weekend and two weeks during the summer up at the lake, and I have my work.

I'm a pretty successful and well off man. I'd give it all up in an instant to have the chance to start over again with that woman and feel the love we once shared.

(Unsigned)

Letter 113

The Old Tree on the Crest

Mr. Garrett,

There is a tree near the crest of the hills across the Carquinez Straits from Benicia. I've seen that tree for over 60 years.

From my distance, now, looking from the front windows of our home, or from our front and back yards, it looks the same as it did when I was a boy. I couldn't see the tree from the sites where I lived then, but would see it when I went around town. I could see the tree from the classroom where I passed the seventh grade. That room is part of the Benicia Unified School District complex now.

The tree bent in its growth through its struggles with the wind over the decades. The lean of the majority of its branches provides more shelter for the creatures, which call the tree home, than it would had its growth not been impeded by the wind.

The branches have offered shady comfort, on a warm day, for the picnic of a couple of lovers, who sat under them. From there the lovers looked across on Benicia, and spoke of their love for it, as they spoke of their love for each other. The tree is part of that love. From Benicia the tree is seen, and from the tree Benicia is seen. I think it is a symbiosis.

That tree has to be made of tough wood to withstand the rigors it has endured through the years. The same can be said of Benicia. It has endured degrees of turmoil. There are good people here, though. They nurture the soil of the community, as Mother Nature nurtures the soil where the tree took root.

Some day that tree will fall. Benicia isn't the Benicia I knew and never will be again. Neither will that tree grow again to show its beauty, show its strength, and spread its shade as I once knew.

Perhaps, though, it has produced seeds which will treasure the earth as some have treasured Benicia. Perhaps the children of Benicia will continue to do the same for this small place on the planet, where I can observe a tree I've seen on the horizon for a lifetime.
Mario

Letter 114

His Roots Are in Benicia

Mr. Garrett,

To love, in my opinion, we must first love ourselves, and then we can love one another. To love ourselves, we have to be encouraged by others to love. It is a circle.

Your advertisement spoke of love, which is in any way related to Benicia. John Wayne does a rendition of a song which includes the words, "my roots are buried here".

The song doesn't apply to Benicia for its location, but the concept is the same. It is the concept, which is important, because having the concept leads to the fulfillment of that concept.

We are all brothers and sisters under the skin.

I was raised here, but not born here. Still, my roots are buried here. One day I will be buried here.

Where we share the good morning hello, where we have shared triumphs and tragedies, the gains and losses, and hope for the future are where our roots are buried. The longer someone lives in a place, the deeper their roots grow.

In real estate, I believe the term is sweat equity. Put in the sweat of your brow, the worry in your belly, and the pain in your head long enough and deep enough and you increase the depth of the roots. There is no magic fertilizer which can be sprinkled on for a short period and have long lasting effects. It takes seasonal commitment. Roots grow strong, deep, and long by commitment.

The same is true for love of a place, a thing, or a human. Some might say the feeling of love for a place, like Benicia, is an anthropomorphosis. I can agree in the literal interpretation, but not the general usage of the word love.

I love Benicia. I love the sights, the sounds, the smell of the air, and the squabbles. They are all part of what makes Benicia, Benicia.

Abe

Letter 115

The Steel-toed Boots

Mr. Garrett,

I have a pair of steel-toed boots. They were a good buy years ago, and I sometimes wear them when I'm doing a job around the house. I wore them a lot when Susan and I were building our home. Any guy knows about a pair of boots and how they become special. You just hate the thought of throwing them out, but with enough wear, they have to be placed in the trash can.

Many, many, many times, when I think of how Susan and I started out, I think of steel-toed boots. Each time I go to put on mine, I think of her.

I wasn't the best dancer in the world, but I got better because of Susan. I think she must have wanted a pair of steel-toed boots the first time we danced.

The only dances I've been to were the high school dances, when I attended Benicia High School. The school was down town then, and the Civic Center Gym was our high school gym. All our dances were held there.

Most of the times at the dances, I stood on the sidelines next to the pulled-out bleachers, talked to some people, and watched others dance. I wasn't as good a dancer as a couple of the other guys, and I didn't want to embarrass myself. If I was ever going to do something, I wanted to do it well. I wasn't going to make an idiot out of myself in front of most of the school, unless I did it on purpose for a joke.

There was a nice guy, with whom I got along well, who was a good dancer. I asked him to show me what to do, and he agreed. I took a couple lessons from him before the next dance. He showed me the box steps, with the start being moving to my left, and how to guide my partner with my hand pressure on her hand and her waist. He said that after that, it was just a matter of practice. He was correct.

It was during the fall semester, and the next dance was the Friday night after the home football game. We won the game, and I held up my end of the responsibilities for the win. I wanted to dance with Susan. She was the one I had wanted to dance with for what seemed like, to me, a long time.

There had never been any problem in me asking her to dance, if I wanted. I just didn't know how to dance very well. I wanted her to think well of me when we finally danced. When I watched her dance, she moved so smoothly and effortlessly. All the time she smiled.

The dance had been going on for about half an hour, when I walked over where she was standing under the basketball net nearest the lobby, and asked her to dance.

She said she would love to dance with me. I could move my feet pretty well in athletics, but I still wasn't very confident about dancing.

Susan took my hand, and we walked out farther on the floor. Maybe she was guiding me, or I was guiding her. I don't know for sure. I do know we wound up as the couple, which started the next dance in the circle "B" on the center of the gym floor.

The center of the gym was a coveted spot for people who wanted to demonstrate their dancing skills. It was also the spot for people, who were couples, to show they were together, or for those who were announcing, to their high school social circle, that they were couples.

I was more interested in holding Susan's hand, and walking with her, than trying to demonstrate anything. There was nothing I could demonstrate. I had asked Susan to dance, she had accepted, and we were walking out to dance. She wasn't my girlfriend. If she was, we would have been walking out to dance a long time before that time.

When we got to the circle "B", Susan entered my arms. It was like she was part of my clothing. From that first touch we moved as one.

Susan asked why I had waited so long to ask her to dance. When I told her the reason, she said I shouldn't have waited. She said that even if all I wanted to do was stand and hold her, and sway with the music that would have been fine. She said she had waited, and waited, for me to ask her to dance. Since I hadn't, until then, she felt I must not have liked her, other than as a friend.

The truth be told, Susan needed the steel-toed boots for the first minute, or so, of that first dance. She could glide, but I didn't know for sure where my feet were going. I tried to say nice, but non-committal things, and move my feet correctly at the same time. That didn't work at the start of our first dance.

Then a change came, and I glided with Susan. In reality, she compensated for every wrong move I made. She reacted to the changing directions of my body as if she knew ahead of time what I was going to do. Susan was a great dancer. I had seen it when she danced with others, and then I felt it as she was in my arms. I had felt attraction for her before that dance. During that dance I felt the first thrill of love.

Susan and I danced the remainder of the slow dances together that night. The next Sunday I telephoned her and asked if she would like to go for a ride, and she said she would love to ride with me.

At the end of the ride, parked in front of her home, I asked Susan to go steady with me. She said she would love to, and had hoped I would ask her.

The next Friday night was our last home football game of the season. Susan and I walked in the door for the dance that night together. We danced every slow dance together, and I tried a couple of the fast dances with her. It was a very good evening. We had won the game, and I danced with my girl. It was high school at its best.

Susan and I danced the first dance at our wedding reception four years later. We have danced many times since at other weddings and in our living room with no one around except us, since that first dance our senior year.

Dale

Letter 116

Liz Was So Nice

Mr. Garrett,

Liz was nice. That is what attracted me to her.

I don't mean only in personal appearance. I mean in her life. She didn't swear, didn't smoke, and the only alcohol she had tasted, until we were both adults, was wine. The drinking of the wine was only at some special family gatherings each year. She wasn't a prude, or she wouldn't have been so popular. Liz was simply a good, sweet, young girl.

There were some girls who were the date-a-month winners of the girlfriend exchange lottery. Liz was never one of them.

Liz dated a number of guys, but never went steady with any of them, until she accepted to go steady with me. Before that, about every other week in the gossip column of the Prowling Panther, one boy, or another, was listed as liking her. One time the name stated was mine. It was shortly after that she became mine.

So many people don't understand the word "mine", in connection to relationships. She wasn't my property. I didn't own her. In my heart, she was part of me, but that part was free to fly, if it chose. Grasping something to keep it only increases the chance you will fail to retain it.

What was printed in the Prowling Panther about me liking Liz was true. I liked her then, just as I had for a long time. There was something which kept drawing her to my attention.

It came to form in my head that the something was that she was nice. She was quiet and demure, but also a willing, and happy, participant in many of the activities at the old Benicia High School.

If there was a theme day activity, she dressed the part with style. She was doing nothing more than reflecting her daily success in selecting her attire.

Liz always dressed nicely. There was nothing gaudy or suggestive. She dressed with charm and grace, while still being a teenage girl. When saddle shoes were what were needed as part of the balance to her apparel, she wore them. When high heels were part of the social requirement of the evening, she was just as lovely.

Her parents cared for her, and gave her what they could. Other things she bought with her own money on one of her shopping forays, alone or with friends, down First Street or to Vallejo.

Guys talk, and girls talk. I don't know for sure exactly what girls talk about, or when, or how they say what they say. Maybe no guy does. I do know what guys often talk about, how, when, and what they say. Sometimes it is flattering to the opposite sex, and sometimes it isn't.

For all I know, some guys spoke some unflattering comments about Liz when I wasn't around. No guy, in my presence, ever said anything derogatory about Liz, either before or after we started dating.

All they ever said about Liz was she was a real nice girl. When we started dating, some of them said I was lucky to be with her. That means a lot in guy talk. I was lucky to be with her. I was lucky she selected me.

I didn't care who she had dated before me, and she didn't care who I had dated. I think that is rare for people, especially teenagers. When we started dating, it was as if it had always been only her and me.

I've traveled over half of the world. In every part, from here to far distant shores, I've seen girls, and women, who were whores, prostitutes, ladies of the evening, soiled doves, or whatever else you want to call them. I'm not begrudging them what they do. Maybe they enjoy their trade, maybe they are forced into it by unscrupulous people, and maybe they are forced into it by economics. In some cases, that is all on them, and who they are with, if they are adults. In other cases they have no choice.

So many of the young girls, and women, I see today have no respect for themselves, their reputations, or their bodies. I see, girls and women, on television, and around town, and other places, who dress, and act, like whores. I think some of them don't know what they are doing, and others know very well what they are doing. How many of the women on television, and the movies, have been married and divorced one or more times? How many belong to the boyfriend-of-the-month club?

A young woman once asked me if I thought another woman, who is very popular in the entertainment industry, was pretty. I answered I had no way of knowing. I said she had so much makeup on, if a guy snuggled up next to her he would slide down to the floor.

Then the young woman asked if I thought men would like to date the other woman, and have sex with her. I said a lot of men would, but a lot of those same men would never marry her.

I told the young woman I had read somewhere that a famous actress once said it isn't what the woman has that is important. It is what the man thinks she has that is important.

When the young woman asked if I believed that, I said I definitely did. It isn't necessary for a woman to expose her navel, or have a tattoo on her spine, to be pretty, beautiful, or sexy. All of that comes from within, but is expressed in many forms on the outside. The walk, the talk, the apparel, the scent, and the smile, are all part of the appeal any woman possesses.

The young woman has been in the lives of Liz and me for many years. She has seen Liz and me interact from dawn to dusk in our home and away. When she asked why Liz and I get along so well, I told her Liz just puts up with me and my ways.

For my part, I said I treat Liz as my Lady, for the lady she is. She deserves, and has earned, to be treated as a lady.

I think the young woman was asking for help in clearing up some questions in her mind. She is a very intelligent young woman. She knew the answers all the time. She simply wanted to hear her thoughts supported. Like many others in the history of the planet, the young lady felt the need to be accepted by her peers. As the years have progressed, she has long since passed them.

Our conversation ended after she asked me how I thought her life with the opposite sex would go. I told her she would keep dating good young men. One day the special man, with whom she would share the remainder of her life, would appear. Maybe he already had, but all the factors hadn't aligned yet, for the fall each of them would take.

I guess this has been old "Father Eddie" preaching the sermon. I don't mean it to sound that way, and I don't live in the past. I just don't like to see so many females degrading themselves for a temporary gain of any kind, or because they think they can't feel wanted any other way.

I love my Liz. She has always been a lovely and appealing lady. She is nice. I'm a very lucky, and very happy, man.

I also love the young woman. She is also nice.

Eddie

Letter 117

For Years I Hated Him

Dear Mr. Garrett,

For years I hated him. He knew it, and came to understand. Then we came to truly love each other. It took me awhile to understand it was a mutual attraction and youthful lust gone past limits.

If innocence is a state of mind, or period of time, or if it is naiveté, or ignorance, each definition applied to me at one time. At first I thought I loved him and he loved me. I didn't know what I was doing or supposed to do, and he didn't know much more. We had sex for the first time, for either of us, on the grass in the city park on First Street.

It was late afternoon, on that warm day in the past, when things were far different than they are today. The park had no Playground of Dreams. Hedges, which have long since been removed from alongside the pathways which are now also gone, blocked much of what could be seen from the surrounding streets. There were only about six thousand people living in town then, so that made the chance of being unobserved even greater.

We started kissing and then lay on the grass out of fear of someone seeing us, I guess. The grass was dry. What happened is something I later wished hadn't happened, but such is life. At the time I was in total agreement with it. Youthful innocence was in love, but it was shattered innocence. He said he loved me. I said I loved him. He was confused. I meant it.

I was lucky. I never got pregnant, and it was in the days when protection, of any kind, was rare. I didn't know that then, but I since learned, along with a lot of other things.

I think what happened scared him. Maybe he thought he was going to get stuck with me, and it would ruin his life. He was a very motivated and driven young man. He had a natural tendency that way, but I believe his parents added too much fuel to the fire.

It was difficult to avoid someone at a high school with 350 or so kids enrolled, as Benicia High had in those days, but he worked hard at it. The next week, I hardly saw him at all. I was never alone with him during that time. I wanted to be alone with him to talk. I knew he had fourth period woodshop. On Monday, of the following week, I hurried down the stairs from my homemaking class which exited into the quad. Homemaking class was above the western end of the woodshop. What was the woodshop is now the place where people go to get building plans approved by the City of Benicia.

I didn't see him come out, so I waited outside the door for a few minutes. When he didn't come out, I thought I must have been too late to see him, and he had gone home for lunch. Each of us lived only a few blocks from the school and usually walked home for lunch. We had no cafeteria and many of the kids, who didn't go home for lunch, brought a sack lunch. It might seem quaint now, but it was a nice time to grow up in Benicia.

We had history together the last period of the day. It was in the room to the left of the entrance to the police station now. Maybe some kids thought of it as a police station then. I didn't, it was a fun class.

When the bell rang, I left the room as quickly as I could and waited outside the door for him. When he stepped out of the doorway, I grabbed him by the arm. He didn't resist as I guided him outside to the sidewalk. I think he accepted that we would talk. Maybe he was tired of avoiding me.

He said he wasn't ready. I told him I understood, but because he wasn't ready didn't mean he had to avoid me. When I asked him if he still loved me, he said he didn't know if he did or not. Then I asked if he didn't at least like me, he said he still did.

I about popped my cork. Ten days before he had told me he loved me and just then he said he still liked me. Buzzers and whistles were going off in my head. In a moment that feeling vanished and I was looking at a sad boy. I told him neither of us knew what the future held.

In all my worldly wisdom, at the time, I told him I hated him. Not for what we had done, but because of his attitude then. He said he was sorry he had hurt me, and I said I was sorry, too. Then I turned and walked away.

We finished out our senior year like strangers. I dated a nice guy and, believe it or not, he dated one of my friends.

The following September, I enrolled at Vallejo Junior College. The drives to Vallejo and back with my friends were fun times. He enrolled at Sacramento State to start what he hoped would be a career in politics.

Mrs. Hyde taught me to type well, and Mrs. Chorley and Mr. Simons taught me to write well. JC was interesting, and I did well, but I had no desire then to go farther with my education. I got a job in personnel, at the Arsenal, after graduating from the JC. I had the educational background and the English/typing skills. I guess I was one of those cute, perky types and that helped. I like people. Years after being hired at the Arsenal, I saw a familiar name in some papers with which I was working. It was him. We hadn't been in contact since high school. By the time I saw his name in the papers, I had an office of my own. As part of my duties I reviewed files. He would be working in my area.

When I knocked on the door of his office, I could read surprise, then curiosity, and then friendliness in his expressions. He stood and walked to greet me. We shook hands, and he asked me if I would like to sit down. He asked how I had been and about why I was there. I told him I was fine and that we worked in the same building. When I asked him how his journey into the world of politics had gone, he said it had been a huge mistake, but it did teach him more about people.

It was approaching lunch time. He asked if I would join him in the cafeteria, if I wasn't committed to someone else. When I told him there was no one in my life to which I was committed, he looked at me with a look of someone who is nearly startled. Then he smiled.

After work he was standing outside my office, as I prepared to leave. He knocked on the door and asked if it was OK with me if he came in. I told him it was fine with me, and that I had enjoyed having lunch with him.

It was a Friday afternoon. He asked if I would have dinner with him, that evening, at Spenger's Restaurant. That restaurant in the old ferry boat at what is now the eastern entrance to the State Park is long a distant memory. At that time it was a good place to eat. I told him I would enjoy having dinner with him and said where I lived. He picked me up about two hours later.

At dinner he told me he had never married. Then he asked if I had. When I told him I had never married either, he asked me to forgive him for being so foolish so long ago.

I told him there was no need to ask for forgiveness.

There are circles in life which are meant to be. He and I held hands across the table. The connection had been made again. I had stopped hating him long ago, though I had loved him all along. He loved me all along and had come home hoping to find me again. He had.

M.

Letter 118

Ada is Always Pretty

Dear Mr. Garrett,

The love of my life, Roger, thought he was a small, ugly duckling until he entered the eighth grade. He blossomed that year, to become one of the biggest boys in the class, and the handsomest. I know, because I later married him.

We had flirted in the eighth grade. Anyway, I flirted. He was probably just being polite. He seemed to have more interest in sports then, and for the next two years, than he had in girls. Roger became mine as a junior. All along he had been a good boy, and continued to be that, and grew into a good man.

I wasn't the only one "hot for his bod" as one of the expressions was then. He was so handsome and nice, the girls seemed to flock around him like they were pigeons and he was tossing out croutons.

When we became juniors at Benicia High School, he started to officially date. He had often been with girls at parties, in accidental, or impromptu, meetings, or had joined up with a girl at some function. Through the first part of our junior year he would ask a girl to go to some special event, but he didn't do it for all events. He would also, sometimes, ask a girl to go to a dance, but he didn't do it for all dances. It was like he was picking and choosing, or testing the water before diving in at the pool.

He was fun to be around. When I saw him at school, or around town, I teased him. Roger never asked me for a date until it was towards the end of that year. When he did, it was to the prom. At first I thought he was joking, and I told him so, but he said he was serious.

I told him I would very much like to go to the prom with him, but wondered why he would ask me, and not one of the other girls, since we had never dated.

If I hadn't fallen for him before then I couldn't have helped myself after what he said next. He said he had watched me since we were in the sixth grade, and liked what he had seen. Over the years we had shared a number of classes. He sat behind me in some, in front in others, and at my side, or in a far corner, in still others. He spoke of me talking with him, helping him with his school work, dancing with him, watching him play sports, and being his campaign manager when he ran for a school office. He told me of teasing him. He said he liked my sense of humor and intelligence. He watched me act in plays and play sports. He said he was impressed that I was intelligent and that I helped people and had friends. He said I was very pretty, and got prettier every year. He said I was as pretty in a sports uniform as I was when I was dressed for a dance.

I cried in front of him then. No one had ever talked with me before as he did then. Tears came down my cheeks as he kept speaking.

He said I wasn't like most of the other girls. They were all nice, he said, but there was something in me that appealed to him more.

I didn't know what to say, or do, so my heart spoke for me. I put my arms around his neck and kissed him. He kissed me back.

That prom was the best dance of my life. When Roger came to pick me up, my dad said I could hardly wait to see him. He said I had been prettying myself up for the last two days. Normally I would have been embarrassed and joked with Dad. I wasn't embarrassed at all. I had spent all the time because it was for Roger.

Roger's reply to my dad will stay in my heart forever, "Sir, Ada is always pretty."

Ada

Letter 119

Janet Is My Angel

Mr. Garrett,

Janet has those silver threads among the gold, of which song composers write. They were a long time in coming, and I love them as much as I love the gold.

Helen of Troy may have had golden hair, for all I know, but she couldn't have been lovelier than Janet. Some women disappear into another person as they age. Others grow lovelier, and continue to live all of their years in grace. Janet is one of those women.

Janet has produced three little curtain climbing, "rug rats", who have brightened our lives. Our daughter has the same color, and texture, of hair as her mother. The two boys are older than our daughter, and they were stuck with Dad's hair genes.

Janet and I have become what our parents once were. We are of that age. We follow the lives of our children, and grand children, and their adventures, in various parts of the country, as our parents once did with us. Our kitchen calendar seems to have every day, of every month, covered with some birthday, anniversary, event, or another.

Our children have now seen the times when their children are expanding their horizons and meeting others. In time, they may all meet a pretty woman, or a handsome man, who will make their hearts skip a beat. Some already have, and those fine young people have been willingly, and readily, accepted into our family.

That is what happened with me in Janet's life. She was a USO worker at a hotel in Vallejo when we met in 1945. One look at her and I knew she was the one for me. I'm glad Hollywood didn't get her.

At the time, I was a Marine stationed at Mare Island as part of the security force. It was a much more pleasant time than the previous two years, which I had spent in the western Pacific. I was lucky the Corps sent me, and some others, back to the States when it did.

Janet told me we couldn't date, because of her job, but she gave me her telephone number.

Then she got a job at Mare Island. The time had come when we could date. Whenever possible, I took the bus to Benicia to see Janet. I stayed as long as I could. Twice I missed my ride back, and had to walk into Vallejo to catch another. It was an easy seven mile walk, compared to what I had been used to in the Pacific.

As Janet and I got to know each other better, I felt so comfortable with her. I opened to her as I had never opened to anyone, nor ever would. Janet became my angel in time of need, my confessor, and my comfort when bad memories of the Pacific flooded my mind. At the times when all I wanted to do was drink my brain into oblivion, to forget what I had seen and done, she stood by me. She saw through the hurt.

We were married in the chapel at Mare Island. Janet's family had to make a few trips from Benicia to get everything set up like they wanted. All I had to do was tell my buddies I was getting married, and everything on my side was done. They were a great bunch of guys. Most of them are gone now, as are many of Janet's family.

As I write this, one of our grandsons is in Iraq as a young Marine. His lady waits. She is to him what Janet is to me. Our grandson is "career gear", as we used to say when I was in the Corps. He is good at his job, and we need him to do it, but I wish he didn't have to do it. I pray for him each night. When

Janet and I are down town, for the Fourth of July celebration, we always walk to the front of the Veteran's Building. We look at the monuments there for a few moments, then Janet squeezes my hand and we walk away.

I wouldn't have that grandson, if I had never had Janet in my life. I am so thankful to God, for letting me have her. God held me in the protection of the palms of his hands, through some strange times, to allow Janet and me to be together. I am very grateful to them both.

Semper Fi
Walter

Letter 120

Juanita Has Beautiful Hair

Mr. Garrett,

I had no car in high school. My date and I had to walk to the school dances, and to the movies down town. There were a few times we double dated with my brother, when we went to the movies in Vallejo. Carlos is four years older than me. At the time he worked as a mechanic in the Arsenal.

Juanita was the girl, who went with me on those dates. We only dated a few times. The love we shared was more friendship love than romantic love, but it was still love.

She is the only girl, I knew in high school, who I thought I could ask for a date. We came from the same cultural background. She also understood me.

Juanita had the longest, darkest, and most beautiful hair I've ever seen. When she moved, if she had it hanging straight down, it flowed like a black waterfall. When we were younger, she often had her hair in two long braids, or had the braids coiled on each side of her head.

We loved Mr. Leo Giogerini's class because he was a good teacher, and he joked a lot.

We have some good memories.

I've lived in the Castro District, in San Francisco, for almost twenty-five years. Juanita, and sometimes members of her family, have come to see me over the years. As the children have gotten older, it has usually been just Juanita who visits.

On her last visit, Juanita told me her youngest son reminds her of me at that age. We talked for about two hours of those early years of our lives in Benicia, and how times, and acceptance, has changed. I wished good things for her son.

When Juanita left I wished her well, and told her I loved her. Juanita still has beautiful hair.

Julio

Letter 121

The Gold Wedding Bands

Dear Mr. Garrett,

When I was small my parents seemed so big. In time, I grew to be my mother's size. My brothers grew to equal our father in size.

Somewhere along the way, the wedding rings my parents wore twenty-four hours a day seemed to be increasing in size. They were simple gold bands.

Mom and Dad never had engagement rings. They waited for, and wanted only, the gold bands they would one day exchange. I have always thought that was very romantic. My parent's tastes in much of what life offered were reflected by the type of wedding rings they each wore.

Both my parents were active people. People had a hard time guessing my father's weight, because the muscle he carried kept him trim. Mom had a bounce in her step, which brought envy to the voice of some of her friends.

As the rings kept increasing in size, I accepted what I had known. My parents were getting older. Each time I visited, the process had made another steady entry into their ledger of life.

Dad was the first to go I had come to their home to visit and take Mom out for tea on First Street. When we got back Dad didn't greet us at the door like he usually did. We thought he must have been in the backyard.

When we passed through the living room, we saw Dad leaning back in the sun room in a recliner. Mom knew right away that Dad had gone.

I checked his pulse, and then turned and looked at Mom. She nodded to me, and then we hugged.

I telephoned the fire department, and then as many of the family members as I could at that time. It seemed the paramedics were in the room in seconds. They were very efficient in their jobs, while being very caring.

Shortly after the paramedics left, the coroner came. Mom told him she wanted to remove Dad's wedding ring before her husband's body was taken away. She said his ring had only been separated from hers for five nights in their married life. She didn't want it separated again.

After Dad's body was taken away, Mom went to their bedroom. I didn't think I should follow. I thought she needed that time for herself. The house was silent, but the warm sun shown in brightening it like it was glorying in a wondrous time. The house didn't feel sad. It was as if Dad's spirit and energy was warming our hearts.

A few moments later Mom came back with a delicate, yet strong looking, gold necklace. As she stood in front of me she un-hooked the clasp, ran the chain through the opening in Dad's ring and re-connected the chain. Then she placed the chain, which held Dad's ring, around her neck.

Mom looked up at me and said when Dad asked her to go steady he gave her his class ring. He placed it around her neck on the same chain she then wore. They kissed. Mom said she never kissed another man in her life after that except her sons and the men her daughters married, who also became sons to her.

She kept Dad's high school ring around her neck on the chain until Dad proposed to her. Then she placed them both in her jewelry box. She said she told Dad she would wait for the time he would put on her finger the only ring she would ever wear after her wedding day.

For awhile, Mom said, Dad kept her ring around his neck

on a gold chain. He had purchased the chain in anticipation of Mom's acceptance of his class ring.

Dad was an athlete, and a very active guy, all of his life. He didn't want to take the chance of having the chain break, and losing the ring and chain. He had it on his key ring most of the time before they were married.

Whenever they went out, though, the ring was on the chain around his neck. When Mom accepted Dad's marriage proposal, he placed the ring, and chain, in a metal dish on his dresser. He would wait to have placed on his finger, by his betrothed, the only ring he would ever wear after that moment in the church when they became one.

Four months after Dad passed, Mom also went on ahead of the remainder of her family and friends. I had come by to take her shopping, and found her sitting in the same chair in which we had discovered Dad. She held Dad's high school ring, and the chain on which she once wore it, with Dad's wedding ring, clutched in her folded hands. She was smiling.

I felt happy for Mom. She was with the only man she had ever loved, or could ever love. Her love for Dad had been total and unconditional, as had been Dad's for her.

Passalacqua's Funeral Home handled everything for Mom's services, as they had for Dad's. My husband, David, and I, have attended many funeral services, over the years, here in Benicia and elsewhere. Most have been in Benicia with Passalacqua's being the director. Father Passalacqua, and son, have been professional, and caring, for those in their responsibility and the proceedings. I believe one day the son will direct services for my husband and me.

I keep all of Mom's and Dad's rings, and chains, in a box in the right front of the top drawer of the dresser in the bedroom, which my husband and I share. The box is lined in red velvet. I gently intertwine the chains each time I replace them in the box. Mom's ring snuggles up to Dad's, as they did so often when the two wearers were alive. They are the only items in the box.

I sometimes think of the time when my husband's rings, and mine, will start to enlarge. In time we, too, will pass. When that time comes, and our rings are passed to one of our children, I know we will be together, as our parents are now.
Beverly

Letter 122

Slow Learner

Mr. Garrett,

Seeing her with him, I realized what I thought had been ugly lies, and rumors, were the truth. The love I had given to her hadn't been returned. It had only been used.

A couple of my friends told me she was only using me, but I was too blind to see. I gave her everything she wanted, or I thought she needed. She kept saying she needed more. I kept giving. I guess it just got to be a habit, and I was afraid of losing her. She taught me a lot.

My friends told me she saw other guys, but I didn't believe them. I had suspicions, but I kept thinking everything I suspected could be explained. She had known some of the other guys as long as she had known me. I guess there is nothing as stupid as a guy in love.

In my job, I basically set my own hours. When one appointment is completed, I go on to the next one scheduled for that day. If there are no more scheduled, I can make a call and try to change an appointment, or make an early day of it and go home.

That day I finished my appointments by 2:00 p.m. and headed for home. Along the way I stopped at the florist and bought her a nice bunch of mixed flowers. I thought I would surprise her and we would go out to dinner.

We weren't married. I had no legal hold over her and

wouldn't want one. I don't think relations between a man and a woman work that way, though I do believe in marriage.

I definitely surprised her. I also surprised him. The light finally came on, in the cave which is my mind. I gave her the next day to clear out. My night was spent in the motel on East Second Street. When I came back the next morning, she was sitting in a chair on the porch with her keys to the house in her hands. When she asked me if I really wanted her to leave, I told her I sure did. Then she asked me about the car and the other things I had given her. She wanted to know if I expected her to give them back. I told her I didn't want anything back from her. What I had given her had been gifts to a young woman I had once loved. I no longer loved her.

I thought she might laugh, but she didn't. She did look at me like she thought I might have been joking, but wasn't sure. Then she tried to lay on the charm and told me how much she loved me. She said she hadn't packed anything, because she was sorry for what I had seen and she hoped we could get back together.

I told her I would help her pack, but she was leaving and she could keep the keys as souvenirs. Before coming home I had gone to a hardware store and bought new locks. I was going to change the locks as soon as she was off my property.

Maybe I was too harsh or cold, but I don't think so. If I hadn't seen and heard other things over the past year, I think I would have forgiven her, and even asked her to marry me. By seeing her with him, too much had fallen into place. I knew I had been an idiot and she had been laughing at me. The love I had felt didn't last longer than a little over a year, but it felt true to me so I think it was.

The nice thing about all of my experience with her is that I had a couple of friends who stood beside me. My best friend let me talk it out. He hardly said a word. He is a smart guy. He just let me vent and say how stupid I had been. It was what I needed.

Loving her, and losing her, opened my eyes a lot. I think I understand more about long lasting love. I hope to find that love some day.
Slow Learner

Letter 123

My Secret Love

Mr. Garrett,

My secret love is locked away in my mind and my dreams. I have no photos or letters, no scented perfume lingers on a pillow.

She was from another time and another place, and passed through my life. Left behind in my brain is the look of her face, the sound of her laughter, and the aroma of her body the one time I held her close to me. A New Year's kiss is a memory I'll always cherish.

My secret love knew us only as friends of youth. It is hard to hold back what I feel for her, but there is no way I can show it. She is the lady in the life of another man. She chose. I'm happy for her, and the happiness, which I hope is hers.

I've been told that I am the happy, care-free bachelor with no worries. I can do what I want when I want. Most of that is true.

When vacation time comes, I can, and do, go anyplace I wish to go on the planet. I've been to a lot of places. Most of the time, I travel alone. I can still get a date, or a traveling companion, without too much effort, if I want to be with someone. At the times I'm with another, I give her all the attention she deserves, but at the same time I think of the one with whom I'd rather be. There are some places I'd never want to go without the woman I truly love.

I'm as happy as I can be. A number of people seem to like me. My career is successful in any of the ways success can be described. I'm upwardly mobile, but not pushy about it. I have ready cash and invested money.

What I don't have is the woman I love. I've seen her three times in the last five years. I could describe when and where, and what she was wearing. Each time was at a distance. Once, I know she saw me. I wonder if she recognized me.

(Unsigned)

Letter 124

What Memories!

Mr. Garrett,

Your advertisement took Elizabeth and me back once more to looking at many of our photos. As we can see growth and change in people, and their lives, through viewing them, so we can see growth and change in the life of Benicia.

My God, Elizabeth and I were young then in those first photos we cherish. I feel almost as young now in my mind, but my body knows the truth.

My love stays the same for me as when we met in the sixth grade in a classroom which is now part of Liberty High School. Elizabeth's features have changed with the blending time gives to all of us, but she is still the person with whom I fell in love and will always love.

Elizabeth and I have taken thousands of photos over the years of our times together and with friends and acquaintances. Many of the photos are kept in albums in a floor to ceiling bookcase which stands at the end of a hallway.

What memories! Times at the swimming pool, times flying kites where homes now stand, and sitting on the trunk of a fallen tree in a place where a highway overpass has been built, are all time capsules of the past.

The photo albums are aligned in chronological order and are dated. We can go to any part of the time of our lives together and pull down pictures of our selves and others as they were. It is kind of like a time machine. We can follow individuals from when they first started dating to the present day, in some cases.

We have photos of the last day of the Arsenal, and the last trip of the ferry from Benicia to Martinez. There are photos of celebrations such as Benicia's birthday, and the opening of the highway bridge between Benicia and Martinez. We have photos of parades, the Peddlar's Faire, the U.S.S. Iowa moving up the Carquinez Straits, and special summer events in the City Park. It is a cornucopia of the life and times of Benicia.

In a second bookcase, at the other end of the same hallway, are the yearbooks from the time when Elizabeth and I were students at Benicia High School. We have also collected many yearbooks from years prior to and following our matriculation at B.H.S.

In one way, it is so sad to look at those yearbooks. Each time we do, it is to reminisce on an old thought. That thought might be because another of our classmates, or one from another year, has passed on from our lives. It is almost like placing black wreaths around the photo of each of those young people, who has gone on, when we once again view their face and speak of them.

In a far greater way, the opening of our yearbooks is a reminder of the good times we had at B.H.S., and giving thought to other good times others are depicted as having. Stories of favorite teachers who were institutions unto themselves never fail to surface when Elizabeth and I, or our friends look at the old yearbooks.

"Didn't he...", "Did you know...", "She was such a pretty girl, and so nice", "That guy was an outstanding high school athlete", "Didn't you go to the Beatnik dance with him?", and other words of fond memories are welcome and accepted points of conversation at those times.

I think time, and interest in Benicia, have given Elizabeth and me much more insight to Benicia's past and present than many others in town possess. The passing of that same time means fewer know of the past of the man with the skilled hands, or the one who walks down the street and sees things no longer there, or the couple at the same place at the same time each week, or the slow walking man, who was once the fastest guy around, or the woman whose natural charm has never faded.

Not all of the photos for which Elizabeth and I care are in albums or yearbooks. Others are framed in various locations around our home.

The photos I enjoy the most, are three which are in our living room. One is of a sweet little kid, the second is of a cute young girl, and the third is of the lovely woman I married. Each has the same name. Each is my Elizabeth.
Doc

Letter 125

We Will Be Here a Long Time

Mr. Garrett,

When we met, Carrie and I were just two people, who were searching, without knowing we were searching. We both sought love, without knowing that was what each of us had searched for all our lives. We found each other, and will keep what we've found for eternity.

Neither Carrie's family nor mine was very close knit. They each did their thing, as the saying goes. Perhaps that is how Carrie and I gained our wandering feelings, and didn't feel the gain of love. Each of our families exchanges the social pleasantries, and gets along well, but there is no dedicated closeness.

I think there is truly a grand scheme in life, and to life. Carrie and I each had others in our lives with whom to share a period of time. Things didn't work out. I think they didn't work out because they weren't meant to work out. I believe an unseen hand was guiding us towards each other all along while giving us challenges to make us stronger.

Both Carrie and I could have settled in many other places. With our careers, we can work almost anywhere. There is a good amount of traveling in the lives of each of us, but that comes with what we do.

Career, and travel, is what first brought each of us to Benicia, though at different times. I went for a drive one

Saturday morning. I followed the hood ornament on the car and wound up in Benicia. Carrie was visiting Benicia the same day, with some friends from the Silicon Valley, and we all met at lunch.

Carrie and I liked what we found in Benicia, and what we found in each other. We got married in the San Juan Batista Mission and stayed at the Union Hotel during our honeymoon. We spent a lot of that time exploring Benicia.

If you drive out Second Street, make a left on Rose Drive, proceed about half a mile, and look off to the right you'll see where our new home is being built. We're going to be here for a long time.

Matt

Letter 126

Sometimes I Need a Hug

Dear Mr. Garrett,

I don't need much in life. I've always been tough when I had to be, but I still need to be held. Sometimes that is all I need, and only for a few minutes, as my batteries get charged once again.

There is one guy who does it for me. Maybe that is love.

I know I can telephone him any time of the day or night and tell him I need a hug. He'll tell me to come on over, whether it's at his business or at his home. He doesn't care, and neither do I.

When the man hugs me, I feel safe. At those times, his arms present the strength of the world. I feel the monsters held within me can't escape to hurt me or others when he holds me.

He hugs me when I arrive, and he hugs me when I leave. Neither of us cares if it is in the heat of the day, or if anyone else is present.

It has been that way for years. When we lived together, it was the same. If I needed to be held, he held me. He got me through whatever was bothering me and he let me express myself with the contact of another person.

When I was younger, and he hugged me in public, I think some people must have thought we were a little different from most people. When I told him that, in a store on First Street one afternoon, he said, "The heck with them. Let 'um think what they want."

Knowing I can still get that hug means the world to me.

My dad has always been there with a hug.

Paula

Letter 127

Summer-time Love

Dear Mr. Garrett,

Some of us girls from Benicia went to pick fruit in Fairfield during the middle of summer between our junior and senior years at Benicia High School. There weren't many jobs for kids in Benicia in those days. When summer came, we always knew we could pick fruit, if we could get rides to the orchards and back.

Three of our parents worked out schedules where we were assured of rides, so we had set off to earn our spending money by picking fruit. I think it was really more to have some time away from home, and to be with our friends. It was always great fun.

When we signed up at the orchard office the first day, we all met a boy who attended Armijo High School. Andy was good looking, charming, and friendly. It seemed like every time I looked up that day Andy was nearby. My friends started giving me a bad time and saying I had found a boyfriend.

About halfway through the morning of the second day Andy walked over to where I was picking and said he had looked for me that morning. He asked if it was OK with me if he worked near where I worked. I told him I wouldn't mind working by him at all. I didn't know at the time that his family owned the orchard. That was why he could be just about anyplace on the property he wanted, whenever he wanted.

It took almost two weeks for the orchard to be picked. At the start of each day Andy met all of us at the office and then walked out to that day's harvest area with us. Each day we seemed to spend more, and more, time together. My friends were always nearby, but they accepted Andy and me working as a team.

The rides to and from the orchard each day became not only times to talk about what was happening in our lives in general, but times for my friends to tease me in particular. I didn't mind at all. It was fun. I started dressing much better than I should have to pick fruit. That only brought out more razzing from my friends, but Andy noticed, too. I was glad he did.

The last day we were to pick at that orchard began with a lot of clouds. They seemed to hang low in the sky. It was like they were pressing down on the earth. By about 1:00pm the air had become heavy. It was one of those muggy afternoons when it might rain, but then again it might not. That sounds like a weather forecast on television these days. I had the feeling something was about to explode. It did start to rain, but it wasn't a drizzle or a shower. The rain came down in buckets. I don't know if there were cats and dogs around at the time, but if they were, they must have fallen from the sky.

Andy and I ran for shelter in a shed, which had a corrugated iron roof. We stayed there until the rain stopped. He held me all that time. We never kissed. He just held me.

I think Andy didn't know if he should ask me for my telephone number and address. He may have thought it would be a gamble for him to ask. He did ask, and I gave him the information. I gave the information too quickly to be lady-like, but I didn't care.

Andy and I dated a few times during the remainder of the summer. Roads weren't the same then and distances were longer to travel. I didn't have a car and my parents wouldn't have let me drive to Fairfield anyway. Times were different then. Many people don't understand that now. School started again and we each gravitated back to the lives we knew before.

We kept in contact for a few years. We haven't seen each other in a long time.

Though it lasted for such a short time, my summer-time love with Andy is something I cherish. Whenever I hear rain on a metal roof, I think of that time with Andy.

Karen

Letter 128

It Wouldn't Have Worked Out

Mr. Garrett,

Maybe I was just a coward. If she had shown me in high school, in any way, that she was interested in me, I would have told her my feelings. But, she never did until the night of our ten year reunion. By then, we were both happily married.

We made time, at the reunion, to be with each other to talk. While we talked we wondered how things would have turned out, if she and I had gotten together in high school. She is what is called today, a black woman. I'm white.

In those high school days, blacks usually socialized in Vallejo, or the Richmond and Oakland areas. Sometimes it was in San Francisco.

There wasn't much open discrimination around town against blacks. The fact is there weren't many blacks in town. A number of adults, from out of town, worked at the Arsenal. That was about the only time most of them spent in Benicia.

It wasn't accepted, by most of our friends in Benicia, that blacks and whites would date. I don't think it was accepted by most of the people in Benicia then. It is now. When I go to games at the high school, it is apparent the acceptance of change has come about in society. It is seen in the youth, and in the adults. The acceptance is a good thing.

That young lady, of whom I write, is very attractive and very intelligent. I think if the times had been different, she would have been Queen of the Winter Ball. I very much enjoyed being around her, for the one year we shared together in school.

When I told her, that I was in love with her in high school and had wanted to ask her out, she smiled. Then she said it wouldn't have worked out. She was correct.

Our families get together regularly now. People are people.

Homer

Letter 129

The Old Hat

Mr. Garrett,

I think love can be expressed in many ways, but we have to be open to seeing those many ways. One way it was expressed to me was by my father giving me a hat.

My dad gave me the hat when I was just big enough to remember. He put it on my head and said it was just an old hat. He told me he thought a young man needed a hat he could grow into, but that it should be one which already had a little experience in it. The hat was olive drab in color and was soft so it could be folded and put in the pocket of a man. My pockets didn't get big enough to accept it for many years.

When Dad put that hat on my head, the only thing which kept it from hitting the floor was my ears. I must have looked like a small green hill. The government could have put antennas on top of the hat, and used me for a mobile sending station.

The hat's two inch wide brim kept the sun out of my eyes. When I was smaller, I overcame the obstacle of size by tilting the hat back on my head. That made it resemble a fireman's helmet because it protected my neck so well from the imaginary rain I might encounter. Sometimes I tilted the hat too far back, and it fell off my head and down my back. As I got older the hat seemed to magically start to guide itself to the position on my head for which it was designed. It was a slow process, which went unnoticed by me. It didn't go unnoticed by Dad.

The hat rode snug on my head when I started riding my first bike. Dad ran alongside me for support, the first two times we went down the block, as I learned balance. I didn't realize at the time that Dad was teaching me more than balance on a bike. He was, once again, showing me balance in life. He did that often, but I sometimes didn't understand at the time.

There was a period of time when I wore the hat every day when I played. One day I wanted to go on a great camping and exploration trip, but it was a cold and rainy Saturday morning. When I told Dad, he said that he and I could go on that trip together right then.

I followed him to my parent's bedroom, where he got a blanket, and then we returned to the kitchen. Mom was standing by the sink when we entered the kitchen again. He told Mom that "the men" were going camping. Then he, very carefully, picked up the vase of flowers Mom had placed on the table for a decoration, and set it on the counter. Then he put the blanket over the kitchen table, and our tent was erected. For what may have been the remainder of the morning, or just half an hour I don't know which, Dad and I shared that tent on the kitchen floor. We lay on our backs, with me snuggled in the comfort of his right arm. As we lay there, he told me I was his right-hand man. I didn't understand what he meant, so I asked him. I didn't know what pride and ego was then, but I know I felt both of them when he told me what he meant.

In that time under the tent, Dad also told me the stories of the purple elk, the tree which grew upside down, and the bush which grew bite-sized pieces of chocolate candy. I can hear his voice speaking of them now.

Another day, hat on head, I journeyed around the great world of wonder which was our backyard. Theoretically I was helping Dad do yard work. Anyway, that's what he said I was doing. I think I was just being his son, and he enjoyed that, but I helped out the best I could. He would ask me to get him the loppers, or anvil clippers, or a spade, and I would go to the shed and get them. He was always precise in what he asked me to get. It was the same when he showed me how to use them. All along, like usual, he was teaching me in the only way he knew.

After a time, we sat down together. Dad asked me if I remembered that wet morning when we had camped in the kitchen, and I said I did. Then he said he couldn't show me how to make a campfire at that time, but now he could.

I followed Dad as he gathered a small number of twigs, and a handful of dried grass. Then he showed me what would be a good place for a campfire, if we were camping, how to align the material, and where to place the match. He took a box of matches from a pants pocket. He told me the matches in the box would light when they were wet and would resist a slight breeze.

Next Dad told me we wouldn't be lighting the fire. He said that would come later, and at a different place. I was a little disappointed. I thought we were going to have a real campfire in our backyard and that I might even get to light my first match. Dad explained why that couldn't happen. He said he could only take me so far with some things at that time. I didn't understand. In time I came to understand many of Dad's lessons.

Then I thought I had gotten too old for the hat. Without telling Dad, I put it on a hook in the closet of my room. It hung there until Dad passed.

The day Dad died, something drew me to that closet hook, and the hat he had given me so long ago. I hadn't treated the hat well by leaving it hanging all those years. Dust had formed a slight patina on the hat, and it had been stretched out of shape by the pull of gravity and time.

I immediately tried to correct my neglect of the hat. I found a box which would hold the hat, as if it were still sitting on Dad's head, or mine. I wadded up some paper, in as close to a hemisphere form as I could, and stuffed the hat to help it keep its shape. Then I placed the hat in the center of the box and surrounded it with other pieces of wadded paper.

The safest place in the closet, of which I could think, was the left side of the shelf. I had to get a stepstool to reach the spot. For some unknown reason, in my young mind, I had to put the box away. Looking back, I think I was saying goodbye to my father, while keeping his memory alive and a part of him, and us, close.

One day, in my late teenage years, my mother told me the history of the hat, and why it had been important to Dad. I went to the closet. I didn't need a stepstool anymore to reach the shelf. As my hands moved towards the box, it felt as though my dad was standing behind me with his arms encircling mine. It was as if they were guiding me toward the box and giving me a loving embrace at the same time. He was telling me it was OK. I took the hat out of the box in which it lay in the wadded up paper. Next to it was a second box with mementos.

When I placed the hat on my head, it fit perfectly. I understood. Dad had been passing on the torch all along. He had been preparing me, the best he could, for what lay ahead when I became a man. He couldn't express himself in some of the ways other kids' fathers did, but what he gave was still always from his heart.

The hat smelled of my dad, I loved that smell. That may seem gross to someone, who can't understand, but it doesn't to me. It is the aroma of my father, and it is the aroma of when I was a young boy. Dad never smoked and didn't use anything on his hair except baby shampoo or shower soap. Some cynical doctor will probably say the hat contained dandruff, dried perspiration, and whatever. I don't care. The hat was mine, and had been my dad's. Dad gave me love when he gave me the hat.

I've passed that hat on to my young son. He'll understand one day. He doesn't understand yet. He thinks it is just an old hat, like I once thought.

Sean

Letter 130

I Want To Be With Shannon Again

Mr. Garrett,

For almost a year we lived together in a condominium by the Middle School. She and I both liked softball and we met on the fields there.

I've kept the bed as it was the last night we slept in it. During the time since then I've slept alone in another bedroom. That is probably very foolish of me, but it is the way I feel. Tonight I'm going back to our bed. I want to lie with Shannon again.

I've prayed, and hoped, that she will come back to me. I know I can't bring her back. If she wants to come back, she will. I'll wait to try to be with her again. She had to leave, to be who she wanted to be, for her career, and to see what she had to see. I stayed here in Benicia.

Did you ever question how much you loved someone? Did you ever question how much, or what, you would do for them? I have many times. I would have done anything she asked, and I mean that literally, because I know she would never ask me to do anything that was wrong. I checked that we were of compatible blood types, so that if she ever needed anything, which my body could provide, I could give it.

I told her I needed her to stay here. But, if what she needed to make her happy was to leave, I wouldn't try to stop her. I wanted to keep her happy, because I wanted her to be happy. I think that is love. You want more for someone else than you want for yourself.

Though I want her here with me, she stays away. But, at least I had her in my life for a time..."better to have loved and lost" etc. Where there is life, there is hope, though.

I keep picturing scenes of two, her and me. In time, the pictures in my mind may become reality again.

Pete

Letter 131

He Saw a Lot

Dear Mr. Garrett,

When I watched the airplane, in which Dana was a passenger, fly away from the San Francisco airport that night, I didn't think I would be able to walk back to the car. The thought of him dying filled my mind. I had been able to handle it the first two times he had flown off, but I felt different at that time. Thanks to God, his determination and skill, and luck, he didn't die. He came back to me. He was scarred a little in his body, and in his mind, but he came back.

Each time he was gone from me, I sent him letters and packages. Dana likes to joke about how hard my chocolate chip cookies became by the time he received them. Actually, he said they were cobble stones with the chocolate melted out and stuck to the bottom of the paper in which they were wrapped. He says he loved them, just the same, and shared them with his buddies.

He sometimes received a number of letters and packages at one time. It wasn't like he was part of a civilian postal worker's regular route. Sometimes it just took a while for the mail to catch up with them.

Dana said it seemed like the only manner in which the local Benicia paper arrived was in bunches. The guys were so hungry for news from the world, and in need for any respite from the emotion in which they were involved, they could have come from any state. They shared the papers and read them as if the newspapers were from their own home town.

Sometimes the mail was all they had as a break from what they endured day and night. He told me all he had one Christmas Eve was a fairly clean shirt, a pair of socks, and a letter from me, which arrived that morning.

Dana wrote back to me as often as he could. I still have all the letters he sent me. To me, they are treasures. He wanted to know what was going on back in "the world", as he, and so many of the other service personnel, came to call the United States. He ended every letter by telling me he loved me, and was looking forward to the time we would be together.

Dana and I weren't married, but he had told me he would marry me, when he was free to do so, if I wanted to marry him. I told him I would wait for the time when he was ready.

During his first tour, something started changing in Dana. At times he was cynical, in his writing, because of what he saw "in country", the foreign lands where he spent part of his youth. Still, in those times he didn't lose his sense of humor, or his appreciation for the beauty he saw in the landscapes and the people.

Dana reentered the United States, after his last tour, on a flight which landed at Travis Air Force Base. It was also the last flight the pilot would make before retiring.

As soon as the plane came to a stop, the pilot walked back to the passenger area and played the song "California, Here I Come", on a battery powered tape recorder. Dana told me he thought that was a nice touch.

In Dana's tours, he had stops for different amounts of time in a few, then, far distant places. Each of those places is much closer now, and easily accessible. Time, and technology, does that, along with politics, and human nature.

Dana says he saw a lot, for a "dumb kid from Benicia." Part of what he saw made him love Benicia even more. In his time serving our country he saw about half the world, in one way or another. It wasn't always the scenic route. Sometimes it was high in the sky in an airplane, or lower in a helicopter.

It was about ten years after Dana came back the last time that he started talking with me about some of the places he had seen. He could have been a prophet for real estate in his words of praise for some of the beaches in Vietnam. He took me for a sea cruise vacation last year which included the sight of some of them. We also stopped in Japan, and I understand his appreciation and love for the beauty of that country.

Some philosopher said that we live our daily lives as who we actually are. I believe that. Dana loves me with all he has to give of love. I give all I have to give to him. Thanks for giving me the chance to share.

Beth

Letter 132

They Gave Us a Car

Mr. Garrett,

A loving couple gave Sonya and me their honeymoon car. That may sound strange, or unbelievable, but that is what happened. It is a classic car which turns heads if it is parked or being driven. He had purchased the car shortly before he proposed to her. They drove away from her parents' home to start their honeymoon in that car. Their only child came home from the hospital in it two days after his birth. Their big, friendly, protective dog came to their home from San Francisco in that car. Dozens of kids had rides to practices, games, and trips in that car.

One day when Sonya and I were visiting them he told us, as his wife stood by his side, that when the time came, they were going to give the car to a young couple, who would appreciate it. I didn't realize at the time that he spoke of giving the car to Sonya and me.

One day that time of which he had spoken arrived. They invited Sonya and me to go for a ride with them. Their home was a short distance away, and Sonya and I enjoy walking, so we walked over as we often had.

At the end of the ride he parked the car by the curb in front of their house instead of in the driveway. We all got out of the car and stood on the sidewalk talking and looking at the car. Then he handed me two sets of keys and his wife reached into her purse and handed Sonya an envelope. Then he said, "The car is yours now."

There were some long moments of silence. Then we each hugged. Finally all I could say was "Thank you. We'll take care of it as you did."

We plan, in time, to give the car to another young couple who will appreciate it.

None of us will live forever. It is the duty of all of us to leave this place we call Earth better than when we arrived. That is a belief Sonja and I have nurtured over the years, and have tried to instill in our children. It is a love of life, honor, and tradition.

The story of the transferal of the property is simple in its beauty, care, and love. The previous owners of the car searched for a nice young couple, just starting out in their married life together. They asked friends to let them know of people, who met the qualities and requirements, for which they searched. They wanted to leave the car in loving hands. I think they have.

I still don't totally understand why they selected us. Neither Sonya nor I had ever felt we had done anything to deserve the gift of the car. He often spoke of chemistry between people. Perhaps that was what it was all about.

Each of the owners loved each other so much that they wanted to share something they together loved with still others. Sonya and I will one day have that time of which he spoke.
Ronald

Letter 133

The Tree Reminded Me of My Grandfather

Mr. Garrett,

The trees the original owners planted in the yard at the house where I grew up have all died out. They had been there for many years. As I grew up, Dad planted a tree to replace each tree which died.

I think it is a good tradition. It is a policy my wife and I have followed as part of raising our family. The trees are good for us, and good for this area. The seasons provide them, and they provide the seasons.

Dad would work, sometimes for days, to get the stump out of the ground, cut up the wood and store it to season. Depending upon when the tree died, it might take over a year for the wood to season. In the first winter, when it could be done, Dad would burn the wood in our fireplace and return its remains, the ashes, to the earth in our yard.

One tree, in our backyard, reminded me of my grandfather on my father's side. For a few years, of my young life, Grandfather lived with my brothers and sisters and me and our parents.

Grandfather had his own room near the back of the house. It was a special place for him, and for us children. The room was a treasure trove of memories. He shared most of them with his grandchildren. We sat and listened to games from whatever sport was in season, and played games. That's where each of us kids learned to play poker and chess.

When I played chess with my Dad, for the first time, he made a move designed to quickly win. I countered it. Then he said, "So my dad taught you that move, too." It made me feel good that I was carrying on what was obviously a family tradition. Dad won the game, but I won the first part by keeping him from easily beating me. He had merely been testing me, and was pleased that I had learned the counter.

Mom and Dad would sometimes talk with Grandfather in his room. Mostly, when he entered his room, it was almost like he had been a guest, who had departed our home.

Both Mom and Dad were employed all the time us kids were growing up. Dad had two jobs. Mom was with us all day Saturday and Sunday. The only time Dad was around all day was Sunday.

The result was Grandfather became, what would be called by many, our baby sitter, when Mom and Dad were at work. He was far more than that. He was protector, teacher, and confidante. He was co-conspirator in some of our devious youthful plots, and an explanation-giver when something went a little off from what we had expected. And, maybe above all, he was a sharer of himself and what material possessions he owned.

Along the way, he was the greatest story teller I've ever known. It started with one, or more, of us kids cuddled up on his lap. He didn't use a book. He merely started talking, and took us on trips of high adventure and drama.

That tree in the backyard was strong, firm, and substantial. It was able to take anything nature, in this part of the world, had to give. In return, the tree gave back its branches for shade, and its leaves for color.

Grandfather had that same kind of strength. It was a supple strength which increased, or decreased, as a situation in life decreed.

Grandfather talked about that tree often when I was a kid. He said people had to be able to sway with most things in life like the tree's branches, but had to hold firm in others. He was talking of life. He meant live and let live, but stand up for something to the point of breaking, if you had to do that to live the life of the person you really were.

Grandfather used analogies often in explaining things, and in answering our questions. I didn't learn what an analogy was until I entered Benicia High School. I thought Grandfather was just talking with us, and I enjoyed hearing him talk. Some things were a little too much for me to understand at times, but I came to know what he meant.

The tree gave sheltered nesting places for birds. The strong arms of my grandfather did the same for me, and the rest of his grandkids. The shelter could have been from a storm of nature, or a storm of anger from someone in our lives. It wouldn't have mattered if either had occurred. Grandfather was a brace against the wind of nature, and the challenges presented by us being human.

Grandfather had a big laugh one day, when Dad told him what a neighbor had said. The neighbor had wondered about our safety, with Grandfather watching over us so much. Dad told the neighbor that we were safe, because we were with his father. Then Dad told the neighbor that his dad could beat the other man's dad. My Dad was right.

I think some grandparents are bitter about being the resident, or nearby, person who must often be the adult present in the lives of their grandchildren. If Grandfather ever felt that way, he never demonstrated it.

Grandfather didn't resent what he was doing. It was shown by his actions. He accepted what occurred as his to do at that time in his life. He truly enjoyed being around us.

We got on his nerves a couple of times, but he shrugged those times off as us being growing kids. Once he said there probably wasn't anything he hadn't done, in one way or another, that wasn't similar to whatever we had done. Only he always said he had done, or would do, it better.

Sometimes Grandfather just sat silently watching us, no matter what we were doing. He would sometimes smile during those times, or nod his head as if he were remembering something, or agreeing with something. More than once I, and I'm sure my brothers and sisters, looked back at him for approval of whatever we were doing.

Never once did he compare us with how his son, our father, had been when he was our age. He would tell us of things Dad had done, but never put any pressure on us to be just like his son. He let us grow as ourselves.

At times, we relayed, to Dad, the stories Grandfather told us about him. Grandfather would laugh and laugh and Dad would humorously admonish us to not do what he had done in his youth. Mom would nod her head and smile. She knew.

There were times when Grandfather was in charge of us kids when he was obviously tired. As time passed, those times increased in frequency and duration.

There were times when Grandfather fell asleep when he was with us. There was never a time then, or any other time, when us kids were in danger. I think he made a judgment call based on the circumstances, to have some relaxation time while with us.

One time at the swings by the tennis courts a car made a noise when it was going down the hill. Grandfather jumped up far too fast for a man of his age, but his eyes were focused on the source of the sound. When he saw we were fine, he sat back down, but he was no longer in relax mode.

I also think, some of the times he only pretended to be asleep to help us grow. It was an extending of an invisible leash, which kept us tethered to him, but at the same time allowed us to explore the world we were coming to know.

Grandfather made sure that we knew he wasn't taking the place of our parents. When there were things, which were our parents' decision alone, he either excused himself or sat silent.

In the evenings he would sometimes go for a walk by himself. At times he would ask if anyone wanted to join him. Sometimes we asked if he was going to go for a walk and if we could go with him. He never refused us.

When we were small, he either walked us to school or drove us there. When needed, he was there to walk us or drive us home. The walks started getting less and less distance from home for him, and the rides became more random. He was letting us know he was still around, but letting us strengthen our wings at the same time.

Mom and Dad tried to be there for anything in which us children were involved. Often, only one of them could make it. Often neither could. Many times, Grandfather was the only adult in our family there at Maria Field for Little League and with my sisters at softball when we started playing sports. His presence followed into high school. The same was true when he watched us perform in the school plays we had rehearsed with him so many times.

Grandfather was almost always there for each of us kids, until the time came when he had to enter a hospital in Vallejo.

When Mom and Dad told us they had to take Grandfather to the hospital, I felt a change was coming to my life, and the life of all of us. There was a change. Grandfather never came back from the hospital.

Every Sunday, all of us would ride over to the hospital and spend a couple hours sitting and talking with Grandfather. We took turns telling Grandfather how our weeks had gone.

Grandfather seemed to smile from when the first of us walked into his room until the last of us walked out. During the time we were with him in his hospital room he would ask about our homework, what we had been doing with our friends, if anyone had a new boy or girlfriend, and what we would be doing the next week. He might not ask about something one week, but he never failed to ask about what we would be doing the next week.

I think his asking about what we would be doing the next week gave him strength. I can picture him lying in his bed thinking about what we would be doing that week and coming up with questions and comments for our next visit.

In what came to be our last visit, Grandfather spoke at

length, and with love, about the tree in the backyard. He said he had been a lot like that tree in his life, but that he had passed it now. He was in the time of his life where he was an "old gnarled tree".

When he spoke of the tree, he said he had moved in the wind, as it pushed on the young sapling he had once been. Most of the time, he moved easily in concert with the wind. At times his resistance to the force of the wind caused him to have a branch or two break off. That was OK. It meant he had stood up for something. Those same branches had produced seeds which dropped on the ground around the tree's trunk, or which were carried away perhaps to grow far from our tree. In time, the branches which remained would stand stark against the sky. At that time the tree would have to be taken down.

While Grandfather had been talking about the tree, he moved his head to look at each of us. When he finished, he turned to look directly at me.

Grandfather said, "After you cut the tree down, make sure you cure the wood well. Then, some cold winter evening, it will give you a warm, clean fire. When the time comes to plant another tree in that area, make sure you prepare the soil well. That tree will grow well if you do. When you plant the tree, think of me."

I told Grandfather we would all do it together like we had with other trees. He looked at me and smiled and said, "I promise I'll be there with you."

Shortly after that we said goodbye to Grandfather. Dad was the last to leave the room, while the rest of us waited in the corridor. I didn't know it would be the last time I saw Grandfather, but I think Dad knew it would be the last time he would see his father.

A year later Dad and I cut down the tree. We cut the wood to fireplace length, split the big pieces, and separated the result by size. The piles ranged from small pieces for kindling to more substantial sizes for long lasting warmth. In a way it was like the projection from youth to maturity, which in turn would turn to ashes. Then we put all the wood in the storage rack, placed a tarp over it, and left it for nature to do its work.

The tree was removed in January. By the following October it was cured. On the second Saturday of that month nature blew in cold wind with rain clouds following. Dad and I brought in some of the wood to have for a fire that night and the next day. The fire burned cleanly and the warmth from the flames embraced us all as if we were held in loving arms. In effect, we were. Grandfather was with us again as we each watched the flames in the fireplace.

The love for the tree had brought enjoyment for each of us in the time we knew it. Each, in our own way, had seen that love. The love of Grandfather was reflected in the love for that tree, and what it meant for each of us.

George

Letter 134

I Sat Next to Juliet on the Bus

Mr. Garrett,

I sat next to Juliet late one afternoon for the bus ride from Vallejo to Benicia after work at Mare Island.

Juliet was the sweetest young lady I had ever seen.

It had been a warm day, and I know I smelled like dried sweat from all the work I had done. Crawling around the insides of a ship isn't the most pleasant way to spend time, but I needed the work and I basically enjoyed the job. I felt sorry for Juliet having to sit next to me, but that is how the seating fell into place that afternoon.

Juliet looked, and smelled, fresh. She had brown hair then and it was cut about even with the bottom of her ears. Getting to know her as I did, I think she must have had it cut that way because of the warmth at that time of the year.

She was friendly, but reserved, at the start. We talked for a few moments at a time, off-and-on, during the ride to Benicia. Along the way I found out where she worked in Vallejo. I had learned, by observation, that she rode the same bus to and from Vallejo every work day that I did. She was a good looking young lady. It was easy to see her in the small crowd waiting for the buses each day.

I didn't have enough time here with Juliet. I wanted eternity here on Earth with her. We had a few years. They were wonderful years.

I wasn't much for religion then. At one time I thought that maybe, if I had been, God wouldn't have taken her so soon. I've come to understand He takes who He wants in His own time and way.

I sit waiting for the time I'll be with her again. I can't commit suicide. She said I could never be with her again, after she went on ahead, if I did. I'll honor that, but I so much want to be with her again. I still hope to have eternity with her.

Johnny

Letter 135

I Had to Say Goodbye

Mr. Garrett,

I had to say goodbye to her. She accepted my words, and wished me well.

Someone can go back, in their mind, to the time of their first love, but they can only go back so far. That first love helped them to find their true and permanent love. That is why that special person was in their life at that time. It was good for both people, at least then, or it wouldn't have happened.

Sometimes, though one may love another, they must shut the door on them, or they will take that person down with them. A person can have done all they could do, but the lifestyle of the other is what they have chosen. If they don't want to be released from it, for anyone, or anything, there is nothing the other person can do. One person tried their best. Perhaps both did.

She whispered, "I love you" in my ear so softly I thought it was only a wishful thought in my mind. Then she said it louder. I know she believed the words she said. I know she meant them. She just didn't understand what she had said.

At least, that is my opinion.

I loved that woman.

What she wouldn't, or couldn't, part with was the lifestyle she led and the drugs which went along with that lifestyle.

I did everything I possibly could. She wouldn't accept

rehab, though I would pay for everything. She wouldn't leave those she called her friends, though she never said she loved them.

When I was informed she had died, I could only guess at the cause. I loved her, and I know I tried. I could only go so far.

Jerry

Letter 136

Hold Onto That Good Man

Dear Mr. Garrett,

It was so easy, in my immaturity, and lack of trust in people in general, to say I hated him. It was also so easy to say I loved him.

The one time I said I hated him, I was being so silly. Larry forgave me and said he knew I wasn't angry at him. He said he knew I had merely been angry at something which had happened in the office that day. When he said that, telling him, over and over, I loved him was so easy.

He has always been like that. He'll let me rant and rave about something that has upset me, until it is out of my system. I think I've increased my maturity level over the years. I don't rant and rave much anymore. I've never again said I hated him.

Larry and I have been married so long now we're looked on as the old couple on the block. Second, and even third, families have moved into some of the houses which we saw being built.

In the time we've been together we've had our little annoyances with each other, but that is part of what is called marriage. Marriage truly is a union of two entities into one.

Girls, if any of you read this, hold on to that good man you find. They are hard to come by, but they are out there. They're looking for you just like you're looking for them.

Put up with any little quirks, or uniqueness, in his personality. Love him all the more for them, because they are all part of what makes him the man he is, and makes him love you. In return, they make him the man you love.

First of all look for a man who likes you as a person. If he doesn't like being with you, nothing else matters. If you're looking for perfection, ladies, good luck! You aren't going to find it.

Carol

Letter 137

I Helped My Father Build a House

Sir,

I think I know every nail in that house. My Dad built it, with me being all-around helper and "boy gopher". I had cut and nailed something during every phase of the construction of what became our home. I also had to go for anything he asked, whether it was a tool or a drink of water.

All along, he was teaching me. He was teaching me so many things. The man could build a house from the ground up, but he taught me more than the skills of a craftsman.

I got my first hammer strain working with Dad on our house. He laughed when I told him my right forearm hurt after I had been hammering awhile. Then he massaged my arm, and it truly felt better after that.

I think he had just been waiting for it to happen. He had undoubtedly seen I hadn't been hammering with the form he had told me to use. He let me learn the skill of hammering through on-the-job training, as he did many other things. He always looked after my safety, though.

Working with his body all his life finally caught up with Dad. In forty-plus years he had slipped, fallen, gotten cut and bruised, and lifted too much, too often. The body wears out like anything else.

He was a stubborn, hard nosed, tough old bird, but in his prime he could work all day. When he felt he could no longer expend the effort needed, he stopped working. He still did projects for friends and neighbors, but his days of going to work for a paycheck had ended.

Mom and Dad retired. They had missed out on some travel they had wanted to do in their earlier years. Dad had needed to make a living for his family, which obviously included all of us kids.

Their retirement is very comfortable. Over the years Dad said he earned the money and Mom invested it. They both did their tasks well. Mom could have been a very successful investment banker, if that had been her calling, and she had been born later. She is simply "Mom" to us kids, and all of us have been very happy with that.

We kids had gone our way in the world by the time Mom and Dad retired. None of us could live in Benicia at that time, because of the commitments in our lives. Each of us had fond memories of the town, and that home Dad had built.

I think I felt the connection to the home the strongest because of the time I had put in building it. My sisters helped, as they could, when it was built, but I was Mom's "Big Boy" and Dad's apprentice.

Mom and Dad sold the house and bought a smaller place. They said the nest was empty, and it was getting to be a handful for the two of them to take care of.

The only things Dad kept, from all the years he worked, were his hand tools, his tool chest, and his carpenter's carry box. Dad had made both the tool chest and the carpenter's carry box.

He kept the tools, and boxes, in the garage of the small place where he and Mom lived. He said, with just the hand tools, a skilled man could build a home for his family. Dad had done it for his. If Father Time wasn't nearing him, he could still do that. The tools were kept clean, oiled, and those with edges always had their edges sharp.

I felt a loss when they told me they were selling. I would have liked to have purchased it from them, but at the time I couldn't manage it.

I kept watching over the house, from a distance, the best I could. The years passed, and Dad telephoned me saying he heard the house was going to be sold. When we talked about the house, he said he wished he was young enough to once more take care of it.

The people who bought the house from Mom and Dad hadn't been kind to it. They didn't perform the regular maintenance a house needs, like a human, to stay as healthy as it could be. The roof, and gutter system, needed replacing. The paint on the south facing walls was blistered and peeling. It was an embarrassment to my parents, and to me. It had been allowed to turn into a "handyman's delight".

I had learned to be pretty handy. Dad had taught me.

When the house came on the market, I was ready. I was standing outside the realtor's door, when she arrived. Right after I introduced myself, I told her I wanted to buy the house. I also told her I could close the deal that day and would raise any offer anyone else might have already made.

My family now lives in the home I helped my father build. In the backyard, my son and I are building a workshop.

Every time Rick and I are going to work on it, I drive over to Mom and Dad's place and bring them over. Mom sits and talks with Georgia, or helps her do things around the house, or they go shopping.

Dad "supervises" and, I guarantee, if he tells me to do something, in a way other than I planned, I usually do it. The man is a natural architect and engineer, and is still, usually, correct in his evaluations. Once or twice, when I went ahead and did it my way, he didn't say "I told you so", but his smile said it for him.

There was a time, in the glory of my youthful manhood, when I had forgotten what Dad had taught. There was too much perfume floating through my memory banks, and too much testosterone in my jeans.

At breakfast, one spring Saturday morning, Dad told me to get the backyard ready for planting. I told him it would be no problem, and that I could get it done pretty quickly.

With breakfast over, I almost hit the backyard running and blazed through what, I thought, was needed. I came in about an hour later and told Dad I was finished. I knew better, because Dad had taught me better. I was young, and in a hurry to do something I wanted to do, so I rushed the job.

At that time, I needed reinforcement of the life lessons Dad had taught me. He gave me one. It was one of the hardest physical experiences of my life, but all I did was sit.

Dad said he, and I, would go out to the backyard and look at the results of the efforts of my labor. We looked at what I had done in silence for a few minutes. It was like the feeling of doom was enveloping me.

Then Dad said, "Son, go sit in that swing, and don't say anything until I get done out here in the yard. It's nice and shady under the tree. You can have a good rest."

He had a controlled anger, at that moment, which I have never seen in anyone else. There was also a look of disappointment on his face. I knew what I had done, or rather hadn't done, and felt guilty as sin.

There were things I wanted to do, and a girl I wanted to visit, but when Dad told me to sit, I sat. I sat for four hours. When Dad finished the job, I should have done, the yard looked like it had the care given to a traditional Japanese garden. I've been to Japan and seen some of those gardens. There wasn't a leaf on the ground, the grass was cut, and everything was neat and in order.

Dad walked over to me and said, "If you're going to do a job, do it right. If not, don't bother. The job you did isn't what I taught you. It's all a matter of pride son. That's what I taught you. Anyone can learn to hammer a nail. You can go do whatever you want now." Then he turned and walked into the house.

From where I sat, I could see Dad through the bathroom window washing his hands. I had just learned more about my father's love for me than in all the time I had known him.

I went into the house and found Dad sitting with Mom. I apologized to Dad, and asked him if there was anything else he wanted me to do. He just smiled, patted Mom's hands, and said, "End of the lesson, kid. Go have fun. Here's twenty bucks." I love him. I love her. He helped make her who she is, and she helped make him who he is.

I've taught my children that, if you have a job to do, a homework assignment, or a sport to play, give your best from start to finish. Dad taught me that, and he taught me the love of a father for his son. By the way, the girl I was interested in has long been my wife. I love her.

Steve

Letter 138

The Neighborhood Couple

Mr. Garrett,

Love takes work and consistent effort. Not, hit or miss, or only when someone feels a need for something someone else can provide.

Through the years, many people visited, telephoned, wrote, and emailed the couple across the street. The numbers diminished with the passing of those years. One day, there were none who kept the contact with the couple.

My wife and I lived across the street from them. I think you could call us all friends. In that respect you could say we all shared a love for each other. We had some kind of contact with them almost daily. There was always a friendly hello, conversation, or just time for a wave in passing. They were good neighbors.

We exchanged flowers, fruits, and vegetables grown in our yards. Christmas saw them mail homemade cards, and give gifts of baked goods and wine. When our children were about to graduate from high school, the couple sent them cards of congratulations. When the day of graduation came they sat in the stands at Drolette Field, and watched them partake in "pomp and circumstance".

If either that couple, or my wife and I, left town for any period of time, the other couple looked after their property.

Over the years, they each told me how much they loved

those they came to, more-and-more, speak of only in memory. It was sad to hear the sense of loss in the voice of the man, when he spoke of those he thought he had known. His words finally gave acceptance that he realized he hadn't known them at all. He had seen what he wanted to be true, but they had passed through his life.

First one of my neighbors passed, and then the other. Within a week both of them were gone. He had told me that if she died before him, people might as well start throwing dirt in his face because he would be done. He laughed when he talked of "pushing up daisies with my face."

When the first passed, it seemed the number of people who visited the one, who remained, was a cross section of the community, and many others I had never seen before. When the second passed, I believe each of them returned.

The couple's children were at the home, as much as they could be, after the first death. When the second parent died, some were still there. After the second death, the others returned. The youngest of them, we had known as children. We had met the older siblings during a Thanksgiving or Christmas season, and reinforced that familiarity over time, as we did with the younger children.

During the visiting time, there was a lot of sitting around, and relating of events from shared periods the couple had spent with their children and with the visitors. Many of the visitors said they regretted not keeping up contact with the couple over the years, and in some cases, losing contact.

My wife and I helped out the best we could during that time of great loss. We observed the property, picked up the newspapers before they were canceled, and generally tried to make the home look like it was still occupied.

We tried to keep watch, when the couple's children were not available, to greet anyone stopping by the couple's home. Some of those people took our offer to sit with us, at our home, and talk about the couple.

In time the home was sold. Many of those visitors we had spoken with months earlier returned over a period of almost two weeks. When I talked with some of them, they said they could only be there on the weekend.

As age was catching up on the couple, they had been designating specific articles for their children, and many of the visitors. My wife and I had never known that.

The couple had told their children what they were doing. They had put tags on items, and also placed information in their wills as to the disbursement of their property. Finally, they gave each of their children the addresses of each person who was to receive an item.

There were many tears, and many somber faces, during that time when people left what had been the couple's home. Some left with an item small enough to be carried unobtrusively. Others had to make repeated trips into the house, garage, or the workshop in the backyard before they drove away.

One woman sat on the steps of the front porch and cried with deep sobs. Those who passed offered comfort as they could. After a time, she walked to her car and drove away with her treasured memento.

One big, strong man stood leaning against a tree and cried. The man enjoyed fishing and hunting. In his left hand was a fishing pole. In his right was a rifle. He had last seen them years before when he and his wife had taken fishing and hunting trips with the couple.

When I talked with another man, he said he had mentioned to the man years before of his fondness for the item he held in front of him to show me. He said he didn't know the man would ever have remembered that time and his words.

The people had remembered, but time had caught up with them, too. They had duties and obligations in life of their own. They hadn't forgotten. They had merely been human. I think the couple knew that all along, but simply missed those they had come to know as the children in their extended family.

Age has caught up with my wife and me, too. My father used to say that if you live long enough, that will happen.

The couple who used to live across the street had a long run, and left behind many good memories for many people. A new family will move into what was once the couple's home. They will make it theirs. That's as it should be.
Nathan

Letter 139

She Left Benicia Many Years Ago

Mr. Garrett,

In time I will totally get over her. That time isn't now. I remember too much. She is as clear in my mind, as if she were in front of me now. I remember how she sounded, her fragrance, and how she felt in my arms.

For mental health, and thus physical health, I have to let her go. I guess I'm like the alcoholic with the maintenance dose. Thoughts of her each day are what kept me going for a long time. I have pretty much gotten over her, but not quite.

Sometimes I've thought I saw her driving by, or walking by a store in town, but it never turned out to be her. I remember her as she was when I knew her, though. Her hair might be gray now, and her figure may have changed for all I know.

She left Benicia many years ago. I now think of her most often on a cool, rainy day. It was a day like that when I last saw her.

My ears hear the sound of the closing of the door, and the click of the lock assembly, but the sounds are long past. It is only my mind which hears the sounds.

We wrote each other a few times, but the times between the letters became longer, and finally the letters stopped. She initiated the letters and I responded. When she stopped sending, so did I.

When I saw her the last time, she told me we could only be

very good friends. It may be impossible to have a squeeze on your heart which breaks its rhythm while keeping it beating normally. I don't know, I think that happened to me when she said those words.

I passed her words off as if I knew what she had been going to say, and that it didn't bother me. I was a pretty good actor. Maybe if I had begged her to stay she would have, but I don't really think that would have happened.
Bill

Letter 140

No One Said: "Welcome Home"

Sir,

I could be just bitter as Hell, if I let it go. That wouldn't be right. People do what they want, and always will. In a way the forgetfulness of the general public, and body politic, is healthy. It's kind of like not remembering a bad dream. In another sense it is terrible. It is like not appreciating a policeman until you need him, and forgetting about him once the need is over.

When I saw your advertisement, my first thought was you had a great idea, and I hoped it would go well. Then I started thinking more about love. It isn't just Mom and apple pie, the love of a buddy, walking down the aisle, kissing your wife, or holding your children. The saying that it takes a community to raise a child is true in its concept. It also takes a community to love those sent, or who volunteer to go, to protect it from having harm march down Main Street.

There was a movie, with Sylvester Stallone starring as the character Rambo. During that movie he said, "We wished that she (America) loved us as much as we loved her." If that isn't the line, it's close.

The meaning is clear. A lot of guys felt that way when they came back from serving their country, and Benicia. They had to keep quiet about some of the things they felt in their hearts, because of the political times. They had to get jobs, or go back to school, raise families, and do all the other things civilians do. Saying what they believed got some of them looked on strangely. They weren't understood. Others said nothing.

High praise should be extended for all of the men, and women, who help keep us all safe by serving their country in the military. Send them packages, letters and emails. Cheer them when they come back home. No one has to agree with why they went, but they did go because they thought it was best. They thought it was best for the country, and thus for Benicia.

A lot of others did the same thing, and didn't even get a simple "Welcome Home". They weren't asked to join any organizations, and they sure weren't given much in the way of pay and benefits. They didn't join to gain college money. Some may have had the choice of the military or jail in those days, and chose the military. There were some, like me, who were told by someone they respected that the military was good for them. I've said the same thing to some in younger generations who have also served.

I loved Benicia long before I turned eighteen. I love it still. I just don't live there. Like volunteering to serve our country, it is my choice. I don't live there because no one had the care, or courage, to give me that simple "Welcome Home". No one even acknowledged the fact I had been gone.

A lot of times, over close to forty years, I was one angry person. Kathleen kept me about as sane as I could be during that time.

As the clock on our lives kept ticking, the anger lessened. I'm not angry any more about not receiving a "Welcome Home". I've come to understand people more. People don't usually see farther than their noses, and many times lack the Christian charity and understanding I've been told of. I say practice what you preach. Those people who served in another time didn't step into a vacuum when they left Benicia.

I moved from Benicia a little over a year after I came back. There is love I felt I gave, which wasn't returned. Unrequited is the word.

People have been good at welcoming home those who have served since, but they sure didn't do it for us. No one in my own town of Benicia welcomed me back. I had played on its fields, marched in its parades, pulled pranks in its environs, and dated daughters of the town in which I grew. I don't think it would have been that hard for someone to say "Welcome Back" to me, but they didn't.

Benicia loves its children. It truly does, but it forgot about some of them. It would have taken courage in those times to extend a hand, and the love behind that needed courage wasn't there.

Shortly after I got out of the service, a classmate of mine passed me on the sidewalk when we were walking on Main Street. When I saw him coming towards me, I thought we'd stop and talk. But, he didn't even look at me. He put his head down, and almost turned sideways to make sure he avoided me as he passed where I stood. I didn't realize until then that I must have had some kind of leper's spots on me. That guy didn't even see me, and we had gone to school together for years.

I'm a civil engineer. The government taught me how to tear things down by blowing them up. I wanted to do the reverse when I got back, and I wanted to do it in Benicia. That didn't happen and probably never will.

At a luncheon, honoring my twentieth anniversary with the company where I'm employed, my best male friend introduced me. We had been in the same part of the world earlier in our lives, though we had different tasks to perform.

While we sat talking, before he introduced me, I asked him if he had ever been given a "Welcome Home". He said he hadn't. I stood, said "Welcome Home", and shook his hand. He said the same words to me. There was a connection, because we each understood what the words meant.

That night, when I talked with Kathleen about what had hurt me so much over the years, she sat and listened. It has been the only time I've talked to her about it. Then she said, "Welcome Home".

I needed that, just that, those two simple words. Neither word was love, but love was in each word. The two best friends in my life said those words to me. At least some of the people in my life understood.
Don

Letter 141

The Uncaring Hunter

Mr. Garrett,

I once found the body of a hawk. It had been discarded, just dumped, after the fool with the gun shot and killed it. I buried that bird on its stomach, with its head towards the top of the hill, and facing east so it could meet a new day.

The place where I buried the bird is covered by a lot more dirt now than I put over it. The spot was once the side of a grassy hill, but homes and asphalt cover it now.

There were once many open spaces, within walking distance, or bike riding distance, around Benicia's periphery, where we kids could play. Those same areas had people, who fired rifles and pistols, walk through them hunting for targets. Even if it were possible today, I wouldn't want my grandchildren to go there now. The world has passed that time by.

I love animals. I also eat meat. The love, and the eating, is acceptable, I think.

I don't believe in killing something to allow me to have a rug to walk on, or a set of horns to hang on one of my walls. We are omnivorous creatures and need a certain amount of animal protein. Farmers, and ranchers, and fishermen provide most of that need for us. If someone hunts, or fishes, to provide added nourishment for their families, I'm in agreement. To shoot something just to shoot it is insanity.

I've often wondered if the hunter could understand how his family would feel, if someone did to him what he did to the hawk. Hopefully his family would have loved him, and would love him after he was gone.

The hunter, too, could have been left to rot in the sun, in a location the family didn't know. They would always wonder what happened. Perhaps the bird's family felt the same.

Gladys

Letter 142

I Asked Shirley If She Was Married

Mr. Garrett,

I put Shirley out of my mind, until I saw her again. One look and all the old feelings returned with one beat of my heart.

It seemed to me like the jump-starting of a car. The battery in the car had been allowed to die. Once the car was jump-started, and ran for awhile, the battery became charged to full strength. That's what Shirley did to me, but she did it in an instant.

We had each grown up in Benicia. It was a funeral which brought us back to Benicia, and got us back together. The services were for a parent of one of our classmates.

I paid my respects to the family, walked back a few rows, and sat down. Shirley arrived at the services a few minutes after me. She stood talking to the family for a few minutes, and then sat in front, and to the left, of me. I had been looking around recognizing some people and wondering if I knew others, though they had changed.

I turned to look towards the center aisle a moment after she had walked by. I hadn't seen her face, but I saw the walk. It drew my immediate interest. I knew that walk. Then she turned to talk with someone at her side, and I knew it was Shirley.

I waited on the steps for Shirley to leave the church. When she did, I made a complete fool of myself, but I didn't care. She walked out with another classmate of ours. After saying hello to each of them, I asked Shirley if she was married, or if there was a man in her life in any other way.

She laughed, and said, "No."

I said, "There is now."

We went to dinner. Things have turned out well. The embers of the love we had held all along resulted in the second, and last, marriage for each of us.

Will

Letter 143

The Journey Continues

Mr. Garrett,

I hope all is well with you and yours.

Last Sunday our family officially gained a new member. I say officially, because Tom has been a combination son and brother to members of the family since he was in high school.

Kids are kids, and always will be. Things happen during that age. When our Connie was with Tom then, I had the same worries any father would have. When you have a daughter, especially if you have only one daughter, I think the worries are natural. Maybe it is sexist, but I never had the same worries with our son.

As time passed, and Connie and Tom saw more of each other, and their relationship grew, I had no worries. It was easy to see the care they had for each other.

Connie and Tom were married in St. Dominic's Church, just the same as Connie and I. During the ceremonies, Connie and I sat where her family had sat when we were married. I think the pews have been changed since others watched us exchange our vows. They looked different than I remembered. I don't attend church services, though I pray many times each day.

The Maid-of-Honor was Connie's life-long friend, Lacey. They met at Joe Henderson Elementary School, and continued their school connection, and friendship, through Middle School and Benicia High School.

Those years saw them playing on the same teams as regular as clockwork during the school years and the summers. Usually, in anything, where you found one you found the other. It was a rare and usually only a special occasion, when either would go on a date if it wasn't a double date with the other.

The boys caught on to that pretty quickly. I think some of them must have worked out deals with another guy to set up double dates. That way they could try to insure their chances of dating the girl they wanted to ask for a date.

The girls' school days separated when they made their choices for college. One graduated from a college in the Southeast, and the other from a college in the Northwest. Through those college years they each worked in visits to the campus of the other.

Through college, Tom became a naval officer. He had spent a lot of good days on boats in the Carquinez Straits with his father. I think the salt spray got to his brain in his youth, as it had to mine during the same period in my life. That salt air can be a clutching vixen. It holds some men forever. For others it is a passage of time. It was that for Tom, as it had been for me.

The bridesmaids were also classmates and teammates of Connie's. In all the years I had known them, it wasn't often I saw any of the young ladies wearing dresses. Seeing them that day was to see them as individuals, and as a group, in a different light. My mind knew they were all young women, but seeing them that day made me feel a little older.

Our daughter wore white, as did my wife on our wedding day. It is a clean color in look, and in spirit. Both wore it well.

The Best Man was Tom's friend, and our son, Charlie. They had been friends since childhood and had often gone to each other's homes. A change could be seen in Tom as time passed and he stopped coming over just to see Charlie, and spent more time with Connie.

Tom and Charlie helped out around our home like brothers. They did the same at Tom's parents' home. If something needed to be done when they were there, they just pitched in and helped out. If either family needed to call on a pair of young strong arms to help out, they were always available. They were simply good young men.

For ushers, Tom chose three teammates from the championship team of which they were all a part in their senior year. Those boys worked hard for the title of champion. Now, they were all young men, and two were married.

There was no stag party, as some men will have before their wedding day. Tom and Charlie spent an evening sitting in his backyard with the wedding ushers, and four others, sharing moments from the past. I thought that was nice. Each of the boys had played in that yard many times as boys. That evening they sat as young men.

One of the three others Tom invited was his dad, another was the man all the boys called Coach, the third was me.

The fourth man Tom invited that evening, and to the wedding and reception, was a man I had never met until then. When Tom had spoken of that man in the past, he spoke almost in awe. His introduction to me was done almost in reverence. The two definitely had history between them.

It was my privilege to meet the man Tom referred to as Chief. Tom's respect, and love, for Chief was obvious. As Tom likes to say, they had "served together in other places and other times". Tom never said much more about his time in the Navy than that.

It was apparent, the clutching vixen of salt spray held fast to Chief. When I talked with him that evening, I felt he would either die in the Navy, or retire from it when they had to finally kick him out.

I was very honored by Tom asking me to join them that evening. Listening to their words was rejoining my youth, as if riding in a time machine, and viewing scenes through a porthole. Perhaps it was a portal. Some of those words came from Chief. He, Tom, and I, had each shared some of the same experiences in our time on the water.

I thought Tom had drawn to himself the male figures in his life he most respected. They were those he thought of as his friends and his mentors. I knew Tom well enough by then to know he would only invite special people in his life to that special evening.

With my daughter's arm linked in mine, as we walked down the aisle, I felt almost as proud as when I stood in that church watching my bride-to-be approach.

Tom was smiling a smile I had come to know over the years when he looked at Connie. It was a smile of pleasure in what his eyes saw and the love his heart felt.

When I was asked, who it was that was present to give the bride away, I answered that I was, as per the custom. I wasn't giving her away. I was freeing her to be in the arms of our religion and the dictates of legal tradition. Her heart was never mine to give away. She is the only one who could have done that, and she had done it years before with Tom.

All brides and grooms are a little nervous, I think. Connie and Tom must have been, too. Far more than nervousness was the beaming love and pride each showed the world. They were standing in front of the most important people in the world to them, minutes before becoming wife and husband. At that moment I don't think either could have been happier.

When I sat next to my wife, I saw in her the pride she felt for her daughter. When I leaned over to kiss her, a tiny diamond of tear was in the inside corner of each eye. She must have seen similar diamonds in mine.

No one got drunk at the reception. I think Chief drank more during the course of the evening than I thought a normal man was capable of doing. It seemed like there were about a thousand toasts during that evening. Towards the end he and I were the only ones I saw drinking anything except water. I think he drank that much because he wanted to match me and because it was one of the few times in his adult life when he saw a time he could relax. I understood, and he knew I understood.

I think at least one romance blossomed during the reception. There are signs to read as easily as observing birds in the springtime. It was good to see.

The wedding ceremony, and the reception, was video-taped by a friend of the family. I viewed it again last night. What a great act that day was in the play of the lives of our daughter Connie, and our new son, Tom.

Circles are circles. The journey continues. The start is the end. The end is the start.

Sincerely,

Tom

Letter 144

The Last Letter

Hello,

My career choice meant Bobbie and I had to live in San Francisco for a few years. The plan always was to come back to Benicia to live.

We enjoy walking. I've run equal to over three times across the United States. I think Bobbie and I must have walked together at least equal to half that distance. We have walked hand-in-hand in sun and shadows, rain and shine, on the concrete sidewalks, and the grass of mountain meadows.

I often joke with Bobbie, and others, that she chased me for six years before we got married. That's the truth, though I did slow down during that time. This thankful guy is very glad she kept after me.

We enjoy being together. Bobbie is my best friend, and I am hers.

Our walks in the evening, I think, have been our overall favorites. We are people who enjoy the twilight time, the cool weather, the rain, the mist, and the fog. It is all cuddly weather time.

I close with, "As always before". "As always B4" was the way my mother closed her letters for many years.

Peace

For my Bobbie, my love, and for me,

As always before,

Jim

CPSIA information can be obtained at www.ICGtesting.com
Printed in the USA
LVOW08s0547130114

369134LV00001B/60/A